Hell's Diva II:

Mecca's Return

Hell's Diva II:

Mecca's Return

www.urbanbooks.net

Urban Books, LLC
97 N 18th Street
Wyandanch, NY 11798

Hell's Diva II: Mecca's Return Copyright © 2011
Anna J.

ISBN 13: 978-1-60162-646-2
ISBN 10: 1-60162-646-0

First Mass Market Printing February 2015
First Trade Paperback Printing November 2011
Printed in the United States of America

10 9 8 7 6 5 4 3 2 1

This is a work of fiction. Any references or similarities to actual events, real people, living, or dead, or to real locales are intended to give the novel a sense of reality. Any similarity in other names, characters, places, and incidents is entirely coincidental.

Distributed by Kensington Publishing Corp.
Submit Wholesale Orders to:
Kensington Publishing Corp.
C/O Penguin Group (USA) Inc.
Attention: Order Processing
405 Murray Hill Parkway
East Rutherford, NJ 07073-2316
Phone: 1-800-526-0275
Fax: 1-800-227-9604

Acknowledgments

Novel number seven . . . Seven years ago, when I penned *My Woman His Wife,* I honestly didn't think I had that many stories in me to write. It started out as just something to do because I enjoyed writing and reading. I wasn't setting out to change the game or anything like that. I never even thought much about writing a book. . . . It just wasn't on the agenda. At the time I was working a night job at a medical billing company and was told that a short story I had written didn't have a market. Around that time Zane had just stepped on the scene, and I'm thinking to myself, *If* The Sex Chronicles *can be on the shelves, with all of that explicit sex, why can't my book be there?* Zane's books were one of the reasons why I went forward with *My Woman His Wife.* Why not test the boundaries and leap over limitations? What did I have to lose?

God has been fabulous in steering my life in the direction that it has gone. Without Him, where would I be? My life wasn't all fabulous and everything as I was growing up, but I've come to realize that even little girls from the projects can make it, too. I've even met some wonderful folks along the way, and whether you were here to stay or just for a season, I thank everyone that I've come in contact with. Your presence in my life was for a reason, whether it was to help me see myself in a better light or to steer me in a better direction. Through the good and the bad, I'm thankful.

Tiffany, I can only hope that I've been leading by example. There is a ten-year difference between us, and in being your older sister, it's hard sometimes to keep it all together when I just want to ball up in the corner and cry. Thank you for just being there. At the times when the world gets too hectic and I just need to do me, you're right there with me. We have a friendship that confuses people, because too often in life siblings hate each other. Did we always get along? Hell no! (LOL) But with age comes maturity, and with maturity comes understanding. We had to grow up fast, and I wasn't too sure about a lot of things. You've been riding this thing with me since forever, through the good and the bad, and I couldn't ask for a better sister. Thank you for keeping me sane and allowing me to be me without having to put on airs and act like I'm invincible. Remember that night at the Econo Lodge? (LMAO) I love you, sis, with all my heart.

Tisha, you know how we do. J I pray a lot for you because I know you're having a rough time right now. We've all been there. Tynayjah and Nyser are a handful, but they are funny as hell! We're all getting older, and I see you trying to get over that hump. It's hard, right? Just keep moving forward; things happen the way they're supposed to. It looks crazy right now, but you'll be just fine.

Janise Bond, my bestie since forever! Thanks for everything, girl. I wish we had more time to hang out, but between school and work, touring and writing, and all that you have going on, I'm glad that I can still pick up the phone at two in the morning and you'll answer. How many years has it been? J I love you, girl!

Melissa Postum, aka Mizzles Fashizells, I remember the first day we met. We clicked instantly, right? Thanks for being my sounding board and a shoulder when I'm feeling emotional about some shit (LOL). We have soooo much in common, and I'm glad to have you as a friend. I can honestly say that out of all the friends I've ever had, you, Chereme, and Janise have always been a constant.

True friendships are few and far between, and I appreciate you being here. We need another shindig. . . . Let's get it poppin'!

Mom, thanks for everything. There have been times with us when we were straight bumping heads and were unwilling to see the finish line. I think we both had to step back and breathe. We have the same personality, and both of us are unwilling to bend. Even though we don't see eye to eye on a lot of things, I'm thankful that I have you here. I wouldn't know what to do without you, and I never tell you that. I worry about you sometimes, and I know it's vice versa. Just know that no matter how pissed off and mad I get, I love you through all of that.

To my family—my aunts Karen and Sandy; my uncles Herb (aka U.F.U.—inside joke, LOL) and Bobby; my cousins Gerald, Dynetta, Shardae, Shalysa (aka Msyumyum Thamadame), Rashun, Delita, Daja, Soraya, Boobie, Kenny, Malik, Keisha, Michelle, Mequilla (yes, you're fam!); my great aunt Pat, my grandmom Anna L Forrest; and all the children (too damn many to name)—we don't all always get along, but we couldn't pick each other. As dysfunctional as things may get, thanks for being there.

To Jerel Brooks, Ed, Stan, Troy King, Eugene Riley, and Henry Govan, all of you played a part in my life that made me into the person I am today. Whether it was disappointment or happiness, an eye-opener or a heartbreaker, without those experiences I wouldn't be and see who I am today. Ed, me and you go way back. . . . Glad you're still around. J Jerel, I know you're happy to have proof that you really do know me (inside joke). Thanks for everything.

Mark Anthony, thanks for giving a sister a chance. When I met you at my birthday bash, I was just a young girl turning twenty-four, trying to make it. Who knew that being the first lady of Q-Boro would lead to me being a bestselling author and household name years later? I thank you and Sabine for the opportunity and the room to allow me to grow creatively. I didn't understand a lot of things at the time, and at the end of the day we all have to do what is best for us. I see you still doing your thing. Keep up the good work.

Carl Weber, I remember when I first met you a few years back at Book Expo America. I think it was in New York that year. I was a little reluctant and hesitant about a few things, but I came to find out you're not as bad a person as folks made you out to be (LOL). On a business level, thanks for continuing to allow me to do my thing. I have been given an opportunity that most people haven't, and I do not take it for granted. I've seen a lot of people come and go in the industry, and I'm grateful to still have a publishing house to call home. Thanks for everything.

Candace K, I miss you, girl! Thanks for the hot covers and all of the phone time. You saw my vision, even when I was painting a picture that wasn't crystal clear. I see you didn't miss a beat, and I'm happy for you. Congrats on all your accomplishments, and keep striving for greatness. You got this whole cover designing, Web page making, Photoshop thing in the bag!

Brittani, I see you doing big things over there! Obstacles come on a daily basis, and I see you scaling hurdles with ease. The industry can make or break you and cut you deep. All of this aids in making us better people . . . hopefully! (LOL) Keep doing your thing, and keep doing it big.

To my industry peeps, M.T. Pope, Dywayne Birch, Allison Hobbs, Cairo, Dawayne Josephs, LaJill Hunt, K'Wan, Treasure E. Blue, Eric S. Gray, Aretha Temple, Keniesha Gayle, Sydney Little, Gayle Jackson Sloan, Marlene Ricketts, Anthony White, Tu-Shonda Whittaker, Ken Devine, Laurinda D. Brown, K. Elliott, Brenda L. Thomas, Victoria Christopher Murray, Angel Mechelle, Beanz, Anthony White, and _____(insert your name here), I love y'all. I see y'all doing it big!

Keep up the good work, and keep those fingers moving across those keys!

To all the bookstores (Maryland is like my second home), book clubs, and fans, thank you!!! Every time I get an e-mail, in-box, or text about one of my books, whether you are just finding out about me or have been through the ride with me, I appreciate you. An author is nothing without a reader, and even if I write something that is not to your liking, stick around for the next one. I got you! Check out my Web site: www.allthingsannaj.com

Thanks for the support and keep spreading the word! A sista got bills to pay! (LOL)

~Anna J.

Also by Anna J.

Novels

Hell's Diva: Mecca's Mission
Snow White: A Survival Story
My Little Secret
Get Money Chicks
The Aftermath
My Woman His Wife

Anthologies

Bedroom Chronicles
The Cat House
Flexin' and Sexin': Sexy Street Tales Volume I
Fantasy
Fetish
Morning, Noon & Night: Can't Get Enough
Stories to Excite You: Ménage Quad

Prologue

A child represents a world from which we have been forever exiled.
— Robert Greene, *The Art of Seduction*

The playful screams and laughter of the children in the playground surrounded by the towering, dingy brown buildings of the Brownsville, Brooklyn, housing projects harmonized with the sound of mothers yelling various commands to wandering, overly playful children. The sound of a bustling avenue, with its buses, cars, and always present roar of police sirens, served as a backdrop. One particular little girl, cute, with long silky hair done up in pigtails adorned with red ribbons at the ends, looked over to her mother, sitting on a bench with other young mothers, and waved with a huge smile. Though in a conversation filled with neighborhood gossip, her mother was always alert to the whereabouts of her only child.

"Be careful on those monkey bars," she yelled across the courtyard at her daughter and just as quickly turned back to the conversation at hand.

The little girl watched as her favorite relative, her aunt Ruby, entered the playground. She stood in front of the little girl's mother and talked using a lot of hand gestures. As usual, she saw her aunt remove a wad of cash from her pocket and hand it to her mother.

Climbing on the monkey bars, where other kids played, the little girl wanted to reach to the top like she saw other brave kids doing. She also wanted to impress her auntie. As she ascended the bars, she looked over to see if her aunt was watching. Disappointed that she didn't notice her, she called out to her. Just as she called, one of her feet slipped off the bar and caused her to fall down toward the black rubber mats placed under the monkey bars. Her small head and body banged off the bars as she fell. Her crying shrieks alerted her mother and aunt, who were seconds late to catch the girl's body, preventing her from hitting the mat.

Before the little girl's mother ran over to her, she felt herself being lifted off the mat. She was dazed, with temporary blurred vision, and it seemed as if the noise of the playground became muffled. When her vision cleared, everything moved in slow motion. That was when she looked into the face of the person who had picked her up off the ground. He was tall and wore a pitch-black trench coat. His Afro was the shiniest and neatest 'fro she ever saw. Even her handsome father's curly, perfectly round Afro couldn't compare to that of the man holding her hand. His bright smile reminded her of the keys on the piano in her music class. As she took in the glow of his dark, rich complexion, she realized that the pain in her head from the fall was gone. Then the man spoke, and his voice seemed to hypnotize her.

"Throughout your life you will fall. What's important is how you function when you get back up."

"Baby, are you okay?" The little girl heard her mother's voice. She was confused as to why she was now holding her mother's hand instead of the hand of the man who picked her up. She looked around the playground, once again hearing the familiar sounds of the ghetto, searching for the mysterious man, but he was gone. Her aunt's cheerful voice grabbed her attention right after that.

"Look, she ain't even crying. She tough like her auntie."

"Let's hope she doesn't follow in her aunt's footsteps," the girl's mother retorted flatly, attempting to deflate the air out of her sister's chest full of pride.

Suddenly the sound of gunshots erupted in the projects. All the parents ducked, running toward their children, who instinctively ducked down as they listened to their parents' yelled commands. The little girl clung to her aunt as the shots rang out for a few seconds; then it ended as quickly as it began.

Mecca jumped out of her sleep. The gunshots in her dream awakened her as her heart beat rapidly. She looked around, realizing she was lying in her hospital bed. After her labored breathing subsided and she could hear the beat of the heart monitor next to her bed, she mumbled to herself, "You were always there, weren't you, Lou? I remember you now." She took the time to get herself together and, after a while, realized that she could hear voices outside of her room. She could hear only a few words that were being said because their voices were low.

Since the fatal shooting at the hands of her ex-boyfriend, Tah, and seeing her entire life with the assistance of Lou, Mecca had to be institutionalized and treated with intensive therapy sessions. She couldn't get over the feeling of wanting to kill her aunt, and any remaining foes from the past that might still be alive. Since she chose not to talk, the doctors thought it would be best for her to stay, much to Mecca's dismay, of course.

"It's more mental than physical," a male voice murmured.

"It's been so long. When can I see her?" a female voice asked in a sad tone.

"I don't think she's ready yet. She hasn't even spoken yet."

When Mecca looked at the door after a face appeared in the entrance, she recognized the face of her once beloved aunt. Now a face she felt sick to her stomach seeing. Mecca remembered there was a time when seeing her aunt was like a child seeing Santa Claus. Mecca was her aunt's little angel, and she could do no wrong in her aunt's eyes. Now her aunt was no longer her personal Santa Claus; instead she was more like Satan in the flesh.

Seeing the smile on Ruby's face made Mecca want to jump out of her bed and choke the life out of her, but that was physically impossible at this point in her life. Even more disappointing, when Ruby walked in her hospital room, she walked in with Karmen. Both Ruby and Karmen smiled at Mecca. A song her father used to play when she was a child came to mind; it was The O'Jays' song about backstabbers. That was exactly how she felt about both of these women.

"Good morning, Mecca." Ruby spoke to her with a hesitant smile on her face.

Instead of responding, Mecca simply turned her face and closed her eyes.

Ever since Lou showed Mecca her aunt's betrayal, she couldn't even stand the sight of her. For Ruby, it was probably a good thing that Mecca couldn't move, because she probably would have already killed her by now. It hurt Ruby that Mecca wouldn't respond to her, but she kept coming back to check on her niece's progress. That was what family was supposed to do.

Lou had been visiting Mecca in her dreams since she'd been out of her coma. He was sitting behind a huge mahogany desk, in a large, burgundy-leather, cushioned office chair, while Mecca lay on a leather chaise lounge, when Mecca asked, "Why can't I get up, Lou? Why are you keeping me paralyzed?"

In a measured tone Lou replied, "Because the revenge you seek is not yours. You've done that half of your life, and it has gotten you nowhere. Be on your best behavior, and you will walk again, I promise."

Chapter One

The most eloquent expression of the unconscious is the dream, which is intricately connected to myth. . . .
—Robert Greene, *The Art of Seduction*

Joseph of the Bible was known for his ability to interpret dreams. It was that ability that caught the curiosity of the Pharaoh of Egypt, whose own interpreters were useless. Joseph interpreted the Pharaoh's dreams and became a powerful man in ancient Egypt. As Mecca Sykes attentively gazed into the bright eyes of Lou, she wondered who could she wake up and ask to interpret her dreams and tell her exactly who Lou was.

"You do not know what vengeance is, because it is not yours to give," said Lou, dressed in a white overcoat, as he held a stethoscope to Mecca's chest. Mecca lay still on a stark white linen hospital bed, with a preoccupied expression on her face.

"You act as if I'm dumb or something. Mind you, Lou, I'm grown. I'm not the child you visit in my dreams," Mecca replied gruffly. Ever since Lou had snapped Mecca out of her coma and had begun appearing in her dreams, Mecca realized that she had become intrigued by his speeches about her doing the right thing in life and letting go of the feeling of getting some payback on all those who had betrayed her, especially her aunt. Initially, she had found him annoying and somewhat cruel for putting her through the grueling task of viewing her friends and loved ones being betrayed and herself as a victim of the double cross.

Mecca no longer had anyone in her life that she could talk to about her issues. She used to talk to Ruby about them or Ruby's lesbian lover, Monique, whom Mecca had confided in more than anyone else. She could rely on Monique to give her motherly advice about men, sex, and feminine issues. After Monique was shot down and killed in the projects Mecca felt like she had no one. She and Ruby had never had that kind of relationship, so she had to learn the hard way about life and trust. As for Lou, he had not only told her that the life she lived was one big lie filled with betrayal, lust, and greed, but he'd shown her how and why.

What could be more interesting than seeing your life played out in plain view, from your childhood to your adult life, and glimpsing things you didn't see at the time? Things like your so-called friends' and family's secret lives of treachery.

"Grown?" Lou questioned, removing the stethoscope from Mecca's chest and chuckling. "Is that what you all call fully matured adults now?"

"What makes you think I want revenge?" Mecca inquired, rolling her eyes at his sarcasm.

Lou looked at the stethoscope in his hands. "If only humans could make machines that could listen to what's in your heart instead of just its beat, then someone would be able to answer that," Lou replied, setting the stethoscope down on a bedside table and rubbing his hands together as if he had a big secret. "Unfortunately, they can't and I can, and your heart tells me revenge is what you seek."

Mecca looked away from Lou and wondered how she could be faulted for feeling angry about being snaked by people she would have risked her life and freedom for. How did he expect her to feel, knowing what they did behind her back? What world did he live in?

"You turn your eyes away so I won't read your feelings and thoughts. Very smart of you, dear," Lou said, snapping Mecca out of her thoughts.

"Huh?" she asked, dumbfounded.

"Revenge doesn't always have to be killing everyone that betrayed you. Karma is nature's form of revenge, and sometimes you have to let nature take its course," Lou preached.

"That 'what goes around comes around' crap? Please!" Mecca said in a tone of disbelief. Lou shook his head. Then Mecca displayed a mischievous grin on her face before saying, "Is this one of those moments where you're gonna show me rather than telling me?"

"Don't tell me you're beginning to enjoy this?" Lou commented, shaking his head at Mecca. If only she could just see what he was trying to get her to see, she would be up and out by now. Mecca smiled. Lou shrugged his shoulders, then placed his hand on her forehead, as if he were checking her temperature. "So be it."

The rapper Juvenile's voice roared through the Brooklyn strip club as the naked strippers followed his orders to "Back that ass up," while ballers, gangsters, and average Joe nine-to-fivers whooped and hollered. Throwing money at big-booty women onstage doing acrobatic maneuvers on poles and erotic dances had them acting a fool. There were even women among the crowd of horny men who were cheering the dancers on and letting go of the cash in their hands, putting it into the G-strings and between the squeezed breasts of half-naked women. In a smoky haze, Mo Blood sat in a secluded booth, sipping on a shot of Belvedere, listening to one of his associates spill some news that made him nervous.

"They gave the green light on Tah. They know you was with him, but it's not certain how they going to play it with you," Mo's associate reported, afterward leaning back in the booth from yelling in Mo's ear over the loud music.

"Tah made an O.G. call and I followed. That can't be my fault, homie," Mo Blood yelled.

"I feel you," his associate said, blowing smoke out his mouth while staring at the girl onstage. "That's what niggas in the mountains is saying. It's the homies on the streets making it an issue with both of y'all."

"First off, that bitch and that cat Shamel had it coming. So what's the beef about for real?" Mo inquired, knowing the associate was just a messenger. Even he didn't understand why the heads of their blood set were angry about what Tah did to Mecca and Shamel.

Luckily for Tah and Mo, the cops were the least of their worries. The cops in the Hamptons made sure that type of news didn't go public, especially in an upscale area of that magnitude. A drug-related homicide in the Hamptons? Property values were more important than some dead drug dealers from New York City. Still that didn't stop the word from getting out on the streets of Brooklyn. When the word got to Shamel's friends, they weren't happy and they wanted heads.

"The dude Shamel had bulletproof love with the homies, and he made a lot of them rich," the associate continued in a somber tone.

"I heard he ain't respect blood. He rocked his own family, and they were blood," Mo countered, wondering if he should get out of Dodge.

Shrugging his shoulders, the associate replied, "I think it got more to do with the chick Mecca's aunt. You know, she was a real live bitch back in the day. She knew a lot of heavy hitters and players, and a lot of them respected her, gee. You feel me?"

"So, what that mean? This ain't the eighties!" Mo Blood responded tartly.

"She back on the streets," the associate revealed.

Just as he finished his sentence, a scantily clad girl wearing a G-string and a pink see-through bikini top jiggled her way over to the booth. She had a dimpled smile on her seductively pretty face. Her five-foot-five frame, with a small waist, flat tummy, and juicy, round bottom, made Mo Blood forget about the nerve-racking conversation he was having with his associate as she approached them.

"Wassup, Mo? You ready for that private dance?" she asked with a forced smile.

Mo immediately felt his manhood come to life. Horny as hell and drunk off the liquor, Mo couldn't wait for this particular private dance. Mo regularly had private dances at the club, but not with the sexy Tasha. She wasn't into the "private dance" thing, because dancing was not what was meant by the word *private*. Tasha had fallen on hard times and had a two-year-old son to clothe and feed. Her reluctance to give "private dances" in secluded rooms in the basement was making her lose money she definitely needed. She had a choice to make, starve or eat. She chose to eat. So when Mo asked her if she was ready, she surprised him and said, "Gimme about an hour and I'll come get you." And wait Mo did.

"No doubt, Ma, I'm ready," Mo Blood told Tasha an hour later. Grabbing Tasha's hand after jumping out of his seat, Mo gave his associate the Blood gang handshake, then spoke loudly over the music. "Yo, Meek. I'll holler at you tomorrow. Talk to them dudes, though. Let them know that was Tah's call, not mines."

"All right, my dude," he answered with a lustful stare at Tasha. "Tear that pussy up, homie!"

Mo smiled while Tasha led him toward the back of the club, to a door leading to the basement. Once in the small room that was decorated with a small bed and a full-length mirror in the corner, leaning against the thin wood-paneled wall, which vibrated from the loud music, Mo got undressed quicker than a New York minute. After Tasha nervously undressed, Mo pulled her on top of him as he lay on his back, dick harder than a baseball bat.

"Don't you got a vest?" Tasha asked.

"Ma, I ain't got no disease. Word to my flag," Mo replied gruffly, ready to go.

Tasha shrugged her shoulders, then straddled Mo. Reaching behind her, she gripped his bulging erection and placed it in her warm, soft middle. Mo held in the urge to moan from the way she made her walls clench his manhood.

Tasha moved her small waist slowly and rhythmically, as if she was moving to the sound of a slow jam. She bit her lip and closed her eyes, feeling Mo fill her insides. Mo squeezed her soft, plump ass as he dug in deep. She felt so soft, he thought his hands would melt into her skin. As Tasha sped up her thrusts, she began to moan.

"Yeah, Daddy, fuck this pussy!" Tasha said into Mo's ear. Her moaning and dirty talk excited Mo, who matched her rhythm with hard thrusts, banging her inner walls as if he was trying to break them down. He ordered her into the doggy-style position, wanting to see her from behind. It was Tasha's favorite position, and once in it, she put her back into it.

"Oh shit, Mo! Yeah, right there! That's it, Daddy!"

Mo didn't want to release yet, but the feeling of her pussy was too much for him, and he couldn't hold it any longer. Tasha knew he was about to release his load from the change in his thrusts.

"Don't cum in me," she grunted. Mo heard her request but paid her ass no mind. Tasha felt his warm juices in her and tried to pull herself out from under him but couldn't due to his body weight.

"Mo, why you do that?" she wailed, pushing him off of her.

"My bad. It's just that pussy good, Ma," Mo replied nonchalantly, while trying to catch his breath. At the same time Mo was thinking, *Bitch, you knew you was going to start selling that ass. Why you ain't got no condoms on hand?* Mo paid her the buck fifty she asked for and left.

*****

At the end of the month Tasha went to the clinic to get herself checked, which was the club's policy, as was using contraceptives. Tasha waited for the results in the clinic waiting room. A half hour later she was called to an office, where a counselor greeted her as she entered, closing the door for privacy. Tasha was a nervous wreck: the unprotected sex with Mo had had her biting her nails for the past three weeks, and she couldn't get it off her mind. The counselor gave her a long speech about AIDS and how people with the disease could live a healthy life if they took the right medication and practiced a healthy lifestyle.

"Please, just gimme the results," Tasha snapped, tired of the anticipation.

"Miss Jackson, you are HIV-positive," the counselor responded.

Tasha fainted in the office.

Good for his ass, Mecca thought as she looked at Lou with an amused smirk on her face. She didn't know Mo Blood personally, but she remembered him from hanging with Tah and had never liked him. Yet she was bored and wanted more.

"Is that it?" Mecca questioned Lou, anxious to see what else was going on out in the world. She could have thought of a million other ways to get at Mo Blood, but what she just saw would do for now. At least until she got better and got out of the hospital.

"I see you're starting to get a kick out of this," Lou replied as he placed his hand back over her head. Silently he prayed for Mecca and hoped she would change her wicked ways.

Tamika heard banging at the door over the sound of the sexy, sultry voice of Aaliyah as she sang "Rock the Boat." That used to be her and Tah's jam, but ever since their son had got there, their favorite song wasn't the only thing they no longer shared.

"I'm coming!" she yelled out to let whoever was on the other side of the door know she had heard their knocking. In a pair of tight cutoff jean shorts and a long white T-shirt, with no bra underneath, she sang along with Aaliyah as she walked to the door, smiling with anticipation. When she looked through the peephole, the smile quickly disappeared. Her son's father was the last person she wanted to see, especially now that she was expecting the company of a danger-ously cute guy she met in downtown Brooklyn.

"What now, Taheem?" Tamika complained after answering the door with one hand on her hip, showing much attitude.

"What you mean, what now? Don't play with me," Taheem growled, pushing past her to enter her apartment. "Where my son at?"

Tamika sucked her teeth, closing the door. *He always pops up at the wrong time, acting like seeing his son is the main reason he makes unannounced visits. Really, he shows up high and drunk, wanting sex and a place to crash when no one else wants his trifling ass in their house. Those days are over,* Tamika told herself, especially after he got his nose wide open off that bitch Mecca, who scarred her face for life. Even though Tamika didn't feel sorry for what had happened to Mecca, it still confirmed to her that Tah was no good.

"*Our* son ain't here, Taheem. He at my mother's for the weekend," Tamika said, watching Tah remove his Tims and plop down on her couch. Turning on her floor model TV, he looked as if he were planning on staying longer than she wanted him in her apartment.

"I got company coming over, Taheem. You got to go. If you want to see your son, walk your ass over to Tilden and spend time over there with him."

"Company? I know you don't be bringing no lame-ass niggas around my son." Tah chuckled, staring at the TV as he channel surfed. Tamika walked over to him and snatched the remote out of his hand.

"Nigga, please! I don't say nothing when you have all those nasty bitches in my son's face. Plus, this dude ain't no lame. You're not the only nigga with a gun, Tah."

"Who is he, then?" Tah snapped as he stood up, walking to the refrigerator.

"None of your business," Tamika snorted. "Plus, you don't put food in this house, so don't go eating everything."

Tah ignored her, pulled a gallon of milk out of the fridge and a box of Fruity Pebbles from the cupboard. To Tamika's annoyance, he used a pot instead of a bowl to eat the cereal. Before she reacted, a knock at the door grabbed her full attention, as it did Tah's. As Tamika walked to the door, she saw the grin on Tah's face and rolled her eyes at him.

"Let's see who Romeo is," Tah mumbled.

Tamika opened the door, smiling at the six-foot, caramel-skinned, big, brown-eyed cutie who favored the singer Trey Songz. He was wearing a tan Yankees fitted cap, which was leaning halfway off his head, and a tan Woolrich coat to match.

"Wassup, Dance?" Tamika greeted.

In a deep baritone voice that moistened Tamika's panties, showing an even white smile, he replied, "What's good, Ma?" Once Dance entered the apartment, his smile vanished as he caught the grinning face of Tah Gunz with a mouth full of cereal. Dance looked at Tamika quizzically.

"Dance, this is my baby's father, Tah," Tamika said uncomfortably, knowing Tah would start trouble. He did that with every guy she dated or attempted to date. His friends in the neighborhood would alert him that she was seeing someone, and Tah would show up every day so that he could see who the guy was. Most of the time he would have his friends or flunkies rob the guy or beat him unmercifully. To this day none of the guys had come back to Brownsville for payback. Part of Tamika's nervousness came from the fact that she knew Dance was the type to come back, and not to fight, either, but to do some damage.

When Tamika met Dance downtown, he was surrounded by a mean-looking crew of thugs from his Lafayette Gardens neighborhood, called "L.G." by Brooklynites. It is one of the borough's most notoriously dangerous housing projects.

Dance and his crew were all decked out in the hottest urban fashion and diamond flooded jewelry. It was obvious to Tamika that Dance was the boss by the respect the others showed him and the way people went out of their way to greet him as he and his crew shopped heavily. After she gave him her number, her panties got wet when he walked to a milky white Cadillac Escalade. She told herself she had to have him.

Dance nodded his head toward Tah without saying a word. Tah's menacing stare didn't intimidate Dance, and he wasn't worried about a possible confrontation with Tah. Dance knew how to fight well and was known more for his itchy trigger finger. He also knew that coming to Brownsville, Brooklyn's grimiest neighborhood, meant that trouble was a possibility. So he had come prepared, toting a twenty-one-shot Glock 9 mm.

"Uh, yo, duke, where you from?" Tah blurted as Dance took a seat on the black leather couch, removing his black flight jacket, which he wore over a tan button-down polo shirt. Tah immediately spotted Dance's icy Piaget watch. Dance ignored Tah's question.

Tah was caught off guard by Dance's display of courage, especially since he was out of his own territory. Dance didn't believe in just being the man in his own hood, though. That made Tah think that either Dance was a good bluffer or he really was a gangster, most likely hiding a weapon on himself. Tah finished his cereal then put his boots and coat on while smiling at Tamika. She knew was a sinister one that meant the episode between him and Dance was not over. Tamika rolled her eyes, then Tah gave Dance a hard stare.

"You a real gangster, huh?" Tah grunted, opening the door. Dance stood up, with Tamika trying to hold his arms to pull him back on the couch.

"You wanna see how gangster?"

"Nah, playboy, I believe you. It's nothing. Meeka, I'll see you later." Tah smiled.

Still holding on to Dance's arm, Tamika mumbled, "Bye, Tah." She knew he would be back, and he wouldn't be alone. He would come back with his goons. Dance knew that also. He was angry at the confrontation, but more angry at himself for not finding out more about this chick. He didn't know she had a kid. He should have gone with his first instinct and had her meet him at the hotel on Pennsylvania Avenue. Blinded by the fact that she had a banging body, he'd rushed to Brownsville to tear the pussy up.

"You wanna go out somewhere, instead of staying here?" Tamika asked, worried. Dance sensed her nervousness. This made him rethink his conclusion that Tamika probably was setting him up.

"Why you ask me that?"

"Dance, my baby father is a lowlife, and he is going to come back to start some bullshit."

Dance could sense the fear in her voice. He wondered whose life she feared for more, his or her kid's father. He knew most likely she didn't want her son to be fatherless, and he definitely wasn't playing stepdaddy. Damn, the things dudes went through just for a piece of ass.

"I'm not worried about dude. I got something for his ass if he wants problems," Dance responded matter-of-factly.

"Please, Dance, let's just go. I don't want anyone to get hurt," Tamika pleaded.

Hearing familiar voices in front of the building, Tamika looked out the window. To her dismay, Tah and his crew were out there, looking as if they were preparing for trouble. Dance got up to look out the window and saw the problem Tamika saw. Sighing, Dance took his cell phone off his waist and dialed a number.

"Yo, son, come to Brownsville Houses. These niggas wanna act up. Come now!" Hanging up, Dance turned to Tamika. "Let's wait here for a minute." Tamika grew more fearful. Dance's tone was calm but sinister.

"Dance, he's my son's father. I don't want anything to happen to him. Please, let's just go."

Her plea convinced him as to whose life was more important to her. Dance didn't know her reason for not wanting her son to grow up fatherless. Personally, she could care less about Tah. She just didn't want her son to grow up without a father in his life, like she did. She knew who her father was, but he disappeared out of her and her mother's life when she was born. He even denied that Tamika was his daughter, all because of a rumor that Tamika's mother was a prostitute before she fell in love with Tamika's father. To add insult to injury, he fathered fifteen kids in Brooklyn and never denied any of them.

Tamika didn't want anything to happen to Dance, either. She was planning on giving him the best sexual experience he'd ever had, hoping he would become her sugar daddy. Tah always seemed to get in the way of her plan, and that was one of her reasons for despising him. The main reason for her disdain for Tah was the fact that he made a lot of money on the streets and gave her nothing. Once in a while he would give her money for their son, and that was only when she fussed about it. Otherwise, he was under Mecca's ass, strung out.

While Dance waited for his cavalry to arrive, Tamika tried to take her mind off the situation by attempting to unzip Dance's pants to give him what she called her "tongue talent" and some goodies afterward. With his mind on the drama about to unfold, Dance pushed her hand away.

"Another time, Ma." Before she could protest, his cell phone's ring tone of the song "Niggaz Done Started Something" by The Lox went off, with him quickly answering it.

"Yo!" he barked into the phone. Tamika watched as Dance got off the couch and looked out the window. "Yeah, I see y'all. Yeah, that's them. I'm coming down now." Dance clicked off his phone and headed toward the door.

"I'm coming with you, right?" Tamika asked. Dance paused, with a thoughtful look on his face, before replying, "Yeah, baby girl, c'mon."

While Tamika got dressed, shots rang out from in front of the building, startling her and causing a smile to show on Dance's face. He recognized the sound of the AK-47 that he gave to his cousin going off. He was proud that his boys came through, representing L.G. Dance pulled out his Glock and cocked it back as Tamika came out, dressed, with a look of terror on her face.

"C'mon, shorty!" Dance commanded.

Tears welled up in Tamika's eyes. "Dance, they shooting. We can't go out there!"

"It's cool. They just wanted to get them dudes from in front of the building. My peoples ain't come to shoot nobody," Dance lied with a straight face.

When they reached the front of the building, Tamika screamed when she noticed that the person lying on the ground, in a pool of his own blood, was none other than Tah, moaning in pain.

"You don't look so gangster now, homie!" Dance taunted while Tamika got on her knees, cradling Tah's head in her arms.

"Taheem, get up. Don't die, nigga. Your son needs you!" Tamika cried as Tah's eyes blinked rapidly and tears flowed down his cheeks.

"Shorty, you coming? You can't help him," Dance said as his crew drove off and Tah's crew vanished into the Brownsville night.

"Dance, I have to get him help. He's dying!" Tamika yelled.

Dance shook his head. "Nah, Ma, he dead."

While Tamika looked down at Tah, crying, Dance placed his Glock to the back of her head and pulled the trigger. The sound of the shot echoed through the hood as Tamika's body slumped on top of Tah's. Still alive, Taheem closed his eyes, unable to feel Tamika's body on top of his due to a bullet shattering his spine from the neck down. Dance walk to his truck, parked in the parking lot in front of the building. He didn't want to kill Tamika, but leaving witnesses wasn't his thing. Charge it to the game.

As sirens roared through the night, Taheem opened his eyes after playing dead. He could hear his own labored breathing among the sounds of the streets. He never thought that things would turn out like this. Why did he allow himself to get caught up in these situations over women who didn't care too much for him, like he didn't care too much for them? Silly pride, he was told by an O.G., could get a man in deep shit. *How true that is,* Tah thought as he lay there, feeling his life slip away.

After being out for what felt like hours, and not satisfied with what Lou had shown her, Mecca woke up, staring into the face of her doctor, who was checking her blood pressure. He smiled at her, and then, after he was done, he left quietly. Mecca stared out the window at the rainy Brooklyn afternoon, thinking to herself, *Lou calls Mo Blood getting AIDS revenge?* Tamika getting killed meant nothing to her, and Tah should've been tortured, not just shot. Lou would have to do better than that to get her to change her mind about seeking revenge herself. She agreed that maybe she should move on, but her anger over how everything went down and what she found out still had her heated, and she wasn't ready to let it go just yet.

"Good morning, Ms. Sykes. Are we going to try and get up today?" the nurse asked her in a friendly tone.

Mecca shook her head no at the fat, redheaded, jolly nurse's irritating voice. It was going to be a long day. Mecca couldn't wait to go to sleep again so she could pick a bone with Lou.

Chapter Two

Length of days is in her right hand; in her left hand, riches and honor.

—Proverbs 3:16

There is a saying among convicts that when asked how much time they are doing or did, the answer would be two days: the day they went in and the day they get or got out. In between is nothing but a blur to some. For Ruby, those days were spent plotting and scheming how she would get revenge on the people who set her up, shot her niece, and killed Shamel. Most important was how she planned on getting rich again.

When Ruby's murder and drug convictions were overturned, and the case was dismissed due to the testimony of an eyewitness, she was given time served for the drug conviction, and began to map out exactly what she would do to get back on her road to riches.

Ruby had many associates and a few lovers in prison, but one person in particular became her confidant. Daphne, a five-foot-five, smooth brown-skinned woman with penetrating hazel eyes, was her favorite. Though no lesbian by far, she had "experimented" with sexual acts with a woman, but it wasn't to her liking. She always told Ruby there wasn't nothing like a hard dick banging up against your walls.

What Ruby did like about her was Daphne's likable personality and her ferocity when she became angered. Ruby saw herself in Daphne. She had a no-nonsense, take-charge attitude that screamed leader. The added bonus to Daphne's repertoire was that she was also from Brooklyn. The women met when Ruby was transferred to the women's federal prison in West Virginia. Daphne had already been there ten years on a fifteen-year stint for being part of a conspiracy to distribute large quantities of heroin. Her boyfriend at the time was a Jamaican-born, Bed Stuy raised hustler who ran a crew out of Tomkins projects. He and Daphne met in 1984, when she moved into the projects with her mother, stepfather, and sister. Afterward, her mother married an abusive man from Bed-Stuy and moved them in with him.

Daphne loved her older brother and was always sad thinking about how much she missed him.

There were rumors about his murder, but nothing ever came of them. He was a drug dealer, so the cops swept his murder under the rug like so many other murders in the ghetto. His presence was greatly missed because he was the man of the house after Daphne's real father was sent to prison for two murders, with a sentence of fifty to life. It was her brother who really took care of the family after making lots of money on the street, which he also used to spoil his baby sister.

He was barely home because he lived mainly with women blocks away from where Daphne and the family stayed. She was protected by the family because she was the baby. Often, she wasn't allowed out to play with kids on her block, and she went to an all girls' school. Extremely smart and an avid reader, she knew things about various topics, from romance novels to black history. Most of all she loved to read the dictionary, because she was determined to learn the meaning of a new word every day.

When she did see her brother, he would give her money to buy candy and toys, and he would make sure she wore the latest style of clothing. Her brother was only about five years older than her, and although she was a teenager, he wanted her to remain innocent. He encouraged her to play jump rope and jacks, and when she got clothes, he made sure they didn't make her look too grown up. The only time she got to show off the clothes was when she went out with her mother to shop for food or visit relatives far away in Queens.

Daphne hated her stepfather, who would get high off ecstasy and cocaine. He also got drunk on hard liquor and abused her mother physically and verbally. Once she was old enough to get out of the house, she began to hang out in Bed-Stuy more than she did in Brownsville. No longer did anyone pay attention to her, like they had when her brother was alive. She figured that the only reason why her mother and sister had been protective of her was to please her brother, because he was her favorite, and if Daphne was happy, then he was, and when he was happy, he gave money to the whole family. Now that he was gone, Daphne could run the streets, and run the streets she did.

Kids growing up in the ghetto tended to get into trouble because of the lack of anything constructive for them to do. With the city's non-caring attitude toward its poor inhabitants and the city's politicians' frequent mishandling of the city's budget, no decent after-school programs existed for the children. The playgrounds were unsanitary due to addicts using them as a place to get high and dump their syringes. The people were too poor to buy things to keep their children's minds from the activity on the streets, so the kids ran them and got into trouble.

Daphne was no exception to this phenomenon. She hung out with the kids in the projects and became amazed at ghetto life, especially at the older guys and girls wearing the expensive clothing and jewelry, like her brother did. The guys reminded her of him; and the girls, of the women he'd dated. These women were the stars of the neighborhood, and she wanted to be adored just like them. By the time she was fourteen, she was well developed and was mistaken for a nineteen-year-old. Still, even people knowing her actual age didn't deter some of the neighborhood hustlers from trying to make her one of their conquests.

At the tender age of fourteen, Daphne lost her virginity when her and a boy from the projects cut out of school and went to his house to do the nasty. It took place on an old, dusty, uncomfortable couch, which made the experience for her unsatisfying. The couch was covered in plastic, and as the boy pumped his dick into her, she stuck to the couch from sweat. It was irritating, and the boy was simply just hurting her. After that she never had sex with him again.

Everyone in the hood liked her, though. She was the nice girl who always smiled. That was a mechanism she used that was taught to her by her brother. She was told by her older brother that regardless of what you were going through, you never showed anger. He told her that when people knew what got you angry, they would use it against you. So, Daphne always smiled. However, when her brother died, she stopped smiling altogether and began to wear her emotions on her sleeve. Her brother was her greatest joy, and with him gone, what did she have left to smile about?

It was her pretty smile that attracted a young Jamaican guy everyone called Marley to her. They called him that because he was Jamaican and he smoked a lot of weed at an early age. His father was one of those Rastafarians, but his real name was Donovan. His almond brown complexion and high cheekbones gave him an exotic look that the girls loved. His eyes were hazel, just like Daphne's.

He was her dream man. He dressed like her brother and made money like him, selling weed for his father. At the age of fourteen he had more jewelry than all the kids in the projects, often wearing diamond rings and necklaces. Nobody dared rob him because his father was ruthless, and so was his crew, made up of family members. All of them were members of a Jamaican crew called the Shower Posse. They got the name because if anyone ever got out of line, as a reaction they would be showered with bullets.

Instantly, Marley fell in love with Daphne and made sure she was the flyest dressed girl in the projects. By the time Marley was seventeen, he was driving a Benz and had his own weed and heroin spots down on Franklin Avenue. Daphne worked out of Marley's uncle's Jamaican restaurant, where they secretly sold weed and heroin. She couldn't have been happier. Soon afterward, both of them moved out of the projects into a two-story home in St. Albans, Queens. They traveled to Jamaica a lot to visit his relatives. No matter what, Marley always treated her the same, like when they first met, and Daphne swore she would never love another man like she did him. She never did.

Her world came crashing down in 1987, when federal authorities raided Marley's spots on Franklin Avenue and their home in Queens. Daphne was working in the restaurant when the raids were being carried out, while Marley was home. She, along with the others, were all arrested and taken to the federal building in Brooklyn.

The next day Daphne received the most heart-breaking news: she found out about her lover's murder. Marley was gunned down by agents during the raid. He was shot a total of forty-one times and died instantly.

After a lengthy two-month trial, Daphne and fourteen other defendants were convicted on various charges under the RICO statute. The only evidence they had on her was her voice on the phone with Marley, talking about orders of beef patties. A government witness lied and said she was referring to drugs.

Daphne was given fifteen years. She knew the Feds were being hard on her because she refused to cooperate. The time did not matter to her. It didn't matter if she got out of jail. As far as she was concerned, life was over. Life without Marley was something she did not want to face. Many days and nights she thought about taking her own life, but she just did not have the courage to pull it off. Even though she was depressed, she tried to take her brother's advice and smile but couldn't. Then she met Ruby.

The two women were inseparable in the prison, except for when they were locked in their cells. Daphne didn't cell up with Ruby, because she celled up with only her lesbian lovers. She respected Ruby because she reminded her of her brother and Marley in certain ways. Ruby was bossy like her brother and laid-back like Marley.

At first she was skeptical of Ruby. All the women in the prison were scared of her, so Daphne stayed away. Ruby was in great shape, with a muscular, well-toned body that was still distinctly feminine, like Serena Williams, the tennis star. However, Daphne was sure that she did not want to get into a confrontation with her, so she avoided her.

It was inevitable that the two would meet due to their being from New York. In the federal system, it was customary for inmates from the same cities to clique up. They sat at the same tables in the mess halls and shared space in the rec yard. In the prison they were at, it was a little different for New York inmates. There New York inmates cliqued up with people from their own borough of the city. Ruby and Daphne being from Brooklyn made it more likely that they would cross paths.

After meeting Ruby, Daphne had a different opinion of her. She understood Ruby's rough exterior was a defense to ward off people who would take her kindness for weakness. Growing up in Brownsville, Ruby learned to take that approach at an early age. Daphne could identify with her, and they quickly bonded, with Ruby nicknaming her "Smiley."

In January 2000 Daphne was released, two years before Ruby's conviction was overturned. They kept in contact with each other, and Daphne made sure that Ruby's commissary account stayed full. Every month she would send Ruby five hundred dollars. Though Ruby didn't need that much, holding down a job as a cook in the prison mess hall, she saved the money Daphne sent her. The only thing she would spend some of the money on was phone cards to call and talk to her niece and her niece's boyfriend, Shamel, who was also her secret lover and who also kept Ruby's commissary full.

Daphne was on the street when Ruby received the news of Mecca lying in a coma after being shot and Shamel's death. Ruby also got the news that two days before she walked out of prison, Shamel's grandmother passed away. To say Ruby was ready for war was an understatement. She already held the guilt of being responsible for Mecca's parents being murdered, and now her niece sitting up in a coma because she couldn't protect her was too much. She had watched Shamel grow from a boy to a man, and even though they were sneaking around behind Mecca's back, she still cared about him. Shamel's grandmother dying was the icing on the cake. They always said tragedy came in threes, and those three events put Ruby on edge. Once she got out, she would have business to take care of. Daphne joined her at the funeral, and afterward, Daphne laid out the beginning of her and Ruby's plan to rule Brooklyn.

"Weed is really popping now. Marley's family in Jamaica gave me two hundred and fifty grand when I came home. I opened a restaurant in Crown Heights, which served to quadruple the money I invested in a short amount of time. I got a weed contact from them also in Texas. If you want, you can fly with me out there this weekend and see what kind of stuff they got. You want the best so you can make lots of paper."

After Daphne gave Ruby fifty grand to go shopping, she smiled and asked, "You ready?"

"You know it!" Ruby told her while they embraced.

They drove from the Brooklyn cemetery in Daphne's 1999 pistachio green 750iL BMW. When they stopped at the restaurant, the rays of the sunny day gleamed off a candy-apple red, two-door convertible Benz with a big purple bow on the hood.

"Somebody about to get a big surprise around here," Ruby said, looking out the passenger window at the Benz.

"I know." Daphne smiled.

Ruby looked at her holding a key in her hand. Puzzled, she looked at the key as Daphne held it out to her. Then she noticed the Mercedes-Benz insignia on the key.

"Welcome home, Ruby."

"Get out of here. No, you didn't!" Ruby screamed out.

"Yes, I did! Now, get in it and go see your niece."

At the mention of her niece, Ruby's smile quickly vanished. She knew she would have to toughen up and face what she felt she couldn't. Her mind was filled with guilt: she blamed herself for Mecca's condition. Every thought made her regret bringing her into this game. It had cost her years of freedom and almost the life of her beloved niece.

"It's not your fault, Ruby. It's about get back. Now it's your time," Daphne said in a measured tone of reassurance.

Ruby simply nodded her head and grabbed the keys.

Immediately, she got in and inhaled the fresh smell of the beige leather interior. When she started the car, she became more excited at the sound of the engine. She hit a button, and the convertible roof mechanically drew back. All the while Daphne kept a smile on her face, happy that her friend was home and excited for her.

Ruby looked over at Daphne, as the cars were parked parallel to each other. "You coming with me?" she asked while Daphne tossed her a CD.

Ruby stared at the Alicia Keys CD while Daphne answered, "Spend time with your niece, and call me when you're done. I'll show you where you're staying."

Ruby nodded. She placed the CD in the system and pulled off. It didn't even matter to her that she didn't have her license. It was the Brooklyn way!

Karmen lay on her back, unsatisfied, as a casual sex partner of hers humped like a rabbit, dripping sweat on her dry skin. This was the last time she'd be giving this dude some pussy. He fucked like he had just lost his virginity! Even his grunting was irritating to her.

"This pussy good, Ma. Who pussy is this?"

"Are you done yet?" she asked instead of responding to his question, her tone filled with irritation.

With his eyes closed, he held on to her thick hips and mumbled. After he released his fluid into the condom, Karmen quickly got up and walked to the small motel room bathroom, slamming the door.

"It's hard to find a good dick these days. All these cats think about themselves," Karmen said to herself while standing in front of the mirror, fixing her long hair into a ponytail.

Ever since her boyfriend was killed and her secret lover Shamel was murdered, Karmen had yet to find a man that could bring her to orgasm. Most of the men she dated were men she dealt with in her new hustle. Credit card scams.

More often, the men in the scam were African immigrants, who were usually in the country illegally and used American women. They would take the women all over the country, getting thousands of dollars of merchandise with other people's credit cards, then selling the merchandise at a cheaper price. Karmen was under the impression that these African men, with their Mandingo dicks, would be good lovers in bed. She was sorely disappointed. A lot of them were a waste of big dicks, and even if they were decent lovers, Karmen couldn't get into it, because the guy didn't believe in deodorant. She held her breath most of the time in bed.

With the credit card scam, the money she made with her partners in crime was decent, but not enough to satisfy her thirst for the hottest and latest in fashion and a means of paying the bills. Gone were the days when her boyfriend, now dead, would give her money and Shamel, after dicking her down, would do the same.

So her choice was easy. At Shamel's grandmother's funeral, Mecca's aunt had offered her a job at a grocery store she was opening up, where groceries weren't the only thing being sold. Karmen didn't hesitate to take the offer.

Meeting Mecca's aunt felt like meeting a celebrity. Karmen had heard so much about her from Mecca and Shamel that she could barely believe it. She was a legend in Brownsville and East New York. She even noticed the resemblance between Mecca and her aunt, and she could also see where Mecca got her swagger.

When Karmen first met Mecca, she immediately took a liking to her. She had style, and she commanded respect from men and women alike. At first Karmen didn't feel guilty about having the affair with Shamel. They had known each other before Mecca met him. She was always at their grandmother's house when she dealt with one of his two cousins, Kaheem and Born.

The more she got to know Mecca, the more she felt guilty, but the good sex and money she was getting erased most of the guilt. Still, she was deeply saddened when she found out that Mecca had been shot and was in a coma. She visited her in the hospital often with Shamel's grandmother, who also loved Mecca like her own. Mecca had tears in her eyes when she came out of it and Shamel's grandmother told her that Shamel was dead. Her eyes just blinked. Now Karmen wondered how she would react when she was told about Grandma's death.

Karmen walked out of the bathroom, naked. The short charcoal black African guy who looked at her with lust in his eyes sat on the hotel bed, stroking his manhood, as if he was ready for another round of skin smacking. His look of lust turned into a gaze of disappointment when Karmen picked up her black thong and clothes and began to dress. He hated to see her cream-colored, gorgeously built body disappear in her clothes.

"You want to leave already?" he asked as his manhood shrunk.

Karmen rolled her eyes. "I'm outta here. Oh, I need that money, too." She pulled her purse strap over her shoulder and placed one hand on her shapely hips, with the other held out.

"We still have three hours left," he sulked in his thick accent.

Karmen walked over to his brown slacks, which were lying on the brown carpet, and went in his pockets.

"Wait. I will get it for you." He jumped up off the bed, but Karmen already held a wad of cash in her hands. She quickly counted a thousand dollars, then dropped the slacks and the rest of the cash on the floor and walked out of the room.

Growing up on the rough streets of Bushwick, Karmen learned at an early age that you couldn't wait around for things to just drop into your hands. You had to go out and take them with no fear. Fear was a hustler's worst enemy. And Karmen, who grew up poor, living in a crowded tenement with four sisters and a mother and father strung out on dope, knew if you let fear take over, you would starve.

Karmen hopped in a cab, smiling. Tomorrow she would head downtown to buy that Dolce & Gabbana blouse she had seen at Macy's. She reminded herself that she would go to a sex shop, too. It was time for her to get a vibrator. If you couldn't find someone to make you cum, might as well do it yourself. Nobody would treat you better than you would.

When she got to her Bushwick apartment building, she rode up in the elevator alone. Once at her floor, she got off and noticed two suited white men in front of her door. Confusion was written all over her round, pretty face.

"Can I help y'all?" she asked. It didn't take a rocket scientist to figure out that they were police, but suited cops usually meant major problems.

"Is your name Karmen Santiago?" one of them asked in a calm and even voice.

"Yes, that's me. What's up?" Karmen asked, nervousness filling her thick Brooklyn accent.

Both men flashed their badges. "Ms. Santiago, we are from Brooklyn North Homicide. We would like to ask you some questions concerning the murders of Kaheem and"—the cop speaking quickly looked at his pad—"his brother, whom they called Born. Can we come in, or would you like to take a ride to the station?"

"I sense you're not satisfied with the karma the people who've betrayed you are receiving," Lou said while sitting with his feet propped up on a large oak wood desk in what appeared to be a doctor's office.

"Lou, how many times do I have to tell you I'm not thinking about revenge? I just wanna move on with my life," Mecca replied, trying to sound sincere as she paced the office, staring at the paintings on the walls. She would say whatever she needed to say to Lou for him to release his hold on her and let her out of the hospital. Intrigued by the paintings, she skipped right by some, while others she stared at a little longer. Some of them, Mecca realized, were of her as a baby, her at eight, then her as a teenager, and finally there was a painting of her as the adult she was.

"Mecca, Mecca, my dear Mecca. Just how am I supposed to believe that after all you have seen and know about your so-called friends and family? That you just forgave and forgot?" Lou asked, sitting up, with his feet on the black carpeted floor.

For a moment, she stood in front of the painting of her at eight, hiding under a bed. "I've always been a grateful person, and now that I have a second chance at life, I want to show my gratitude. And you're just gonna have to take my word for it."

Lou walked over to Mecca. Standing next to her, he stared at the painting. He shook his head before saying, "Childhood is a golden age for mankind. So innocent and full of misunderstanding of this cruel world. To think it was Sigmund Freud who said that childhood is a time of uninterrupted bliss. Don't you wish you could have it back, Mecca?"

Suddenly, her dream state switched to the painting on the wall. Eight-year-old Mecca remembered hiding under the bed, with tears running down her face. She looked back and forth at her mother's and father's eyes, which held fear. Their voices were muffled due to the tape around them. Two men with guns barked menacingly at her father, while her mother cried.

The words the men said couldn't be heard in the dream. One of them removed the tape from around her father's mouth and was talking intimately with him. For the first time in her eight years she saw fear on her father's face. She remembered him as a fearless man who would stand up to anyone. He was their protector, their hero. No one messed with her or her mother because they were Bobby Blast's family.

Her father's fear heightened hers. Seeing the tears in her mother's eyes made her cry even more. She hated to see her mother cry. She could still remember the first time she saw it, back when Mommy and Daddy were arguing and her father stormed out of the apartment, yelling that he would never come back. Mecca cried as she lay in bed with her mother, until the middle of the night, when she felt her father hug both of them. She heard his voice mumble, "I love you. I will never leave y'all."

Then the only sound Mecca heard in the dream was the gunshots that took her mother's and father's life. Little Mecca stayed under the bed, and the two men left. She heard the door slam, then the footsteps. It took a while for her to look out from under the bed when a person's black, shiny shoes and the hem of his long trench coat came into view. She knew who it was. Then his face appeared, and he stretched out his hand.

"Come out from under the bed, Mecca. I will protect you. I will never leave."

Mecca awoke from the dream as the sun shined through the blinds over the hospital window. The rays beamed in between the slats, making lines of long triangular light appear across the walls of the room and on the bed. For a moment, she looked at the print of her feet under the white sheets.

Slowly, she pulled the sheets off of her body and placed her feet on the cold tiled floor. Instantly, she noticed the metal walker in front of a bedside table.

Taking hold of it, she stood slowly. Her first steps after lying in bed almost six months were shaky and wobbly. Her legs responded slowly as she took baby steps, eventually moving quicker toward the window. Parting the blinds, she stared out at the sunny Brooklyn streets and smiled.

"Mecca?" The voice made her turn and face the door. Ruby stood next to Karmen, who covered her mouth in shock. Her eyes watered, just as Ruby's did. The smile left Mecca's face, and she turned to stare back out at the Brooklyn scenery. Her only thought as she looked at the familiar streets was a simple one. These streets are mine.

Chapter Three

For they eat the bread of wickedness, and drink the wine of violence.

—Proverbs 4:16

Daphne hired five trusted women among Donovan's relatives to bag up pounds of weed. She instructed them to put the different types of exotic weed in small glass jars, small twenty-dollar bags, and sandwich bags, which she would sell as weight broken down into quarters, ounces, and halves. After showing Ruby to a furnished brownstone apartment in the Clinton Hill section of Brooklyn, she drove her to a gutted, abandoned store in Crown Heights.

"I bought this place six months ago," Daphne told her as they stood on the sidewalk, observing the bodega with its dirty yellow sign.

"The money clean?" Ruby asked with her hands in her black Enyce velour jacket.

"Of course. You know the Feds still watching."

Both women entered the store after Daphne opened it up. Ruby looked around at the dusty interior. With nothing special standing out, it appeared to be an average bodega, which almost every corner in New York City's neighborhoods had. Taking another step, Daphne crushed glass under her foot.

"With your friend Karmen working here, it will look like any other bodega."

Within a month, the store had been up and running. Karmen had two of her sisters, Maria and Tina, help her run the place. They quickly got a lot of business. Guys in Crown Heights began to frequent the store just to try to kick it with the three Puerto Rican cuties that worked there. Karmen was kind to all the guys and was flattered by their compliments, but she gave none of them the time of day. Her sisters were another story. Not only did they flirt with the guys, but they even left the store at times for quickies in a guy's car or apartment.

Karmen scolded them about their activities, but she knew it fell on deaf ears. She realized they would have to learn how to deal with the opposite sex the way she did. Eventually, she thought, they would get burnt out spreading their legs for everyone that paid attention to them, leaving them with sore pussies and broke pockets. Karmen knew she had to pay attention to business and also the illegal business being run out of the store, in the back. Ruby gave Karmen bagged-up weed to sell with these instructions.

"A person has to buy something like potato chips or a twenty-five-cent juice if they want some weed. Believe me, they will do it! This is some high-quality shit, better than any other spot in Brooklyn. I won't have a lot of it in the store at one time, but before you run out, always call this number," Ruby had instructed, handing her a small white card. "Just say, 'Wassup, shorty? You coming over?' and somebody will bring the next batch."

In no time, the word spread that the store in Crown Heights had some of the best smoke in town. Karmen and her sisters were enjoying the money they were making. The more money Ruby made, the more money she paid Karmen and her sisters, who did little with their money but shop for clothes and jewelry.

"Stack your money. There will always be rainy days ahead," Ruby had informed Karmen one day. Karmen knew that she was referring to her possibly going to jail. Karmen hated to think of that, and she really thought that the day would never come. It was just weed, but the thought of those homicide detectives still bothered her in the back of her mind. The cops found out from the landlord that her boyfriend, Kaheem, was killed in an apartment that was leased in her name, and right after the murder she moved.

"I couldn't sleep there anymore. It reminded me of him," Karmen cried. However, what the cops did not know was that her tears were from fear of them thinking she had something to do with the murders, and were not for her dead boyfriend.

"Where were you?" one of them asked while sitting on a wooden stool in her kitchen.

"I was at a friend's house in East New York," she lied as the scene played in her mind. She hadn't actually witnessed the murder. Shamel had ordered her to wait outside while he took care of his cousins, who were snakes. Murder, Karmen felt, Kaheem and Born deserved.

"Who might that friend be? Can that friend verify that?" the other cop grunted.

"She is in a hospital. She can't talk at this point," Karmen replied, referring to Mecca.

The cops finally left the apartment, telling her that they would more than likely be back to talk to her and giving her their cards, with the usual, "If you find out anything that will bring the killers to Darnell, give us a ring."

"I'll definitely do that."

Karmen figured they wouldn't get anything. Shamel was dead, and the only other person that knew about it was Mecca, and she couldn't talk. Even if she could, Karmen doubted she would talk to the cops about it. Then she figured that, hopefully, that bullet to the head had taken her memory. She was damn lucky that that bullet had only cracked her skull, just barely grazing her brain.

Still, she was shocked when they entered Mecca's room and saw her standing at the window with the aid of a walker. It seemed like a miracle to her. For months now, Mecca had lain in a coma, only to come out of it and not talk or move out of the bed. The doctors said that she wasn't paralyzed, that it was like a person coming out of a mild stroke, and that it would take time for the brain to recuperate from the trauma.

But she was still beautiful. Her hair grew back from when the doctors cut it to operate, but it wasn't long like it used to be. Her skin was no longer too pale and had gained some of its natural color back. Now all she had to do was gain her weight back and the old Mecca would emerge.

Still, this was the hardest time. During the following weeks, Mecca went through physical and speech therapy. She quickly got her swagger back, and though she talked, it was slow and low. Most of the time, she barely talked; she just glared at people. Karmen could swear that every time Mecca looked at her and Ruby, there was a look of anger or hate in her eyes. It was like she wanted to lash out, but something was holding her back. When Karmen brought it up to Ruby, she waved it off.

"She's just stressed and frustrated. That therapy could stress a person out. Can you imagine being a grown person having to learn how to walk and talk again like you're a baby?" Ruby tried to explain to Karmen so that she could understand. Though it made sense to Karmen, the look still left her shaken.

"Watch. The Mecca we know will be back. Did you hear about Tah Gunz?" Ruby asked as she drove her Benz through Manhattan traffic after a day of shopping for clothes with Karmen.

"Yeah, they say he in a wheelchair. That's messed up that Tamika got caught in the middle of that," Karmen replied, knowing that Ruby had never seen Tah face-to-face and couldn't wait to get her hands on him.

"Good for his ass," she growled, "and that little bitch Tamika had it coming too."

Looking over at Ruby, Karmen saw the same facial expression on her face that Mecca had had when she looked at her and her aunt. What was it?

"I have to make a stop uptown before we head back to Brooklyn," Ruby said, snapping Karmen out of her thoughts, but another quickly came to bother her. Now that Mecca could talk, would those cops question her about her alibi the night Kaheem got killed? All Karmen could do was hope Mecca didn't remember, or was she still the same Mecca before she got shot?

Thirteen years ago Alejandro Torres was a thirty-five-year-old Dominican with a medium build. At the time, he was a middleman on the Harlem drug scene. Now forty-eight and weighing close to three hundred pounds, he was an ex-convict fresh off a five-year bid for the sale of a kilo of cocaine to an undercover narcotics cop. His once curly black hair was now gray and cut short. His youthful appearance had gone, leaving a man with a deeply lined face who looked older than forty-eight years.

His Bronx parole officer had explained the conditions of his parole when he was released. The one rule that made him a loner on the streets was not to associate with known criminals or convicted felons. All his associates were criminals, and most were convicted felons. So on any given day, you could spot Alejandro in his everyday attire of Sergio Tacchini sweats suits, either playing dominoes in front of a bodega in the South Bronx or sitting on a park bench, feeding pigeons and ducks in a Central Park pond.

Today, though, Alejandro was in Central Park, lighting a cigar before he began feeding the pigeons. Suddenly a whole flock descended in front of the bench. He looked up from lighting his cigar and saw a black woman throwing down pieces of bread. The shades on her face hid her eyes, but he could tell she was a pretty dark brown lady from her profile.

"For a minute, I thought they were gonna come snatch the bread crumbs out of my hand," Alejandro said.

The woman simply smiled. Her sweat suit couldn't hide her firm, pointed breasts or her shapely body. During those five years in jail, Alejandro had collected a lot of porno magazines, and his favorites were the ones that featured thick black women. This stranger reminded him of one of those fantasies.

"I like the ducks better. They don't fly in crowds like these guys," Alejandro continued, trying to strike up a conversation with the woman.

"And they definitely don't bite the hands that feed them. Right, Al?" the woman said after looking at her Jacob watch. Her tone had a bite to it, which caught him off guard.

Alejandro stared at the woman quizzically, wondering how she knew his name. Since she had called him Al, she had to have known him for many years. Yet the woman didn't look familiar to him. It was the large shades that covered most of her face.

"If you're the police, there is no reason for you to be following me. I've been clean since I've been home. I'm done with the streets."

The woman took note of how well he spoke English now and laughed before pulling out a handgun with a silencer. Then she removed her shades. Alejandro thought he was looking at a ghost.

"I thought you had a . . ."

"Life sentence?" The woman completed the sentence for him.

Alejandro sighed, then proceeded to finish feeding the pigeons. He accepted the fact that she was there for one reason. Revenge. He realized that she must have gotten her sentence thrown out on appeal. Trying to show a brave face, he spoke to her with a surrendering tone.

"Ruby, so many years have gone by. I'm out of the game now. Why don't you let bygones be bygones?"

"I was straight up with you, but you tried to have me killed, like I would rat you out one day. I will never be a rat," Ruby answered.

"How did you find me?"

"I know people in high places," Ruby replied.

Alejandro had no idea that his parole officer, a black woman he sometimes flirted with, was the sister of Daphne's older sister, who had a different mother. In 1998 she became a parole officer after marrying a corrections officer who encouraged her to get into law enforcement. One thing she didn't want to be was a cop, so she chose parole so that she could help criminals stay out of jail by helping them attain employment and stay out of trouble. She was known to parolees as "the people's PO."

Daphne had convinced her sister to give her Alejandro's information by telling her that Alejandro was a friend of Donovan's whom she was trying to get in contact with. Daphne lied and told her that he gave Donovan a good deal on his first car, and she wanted to see if he was still in the car business. Her sister was reluctant because she could lose her job by divulging such sensitive information. Besides all that, it was against the law.

"You're about to visit that high place," Ruby said to him just before squeezing the trigger, sending bullets into Alejandro's chest.

He fell from the bench in a bloody heap, causing the pigeons to scatter from his sudden movement. She slipped away as the birds flew over her head, and no one in the area witnessed anything. Ruby walked out of the park to where Karmen was sitting, waiting for her in the Benz. When she reached the car, she smiled.

"Nothing like a walk in the park to get your blood flowing," Ruby said with a smile as they pulled off. She was cool with the way everything went, and was even happier to learn that Mecca was getting discharged from the hospital the next day.

Mecca found it hilarious that Lou was dressed in plaid pants, white patent leather shoes, and a bright yellow sweater.

"Church?" Mecca asked, surprised.

"Why are you surprised that I said church?" Lou paused from tapping a golf ball into a paper cup to stare at Mecca's back while she stared at a painting of herself as teenager, wearing big gold door-knocker earrings, a small rope chain around her neck, and a green Gap sweat suit.

"Because you're like a demon or something. The devil, right?" Mecca turned her head, looking at him with a grin.

"If I'm the devil, then what are you, Mecca?"

"I believe in God," she answered.

"And I don't?" Lou asked. "The devil does evil deeds, as you were taught. So what do you call selling drugs, killing other humans, stealing, extorting, and all the other commandments that you violated?"

Mecca sucked her teeth and waved Lou off. "Heard it all before, Lou. It's overrated now. I'm not the church-going type, anyway. I can pray at home."

"Prayer means nothing if after you pray, you go out and do the evil deeds again that you asked forgiveness for. Are you that shallow, Mecca?"

Mecca ignored Lou and looked back at the painting of herself in her teens. Then her dream switched from Lou's office to her and her former best friend, Dawn, hanging out at the Albee Square Mall in downtown Brooklyn. They were dressed stylishly eighties as they roamed the crowded mall. Then Mecca came in eye contact with a girl who, she'd noticed, had been staring at her since she and Dawn entered the mall. For some reason, every time they would cross paths during their two hours in the mall, the hazel-eyed girl would glare at her as if she knew her.

"Why is that bitch down your throat?" Dawn asked, noticing the girl staring at Mecca.

Mecca knew it couldn't be jealousy. The girl was dressed twice as nice. She saw the girl's jewelry and knew she couldn't compete with this strange girl, and she had to admit the girl was pretty. So what was her problem? Oddly, the girl would then turn away and walk off with an older girl that looked like her sister or mother.

When she and Dawn left the mall, they spotted the girl. Mecca couldn't tell if the girl was her age or older, but if she guessed, the girl was older. Again, the strange girl glared at Mecca as she and the other woman entered a burgundy Jeep Wrangler. Mecca couldn't read the look, so she simply watched the girl take off a Louis Vuitton coat, place it in the Jeep's backseat, get in, and take one more look at her as the driver pulled off.

"Girl, I know you ain't get another chick's man to like you like that bitch we had to cut," Dawn blurted.

"Can't help it if I'm beautiful. It ain't my fault." Mecca grinned.

A week later Mecca was watching TV in the Coney Island apartment she lived in with her aunt. A woman's face flashed across the screen while the news reporter was talking about a large drug bust in Bed-Stuy. She was sure the woman's face was that of the girl she'd seen at the mall. It just had to be her. Those piercing eyes, she recognized. By the time Mecca turned the TV up, the report of the bust was over. Then his face appeared on the screen. It was the guy with the leather trench coat and neat Afro. He smiled.

Mecca awoke in her queen-sized bed. She looked around the spacious bedroom with all the "welcome home" balloons, cards, and flowers spread around. Just then she remembered she was at Ruby's brownstone apartment. She got up, washed, ate a bowl of Cinnamon Toast Crunch cereal, and dressed.

Realizing that Ruby wasn't there, Mecca decided that she would take Lou up on his advice and go to church. At least that was what she put on the letter she placed on the refrigerator. Mecca had other plans.

Chapter Four

If you seek her as silver, and search for her as for hidden treasures, then you will understand the fear of the Lord and find the knowledge of God.

—Proverbs 2:4–5

When Ruby introduced Daphne to Mecca, Mecca's heart skipped a beat when she saw her eyes. She could not believe how much her eyes resembled the girl's in her dream. Those same penetrating hazel eyes. Mecca wondered what the significance of it all was. Who was she? She could not remember her when she was a teenager; she never saw that girl in her life. But those eyes! Mecca simply stared at Daphne as she smiled, a beautiful display of even white teeth. It was Daphne's smile that made Mecca feel as if she was a kind, cool person who had an inviting personality. She found Daphne's voice soothing and easy. Not loud and ghetto, but confident, with a swagger to her, which made Mecca begin to like her.

Over a soul food dinner that Ruby and Daphne had cooked, Daphne told Mecca all about herself. Mecca could tell she wasn't telling everything, but Mecca respected that. You never put all your cards on the table. Always be mysterious; keep people guessing and off balance. That was what she had learned from her life in the game. When people had you figured out, then they began to plot and scheme how to remove you. When you were mysterious, they didn't know how to plot on you.

Yet Mecca liked the fact that Daphne was loyal and a hustler. Qualities she wished everyone around her could have. Still, she would never put her full trust in anyone again. At the same time, Daphne grew fond of Mecca. She reminded her of herself. She could tell that she listened more than she talked, and she also noticed that Mecca was very observant. Mecca wouldn't open up to her, and like Mecca, Daphne respected her for that. She knew you had to feel a person out, measure them to see what they were fit for. A lot of people put on acts like they were fit for the game, but when things got bad, people put their tail between their legs like scared dogs.

Daphne was a good reader of people, but she couldn't read the look in Mecca's eyes. Especially when she looked at her aunt Ruby and Karmen. She had not known Mecca long enough to read the gaze, but her instinct told her something was not right. Still, the women bonded. They had the same taste in style. Daphne put micro braids in Mecca's hair so her real hair could grow quickly. The scar from her operations was barely visible and was covered by the braids.

One afternoon, as they drove through Manhattan after they ate at a downtown restaurant, the three women silently stared at Ground Zero, where the World Trade Center used to be. They were in their own thoughts at what they were seeing.

Thinking to herself, Mecca realized that in the few months she'd been in a coma, the world had changed quickly. Daphne simply thought about how crazy it must have been for the people who got caught in that mess. Ruby realized that was why the price of weight went so high and there were so many cops. Bin Laden got shit hot!

Daphne showed Mecca her restaurant, gave her a tour, and then drove over to Ruby's grocery store that Karmen ran. Once in the store, she noticed the look again when Mecca saw Karmen behind the bulletproof glass Ruby had installed.

Ruby knew that the stickup men would think the spot was sweet, being that it was run by young women, so she wanted Karmen and her sisters to feel secure. Also it would give Karmen time to toss the stash of weed in a secret compartment under the cash register that led to a barrel of acid in the basement. If the cops raided, there would be no evidence.

"Hey, Mecca!" Karmen said excitedly, coming from behind the bulletproof glass.

"What's up, Karmen?" Mecca simply nodded with a forced smile.

Karmen and Ruby showed Mecca the store and how the whole operation was set up.

"Weed is really poppin' now, Mecca. It's like crack in the eighties," Ruby told her.

"It's cheaper, and you don't get a lot of time in jail," Karmen added.

"That's what's up," Mecca responded but was really thinking how she wanted to put both their asses in a casket.

After the tour of the store, Ruby and Daphne surprised Mecca by taking her to a Queens car lot. As soon as they walked in the showroom, a tall, tanned white man in an expensive suit walked up to Daphne with a hug and a smile.

"Daphne, I was expecting you yesterday. Everything is ready. Here are the keys." He handed the keys to Daphne, who then turned and handed them to a confused Mecca.

"On behalf of me and Ruby, welcome home!" Daphne said.

"What are you talking about, Daphne?" Mecca asked.

"Let's show her," Ruby chimed. They walked out into the lot and pointed to a silver, fully equipped 4.6 Range Rover.

"It's yours, baby!" Ruby pointed to the truck. Mecca loved it, and immediately, she climbed in the driver's seat, took in the smell of the black leather interior, and scanned the features.

"You ready to pull out?" Daphne asked from the passenger-side window.

"I think so."

"I'll ride with you just in case. Ruby, drive my car," Daphne said as she threw the keys. "I'm riding with Mecca."

At first Mecca drove slowly and cautiously. Then the feeling of familiarity set in, and she shed the nervous feeling and cruised to the sounds of Jay-Z's *The Blueprint* CD. Daphne looked at Mecca's expression and smiled. Her spirits seemed to be up, but Daphne knew there was something she had hidden deep within her soul, something she wanted to let out, but she seemed not to have anyone she could trust. That made her confused because in prison, Ruby would be elated to receive visits and letters from her niece. They seemed to have a sisterly relationship. Daphne knew that Ruby took her in after Mecca's parents were killed and raised her like her own. So why the look of scorn? Daphne knew she would have to get to the bottom of this to learn more about her new friend Mecca.

Later that night, while Ruby and Daphne went to a WNBA game at Madison Square Garden, Daphne's restaurant was robbed by two armed, masked men. Marley's sister was closing the place when someone placed something hard against her back.

"What you gonna do is open the place and take us to the safe. If not, you die here," the voice said in a skin-crawling, menacing grunt. She did as she was told. Marley's sister, Andrea, found it kind of strange that the men knew exactly where the safe was and where they had stashed some weed. In no more than five minutes, the two robbers left with two pounds of weed and fifty grand in cash.

Still shaken from the ordeal, Andrea locked the door from the inside, sat on the floor by the cash register, and called Daphne. Sitting courtside, Daphne felt her phone vibrate on her hip.

"Hello?" she yelled.

"Da . . . Da . . ." Andrea stuttered.

Daphne covered one of her ears. "Hello? Who's this?"

"Daphne, it's Drea!" she managed to yell.

"Drea? What's up?"

"I just got robbed!" she cried. Daphne did not hear her clearly and asked her again. This time, she heard every word.

"I'm on my way, Drea. Don't go nowhere!"

"You can't front, Lou. I'm doing good, despite the fact that they didn't receive their karma for what they did to me," Mecca said while they walked through a children's ward at a hospital. Glancing in each room, Mecca saw children suffering from various ailments and injuries. They stared at Mecca as they walked by, reminding her of the hazel-eyed girl she saw in the mall.

"So, all the time your aunt did in jail, you don't consider that a consequence of her acts?" Lou asked, checking the security guard uniform he wore.

"Yeah, I guess so." Mecca shrugged.

"And Karmen has her own problems. Her life isn't peaches and cream, and she is playing with fire by what she is doing right now," Lou said as he walked into a room where a doctor was standing, holding a long needle filled with clear liquid. The sight of it simply frightened Mecca.

"What is he going to do with that?" She looked at Lou quizzically. Lou had a smile on his face.

"Don't worry. You won't feel a thing. You're dreaming, Mecca." The doctor approached her and took a firm hold on her arm. She tried to pull back, but she couldn't move as Lou held her tightly from behind.

"Mecca," he said, "trust me, it won't hurt. Have I ever lied to you?"

"I don't want no needle, Lou. I'm not sick!"

"It's just a truth serum. It will be quick."

He held the needle up before her face and pressed on the plunger, watching as the liquid squirted out of the sharp tip. The pinch of the needle caused her dream to switch back to her teens. She was sitting in Gershwin Park with Dawn, watching a basketball game between a Brownsville and an East New York team. They were cheering for their neighborhood team when a voice from behind startled her.

"Take the necklace and watch off. Don't turn around, or I'll clap you."

Mecca felt the gun against her back. From the corner of her eye she saw Dawn reach over to her and remove the earrings and necklace. Confusion spread in her mind as to why Dawn was helping them rob her.

"You always thought you was all that," she said with a smile.

Then Mecca heard a shot. She ducked as the crowd scrambled and screams could be heard everywhere. When she got up, Lou stood in front of her with a spent casing in his hand. He looked at the bullet and simply said, "A few more inches to the left and it would have pierced your brain. Don't play with death, Mecca."

Mecca awoke with Ruby shaking her arm.

"Mecca, get up, girl. You got to see the doctor today."

"What time is it?" Wiping the cold from her eyes, she yawned and responded in her groggy morning voice. Ruby took a quick glimpse at her watch.

"It's nine o'clock in the morning. C'mon. Your appointment is at nine thirty. Whoever this guy Lou is you're dreaming about must got some good sex," Ruby continued as she walked out of the room.

Mecca was shocked.

The very same morning, Karmen opened up the store, and he walked in. He wore a black, sleeveless Sean John sweater over a white, short-sleeved, collared shirt. Karmen stared at his black jeans from behind, admiring his physique. He was one of the finest men she had seen in a long time. His creamy complexion was smooth and flawless; his jet-black hair was silky and curly, with a sharp line up from his forehead to his five o'clock shadow. His eyes were a pretty brown, and when he approached the glass partition, his voice was harmoniously deep and sexy.

"Do you have any eggnog?" Miguel Sanchez asked. Karmen snapped out of her infatuated daze and answered.

"Yeah, all the way in the back. I'll show you."

She quickly came from behind the glass and walked Miguel to the freezer, making sure she walked in front of him so he could get a glimpse of her voluptuous measurements. It didn't take long for him to assess Karmen's goods. Her blue denim jeans hugged her frame like a leotard on a ballet dancer.

Opening the freezer, she grabbed the eggnog and turned to hand it to him. She almost bumped into him as they came face-to-face. She could smell his cologne, and Karmen felt herself become wet between her thighs. His six feet made his chest come almost near her face, and she could see he was in good shape.

"I'm sorry," he said, stepping back and taking the eggnog.

"It's nothing." She blushed.

She knew she had to say something to him. She would kick herself in the ass if she let him get away. That was her motto in life. "Don't let a good opportunity pass, because you will regret it." The last time a man made her wet just by the way he looked was a long time ago, and he was no longer alive. She had to have this one.

"Are you from around here?" she asked as she was walking back toward the door that led behind the counter.

"Yes, I am. I just returned from overseas, playing basketball," he replied. "By the way, my name is Miguel."

"I'm Karmen."

She was satisfied, she had accomplished her goal. She got him to stay awhile and talk. She learned that he was originally from the Bronx. He was of Panamanian descent, and he lived by himself in an apartment around the corner from the store.

"I heard a lot about this store," he said, giving her a grin.

"Yeah? What have you heard?" Karmen asked curiously. She hoped that he wasn't one of those guys who looked down on a woman for hustling to get a dollar by any means except for degrading herself by selling her body. Though, Karmen didn't knock the hustle.

Miguel's smile grew wider. "I heard good things, and I'm wondering if I can get a sample." His dimples made her melt. She gave him a jar of the best weed they had in the store. "When do you get off of work?"

"Later tonight," she answered.

"Cool. Here's my address. . . ."

Later that night the two of them couldn't wait to rip each other's clothes off in Miguel's simply decorated apartment. They didn't even make it to his bed when they kissed each other passionately, removing their clothing at the same time, stopping only to pull shirts over their heads. Karmen rubbed his ripped abdomen and felt the harness of his athletic body. He picked her up off her feet, kissing her while she guided his thick manhood inside her creamy walls.

"Ay, Poppy!" she moaned as he put her back against a small closet door and slowly moved his hips, feeling the warmth of her insides grip his shaft. The tightness made him grit his teeth. He walked over to a couch, still holding her, and then laid her on her back, pushing himself deeper in her middle.

"Shit, Miguel! I'm coming, baby!" Her juices soaked his pole and pubic hairs. She scratched his back as orgasm after orgasm pulsed through her body.

In every position from doggy style to her riding him, she felt as if she no longer owned her body. It was his to do as he pleased. To spice up the sex, Karmen even let him give her anal pleasure, which she hollered all the way through. After three ejaculations from him and countless orgasms from her, they finally rested in each other's arms on the carpeted living-room floor, with Miguel staring at the ceiling fan .

"Do you have a girlfriend?" Karmen asked while catching her breath.

"No. Why?"

Karmen smiled. "You do now."

Chapter Five

With her enticing speech she caused him to yield, with her flattering lips she seduced him.

—Proverbs 7:21

"Has that ever happened before, Daphne?"

"Not since I been home. The thing is, if it were a random robbery, I would take the loss. But these people knew exactly where the stuff was at," Daphne replied angrily as she and Ruby sat at Ruby's kitchen table, discussing the holdup. Daphne was convinced it wasn't Andrea who had set it up, because when she arrived at the restaurant, Andrea was too shaken for it to be an act. Plus she trusted her. Andrea was extremely loyal to Daphne due to Daphne's loyalty to her brother and family. After seeing Andrea like that, Daphne told her to take off as long as she needed, while she got to the bottom of things.

Immediately word went out around Crown Heights that whoever had information on who pulled the heist would get a hefty reward. The loss was nothing to Daphne; however, it was a matter of principle. A lesson had to be taught.

"Can you think of anybody who would do this? A past enemy or jealous hater that would take it there?" Ruby asked, sipping a hot cup of coffee. Her question reminded Daphne of a lesson Marley had always reminded her of when he said, "There are no friends in the game, baby. Matters of the heart have no place with matters of greed." Once again, Daphne had a feeling that his words would prove prophetic.

"None that I can think of."

Mecca walked in, sliding her slippers across the tiled kitchen floor, wearing a black silk two-piece pajama set and scarf on her head. Instantly, both Ruby and Daphne stopped discussing the robbery.

"Wassup, Mecca?" Daphne asked, happy to see her. "What you doing tonight, girl? You got to go out on the town and hit a club with me! You with it?"

Mecca thought about her invite while looking in the cupboard for a box of cereal. Then, as if someone had cut a light on in Mecca's head, she turned and smiled. "Yeah, let's do it."

That night, while Mecca and Daphne went to the club, Ruby drove over to Crown Heights to drop off a package to Karmen at the store. Listening to Heather Headley's voice bang through the car's sound system, Ruby was in deep thought about the robbery of Daphne's restaurant. The whole thing reminded her of the time her spots in Brownsville were being robbed daily. At one time, she thought it was just random, but she found out it was the old cat named Stone. A hustler turned addict she had employed as a lookout and to give out packages to the workers. He was allowing the spots to get robbed by a crew he feared. Tah Gunz's crew.

The last thing Ruby wanted to think was that Daphne could be behind the setup. Ruby knew you couldn't control the way someone might think, but if you took control of the situation, then you could persuade people to see things your way. She knew that she had to find out who was behind the robbery, for her sake and Daphne's. If Daphne started showing any signs of mistrust toward Ruby, she would act first before Daphne made a move. Damn! It was never a smooth ride in the game.

Ruby walked in the store with a plastic shopping bag containing the package of weed Karmen called for. The store was unusually empty, and

Karmen stood behind the glass partition with a strange look on her face. Her sisters weren't chatting in front of the store with a group of guys, as was their normal routine, nor were they standing around inside the store, watching the small TV they had installed behind the cold-meat counter.

The sound of a gun being cocked was all she heard, followed by, "You want to drop the bag and put your hands up, and don't try to be a superhero, or you'll end up super dead."

Ruby did as she was told.

"Turn around," the voice commanded.

Slowly, Ruby turned around, and she saw Karmen being led out from behind the counter by a man in a black mask, leather peacoat, holding a shotgun to her back. Out the side of her eye, she saw Karmen's two sisters being brought out from the back of the store by another masked man, holding what looked like an AK-47.

"Boss lady, you gonna open up the safe in the back and give us what we came for," the guy holding the gun to Ruby said in a low growl.

Listening carefully, she tried to recognize the voice, but after thirteen years of being off the streets, how could she? Knowing where the safe was hidden was an indication that these guys knew either her, Karmen, or her sisters. They had to know them, because only they knew there was a safe hidden inside one of the freezers, covered by juices and milk. Ruby didn't believe in coincidences. First, Daphne's restaurant, then the store. She ruled out Karmen because she knew nothing about Daphne's restaurant. *Who are these people?* she wondered as she walked to the safe.

As Ruby walked, she mumbled to the guy, "I'll pay you double the amount you're getting out of this if you tell me who sent you."

The guy chuckled and then put the gun to her ear. "Listen, bitch, live or die. That's the only options round here right now."

Since Ruby just got out of jail, she was nervous about carrying guns. Added with the ever-present sight of the NYPD everywhere you went in New York City as a result of Mayor Giuliani's crusade against the city's criminal world, she wished she had hers on her now. These guys didn't even bother searching her. Just another indication that this was an inside job.

When it was over, the guys made out of the store with ten thousand dollars' worth of weed that Ruby had in her bag and thirty thousand in cash from the safe. Not to mention the thousand in the cash register from the sale of groceries. Karmen and her sisters were crying and shaken up, just as Andrea was. Ruby was infuriated.

"Ya'll stop bitching! You're alive! Go home and sleep it off. I'll call you tomorrow, Karmen."

Walking out of the store, Ruby hopped into her whip and sped off. She didn't know where she was driving to; she just drove in deep thought. She guessed it was a natural instinct of hers from the time she ruled the rugged streets she grew up on, but her aimless driving had her wind up in her native Brownsville.

When she looked at the street signs that read Rockaway Avenue and Livonia Avenue , she asked herself, *What am I doing here?* She knew she would need to buy an arsenal, and what better place to get something hot than Brownsville? Someone referred her to an apartment in the Brownsville Houses where a person could buy any kind of gun they wanted. That someone was Mecca.

Being back in Brownsville brought back so many memories for her. The thugs on the corners, the loud young girls on project benches, the kids in playgrounds, and the sight of police cruisers speeding down avenues reminded her of the good ole days.

When she entered the building, a blunt-smoking crew of young, do-rag- and oversized-clothes-wearing guys paused from their animated conversations about the hottest rapper out to stare lustfully, skeptically, and questionably at the thick, sexy Ruby in a pair of form-hugging jeans and a black and blue North Face. The Halle Berry haircut fit her facial features, but to some of the young cats, it spelled *dike*.

Ruby knocked on the door. The sound of music blasted from apartments. The familiar project hallway smelled of customary old urine, paint from a freshly painted elevator door, and burning garbage from the incinerator. Yes, the good ole days. A frail, shirtless teenager answered the door. Looking at him, Ruby thought he was probably five years old when she got locked up.

"What's good, Ma?" the rotten-toothed kid asked, sticking his nappy head out of the door and looking around skeptically.

"I need some steel," Ruby stated.

"You police?" the kid asked.

Ruby smirked. "If I was, I would have been ran up in there. No, I'm not police. Ask an older person in that crib about Ruby from Langston Hughes."

Upon hearing the name, the kid's eyes lit up. Everyone in Brownsville had heard of the notorious female gangster Ruby, and everyone had heard she was back on the streets. He stepped back, holding the door open to invite her in. Entering the small apartment, she quickly inhaled the always present aroma of weed smoke. The house was so smoky, she thought she would be stoned out of her mind by the time she left. There was barely any furniture in the apartment, nothing but a couch that was so dirty, you couldn't tell its original color, a glass coffee table littered with ashtrays and stains from both food and ashes, and a stereo system. Two guys sat on the filthy couch; one was asleep with his mouth open, and the other was smoking a blunt. When he looked at Ruby, his eyes were squinted and as red as a blood-soaked gauze.

"Yo, Mo!" the teen who answered the door yelled.

"Yo, what's up!" A tall, lanky guy entered the living room, looked at Ruby. He immediately recognized her from back in the days when he ran with Tah's stickup crew. He remembered they would stick up her spots, until Tah Gunz fell in love with her niece. She was a legend, but only in the eighties. Those days were gone. Mo Blood wondered what she was doing here. Did she know who he was?

"What you looking for, Ma?" Mo asked, hiding his nervousness with a cocky appearance.

"I'm looking for some guns. I was told this is the spot."

Mo lit up a cigarette. Inhaled and then spoke. "And who told you that?"

"That's not here or there. Y'all got what I need or not?" Ruby replied with a cocky tone of her own. She knew she could have gone to Daphne to get guns, but her pride wouldn't let her depend on Daphne for everything. She was used to being independent and in charge. So she decided to get what she needed on her own accord.

"Any kind in particular?" Mo asked.

When the purchase was final, Ruby, with the help of Mo Blood and two other goons, carried two duffel bags down to her Benz. Mo Blood admired the car enviously and realized that she didn't waste any time doing her thing. Niggas been hustling for years and couldn't even cop a decent set of wheels. Ruby spent ten thousand in cash on two AK-47s, an AR-15, three .50-caliber Desert Eagles, and a .40-caliber handgun.

"If you're with it, I can get you the best weed in Brooklyn. My prices are good," Ruby told Mo before she got in the car.

"We'll talk. You got a way I can reach you?"

Ruby reached in the glove compartment, removed a pen, and wrote her cell phone number down. As she was handing the number to Mo, a man in a second-floor apartment had a camcorder aimed at both of them. Their every movement was captured and recorded on tape. He even caught her speeding off.

"I ain't never been that scared in my life, I swear," Karmen said as she sat in Ruby's living room, telling Mecca the details of the robbery, while Miguel sat beside her on a brown suede couch.

Mecca simply acted like she was listening enthusiastically, but she couldn't get how good-looking Miguel was out of her mind. Being in a coma and recovering from it had definitely put a dent in her sex life. And with so much on her mind, she hadn't had the time to think of a man's company. Yet seeing Miguel made all those feelings of wanting to be held and made love to by a strong man surface.

Even though she was lusting over Karmen's new boyfriend, Mecca didn't feel guilty. Images of Karmen and Shamel sleeping together kept entering her mind, and that made lusting over Miguel all the more justifiable. Now she was thinking of the challenge of getting him in bed.

Her glares didn't go unnoticed by Miguel, either. When he first laid eyes on her, he found it hard to believe that she had just come out of a coma after being shot in the head. She was absolutely beautiful. Yes, Karmen was, too, but in an "around-the-way girl" way. Mecca, on the other hand, had an aura of sexy classiness. When she looked at a person, it was as if she were staring into the person's soul. He admired her ability to listen more than she talked. He couldn't say that about Karmen: she babbled all day long about things that didn't interest him. Sure, the sex was good, but her personality became boring. She wasn't a challenge.

Mecca, on the other hand, reminded him of his mother. Same golden complexion, same sexy eyes. The graceful manner in which she walked and talked. At the same time, she wasn't a pushover. A man had to tread carefully with her. She reeked of independence.

"It's all part of the game, Karmen," Mecca said.

Karmen excused herself to go to the bathroom, while Mecca and Miguel remained in the living room. She pulled out a deck of cards from her pants pocket and looked at him. "Do you play tunk?"

"I'm the best," he bragged.

Mecca grinned. "How much money you got?"

Miguel returned the grin. "How much you willing to lose?"

"Oooh, cocky. There's nothing sexier than a confident man," she cooed.

"Likewise with a woman." Miguel gave her his sexy smile.

In that little exchange both of them knew they wanted each other. With money Ruby and Daphne had been giving her to do as she pleased, Mecca removed a stack from her pocket and held it up before his face.

'That's three stacks. I could afford to lose more, but I doubt I will. You be easy on yourself now," Mecca taunted.

Miguel smiled. He removed a small stack of bills from his wallet. "Not much cash, but I got this." He showed her his platinum Visa card. "I got an idea. Whoever wins the best of five, the loser treats to dinner."

"Ya'll playing cards? What y'all playing?" Karmen asked as she entered the living room.

Mecca rolled her eyes. "It's a bet."

A week later Mecca snuck off to a Manhattan restaurant. The place was elegant and exquisite. It was definitely a place where the rich and famous dined. The menu was made up of Italian cuisine, and everything looked or sounded just as good.

After plates of veal Parmesan, pasta in a delicate cream sauce, a bottle of Krug champagne, and a conspiratorial plan to hang out again a few days later, Miguel told the maître d', "Check please. I'm paying by card."

"Why the truth serum, Lou?" Mecca asked while being strapped down by her wrists and ankles to a hospital gurney.

"It's self-explanatory, my dear." Lou, still wearing the security guard uniform, stood over her in the brightly lit room and smiled.

"Truth about what?" Mecca looked at him quizzically as she struggled with the restraints.

"About what you're up to. Do you think I am a fool, Mecca?"

"I swear, Lou, I don't know what you're talking about," Mecca whined in a pleading tone.

Lou leaned closer to her face and stared into her eyes. It felt as if his eyes pierced her flesh. What was he talking about? she wondered. Was it her lustful thoughts of Miguel? Or was he angered that she wouldn't discuss what she'd been doing while awake? Was Lou feeling left out? Then she realized that he knew only about things that happened, not what would happen, and her silence angered him.

"I thought you knew what was in my heart," she snapped.

"I do," Lou said, turning his face from hers. "Your intentions and actions sometimes conflict. That is human emotions."

Mecca smiled assumingly. "Lou, I've done nothing immoral. I will not lie to you. You have truly been a friend, and I know you care about my well-being."

Lou believed her. He nodded to the doctor, who administered the shot of truth serum. "Release her."

When Mecca's dream switched, she was lying naked on her bed in Ruby's old Hamptons home while gripping the sheets in ecstasy as her lover's face was buried between her thighs.

"Please don't stop," she moaned in euphoric pleasure.

He continued to please her orally, orgasm after orgasm. She felt heavenly as the tension and stresses of her life lifted from her body with every orgasmic release. She held his head as his tongue danced in and around her middle. He squeezed her bottom as she arched her back off the bed. It was too much for her, and she pulled away from his mouth. When his face came into view, she felt sick to her stomach. Tah Gunz smiled at her.

When Mecca came out of her sleep, she wiped her eyes, then stretched. She could feel her satin panties were soaked. Her wet dream was a signal that she needed a tune-up, and fast.

Chapter Six

A gracious woman retains honor, but ruthless men retain riches.

—Proverbs 11:16

"The crazy thing about it is she doesn't know who I am."

"Still, be on point, though. She is a vicious broad."

Mo Blood pushed the wheelchair up a ramp in front of the project building and stopped before the elevator. Tah Gunz was paralyzed from the waist down after spending months in the hospital, recovering from bullets to his stomach that traveled to his spine. The doctors informed him he would be paralyzed for the rest of his life.

For the first two months in the chair, Tah was frustrated and depressed. He hated having to depend on family and the few friends he had to help him with the basic things, like using the bathroom, showering, and getting out of bed in the morning. He woke up every day still in disbelief at his condition. Then there was the responsibility of raising his son. With Tamika dead, it was now his time to be a full-time father. He felt helpless, wondering how he could raise his son when he could barely help himself.

After a while, Tah became accustomed to being in the chair and learned how to get up in the morning, climb in it and the tub. The city paid for the installment of bars in the bathroom to accommodate his condition.

He put the word out about who had done the deed after learning from one of Tamika's girlfriends where the guy Tamika had been seeing was from. The word he put out meant nothing to his homeboys. Unbeknownst to him, high-ranking Blood members had stripped him of his status. He lost points with the gang when word got out that he had shot Mecca and Shamel out of jealousy. He was considered a sucker unworthy of general status.

"Yo, but the weed is official, my dude. We got all the spots in Brownsville beat," Mo boasted as they rode the pissy-smelling elevator up to the fifth floor of Tilden Projects. "We doing like ten Gs a day."

Despite the fact that Tah had lost his status, Mo still treated him with respect. Mo remembered the days when Tah Gunz's name planted fear throughout the Ville. Tah treated his crew like brothers, even though he often treated Mo like a kid. This often made Mo mad, but he was younger than Tah, so he figured Tah was treating him more like a little brother. Still, rules were rules, and when Tah decided to become a Blood while on Rikers Island, he belonged to Blood for life.

Mo Blood made sure Tah's appearance stayed up. He kept him in the latest gear and took him out to parties and clubs with him and the crew. Tah accepted his demotion in rank like night and day. It came and went. The guys he grew up with still treated him with respect. Who cared what some guys in jail that were never getting out thought? Brownsville still belonged to him and his crew.

"Nobody found out nothing about this dude from L.G.?" Tah asked as they entered the small apartment.

Though his crew still respected him, no one was going on a hunt for some guy that shot Tah. There was money to be made, and Tah shouldn't have been at Tamika's in the first place. What was the purpose of starting problems with a

dude just trying to get some pussy from a girl
that shouldn't have meant nothing to him? Pussy
had no face; that had always been the code.

Not to crush his pride, Mo simply said, "Not
yet. The homies in L.G. ain't really saying too
much."

The sound of a cell phone ringing caught Mo's
attention. It was his.

"What's poppin?" Mo blurted into the phone.
Tah watched as Mo's expression changed from
something the caller said. "What! When?" Mo
roared. "I'm on my way now!" Mo slammed the
phone shut and rushed to the door.

"What's the deal?" Tah asked.

Opening the door, Mo turned to Tah and
answered, "Niggas ran up in my spot and robbed
it."

Mo slammed the door shut, rushing off to
Brownsville Houses.

Daphne's Jamaican restaurant was practically
empty as she and Mecca sat at a table by the
window, eating plates of spicy West Indian food.
The more they spent time around each other, the
closer they got. They truly adored each other.
Ruby didn't mind, because she had a lot of things
of her own going on, and to relieve her stress, she
frequented lesbian hangouts for casual sex.

As tempting as it was, Ruby would not go near a man sexually. She knew what a piece of good dick could do for her. She had to think straight and sensible when it came to the game, and she did not need any emotional distractions. She wanted to remain in control at all times, and that was what the lesbian lifestyle afforded her. She was the dominatrix. Not to mention that she had an assortment of sex toys to play with also.

"No word on those robberies yet?" Mecca asked, sipping on a Kola Champagne.

Daphne sighed. "Nah. Not even a rumor."

Mecca still couldn't get over how much Daphne's eyes resembled those of the girl from her dreams. She still could not figure out why the girl in her dreams had stared at her as if she wanted to hurt her. Changing the subject, Mecca buried her head in her hands.

"I'm bored, Daphne. My aunt doesn't want me working or nothing. I'm used to ripping and running."

"You know your aunt still partly blames herself for what happened to you. So she is being protective, and I understand that," Daphne replied.

"So I'm supposed to just sit back and take an allowance from you and her? I sold the house in the Hamptons. I don't need an allowance."

Ruby hadn't argued with her when she informed her about selling the Hamptons villa. Mecca wanted no part of it. It reminded her of a bad time in her life, just like the projects she lived in when her parents were killed. That was the spot where Shamel was murdered. Even after finding out about his betrayal, it still hurt how everything went down. There was no possible way she could sleep in that house with the memories of Tah shooting her constantly on her mind. Selling it was the best thing to do.

"You know what you should do, Mecca?" Daphne asked, as if something suddenly came to mind.

Mecca looked on with anticipation.

"You should travel. Go everywhere. The islands, Africa, Paris. Just travel."

"By myself?"

"Girl, you need a man. Find yourself a good man and see the world," Daphne proclaimed.

Mecca knew she spoke from experience. She recalled the conversations they had had about Marley, Daphne's dead boyfriend, and all the traveling they had done together. The stories of their love life made her envious. Mecca wished she had a man like Marley to treat her like a princess and remembered that Shamel had treated her as if she were his one and only. But she knew now that he was a cheating dog. She watched as Daphne's attention wandered toward the window.

"You miss him, don't you?" she asked consolingly.

Daphne replied sullenly, "Like hell."

"Girl, you need you a man, too!" Mecca joked to bring cheer to the moment.

They both laughed.

"What do you think about Miguel?" Mecca asked.

"Girl, he is fine!" Daphne answered with a grin. "And I see the way he looks at you! Oh yeah, and I see your looks, too. Let me find out."

Blushing, Mecca looked down at her food.

"Oh no, you didn't, Mecca!" Daphne snorted.

"What?"

Daphne waived off. "That girl Karmen is a bird, anyway. Do you, Ma!" Pausing for a moment, she looked at her with a serious expression. "Speaking of Karmen, let me ask you something. There's this look you give her every time you see her, I noticed. And the look isn't the one that says ya'll have good history. What's up, Mecca?"

"Isn't it obvious I hate the bitch?"

There was no way Mecca would or could explain to Daphne seeing Karmen having sex with Shamel in a vision showed to her by Lou, the devil, or whoever he was. How would that sound? Yeah, I hate the bitch because a man in a vision showed me her fucking my dead boyfriend?

"She's an ass kisser. A flunky. I can't stand flunkies," Mecca answered.

Then Daphne stepped on dangerous territory when she asked, "Why do you give your aunt the same look?"

Mecca was stunned. After inhaling deeply, then exhaling, she replied, "It's long story. Let's take a ride to Coney Island."

That night, while Mecca and Miguel ate at a City Island restaurant, Mecca couldn't get the conversation she had had earlier with Daphne on the Coney Island boardwalk out of her head. Men had stared at the two sexy sisters with the glittering diamond earrings, expensive designer clothes, and perfumes that gave the fishy-smelling beach a mixture of good and bad scents. Daphne was shocked and angered by what Mecca had revealed.

"On the visiting floor, she would sneak in the bathroom and fuck my man," Mecca had told her.

"She's into woman, though. At least that's what I thought," Daphne had murmured.

Still, Daphne couldn't understand why Ruby would do such a thing to her niece. As much as Ruby claimed to adore and love her niece, how could she backstab her like that? Now Daphne began to doubt Ruby's loyalty. She couldn't imagine how she would feel if one of her friends or family members had betrayed her like that with Marley.

"Mecca . . . Mecca!" Miguel snorted.

"Yeah."

"Where you at, Ma? You were in a zone. You must have a lot on your mind."

"Let's go to your place and help me take my mind off of things." Mecca smiled.

"Check please!"

Later, as Gerald Levert's "My Kind of Love" played, Mecca and Miguel locked lips and tongue kissed passionately.

"God, I want you so bad," Miguel whispered as he lay in the bed, watching Mecca do a striptease out of her red lace thong and matching bra. Miguel couldn't believe how in shape she was after coming out of a coma. Her tight stomach went perfectly with her small waist and rounded hips. Her breasts were the perfect handful, with pointed nipples of a golden brown hue. She crawled between his legs, taking his stiff manhood in her soft hands, softly stroking him while giving him a seductive smile. "You're so beautiful," he mumbled.

"You are too," she replied seductively.

They began to kiss again. The taste of cinnamon-flavored toothpaste invaded Miguel's mouth as she straddled his stiffness and let herself down slowly. So many months without sex had made her vagina tight, and looking at his size, she knew she had to be easy. A sharp gasp slipped out of her lips as she slid down his pole. She rubbed his chest, biting her lip as she felt herself become filled with Miguel and a pleasant feeling. She couldn't believe how quickly she began to orgasm.

"Miguel, it feels so good," she moaned. He laid her on her back and explored her gorgeous body with his tongue. When his tongue introduced itself to her clit, she lost control.

She squeezed his head and tried to get up. It was too much, but Miguel held her down firmly and continued to please her. She felt so good, she thought she would faint. Once again, he entered her while she lay on her stomach. Miguel kissed the back of her neck, then nibbled on her ear as he stroked slowly, letting himself go deeper within her confines.

"I'm coming, Miguel!" Mecca moaned as she released her cream all over Miguel's dick. Miguel also couldn't hold back any longer, and he felt his balls tighten, pushing the baby-making fluid through his shaft into Mecca. Afterward, they lay in each other's arms, exhausted and satisfied.

"I'm coming to see your first game," Mecca said while looking into his eyes.

"My first game is in Italy."

"I know, Miguel. I wanna travel with you."

When the hunger built within them again, they made love into the wee hours of the night, until they both fell asleep in each other's arms.

"Idle time is the devil's workshop."

"You should know,'" Mecca said sarcastically to Lou while she sat in his office lounge chair, watching him pace back and forth behind his desk.

"Ha-ha, very funny," he snorted. "On a serious note, this is a time to find out what your talents are. You ever thought about finishing school?"

"For what? I got enough money to live a comfortable life," she answered.

"Oh, I forgot you sold the villa. Money isn't everything, Mecca," Lou growled.

"It is when you come from nothing. And I don't just have money from the villa. I'm getting SSI from the state for the shooting."

"So that's it. Sit around, collect money, and do nothing? Sounds like heaven in the Bible. You do good on earth, then sit around in heaven, doing nothing forever."

"Take your frustrations out on someone else, Lou. I have heard these sarcastic Bible complaints before," Mecca retorted.

Lou cleared his throat. "Anyway, love . . ." Lou pointed at the wall. "Look at that picture."

Mecca did as she was told and turned to see what Lou was referring to. Her eyes went wide in shock as she looked at a picture of her and Miguel making love. Then she awoke out of her sleep, staring at a sleeping Miguel. For some time she watched his soft breathing and smiled to herself. He was definitely a keeper.

Chapter Seven

I will also laugh at your calamity; I will mock when your terror comes.

—Proverbs 1:26

Karmen knew the signs well; she's been through it before. When a man started messing with another woman, he started becoming distant. He started making excuses as to why he didn't call or why he stood you up. He became less talkative, and his mind always seemed to be somewhere else. She just wished it wasn't Miguel. For the first time in her life she thought she'd found a good, honest, loving man. He was everything a woman could ever want: sexy, successful, and good in bed.

Karmen knew the odds were against her. The ratio of men to women was ridiculous in her city and, she imagined, all over the world. Men were outnumbered at least ten to one, and that meant competition. Karmen wasn't about to get bent out of shape, lowering her self-esteem over a man. She would just confront him and tell him to keep it real. The truth of him messing with another woman would hurt, but it beat being lied to and treated like hand-me-down clothes.

She told herself over and over again that if he was messing with another woman, or several, for that matter, she would either have to step her game up and make him want her more or just walk away. She wished she had another option, because she didn't want to take the latter.

"Just tell him it's you or her. Let him feel like he's losing out. If you let a man feel as if you're in need of him, he will step all over you," Mecca explained while Karmen removed the micro braids out of her hair. Daphne was out of town, handling business, so Mecca had opted to go to Karmen's Bushwick apartment to get her hair done.

Talking to Karmen about her problem with Miguel made Mecca feel in control. She felt as if she had Karmen's emotions in her hands. She couldn't have been more elated about it. It made her secret affair with Miguel much more exciting. She couldn't wait to travel with him to Europe, where he was a star, to be seen in photos taken by paparazzi, and to send them back to

Ruby, who would probably show Karmen. Mecca laughed inside.

"Anyway, what's up, Mecca? You trying to hit Speed up tonight? I'm putting my 'fuck 'em, girl' gear on and enjoying myself," Karmen uttered. Mecca knew it was a front. Women that were hurt usually tried to hide the pain by hanging out with the girls, getting drunk, and sometimes waking up hungover in some strange man's bed, feeling disgusted at themselves. To watch Karmen act a fool over her broken heart would be entertaining.

"Yeah, why not?"

Later, they showed up at Club Speed, fashionably late, of course, and Karmen had definitely thrown her "fuck 'em, girl" dress on. The strapless, formfitting Donna Karan dress, reaching just below her shapely hips, made men almost catch whiplash as she cat walked by in the aqua blue piece. There was no mystery to the fact that she wasn't wearing full panties that covered her ass; instead, she wore a scarlet lace G-string.

Mecca's attire was much more classy and expensive. Her black, spaghetti-strap Versace knee-length dress fit nicely, showing her curves, but not fitting like a glove. Her princess-cut diamond earrings complemented the small diamond tennis bracelet she had adorned her wrist with. She realized instantly that she was dressed too classy for the club; it was more of a hip-hop crowd. There was a mixture of casual dressers among the baggy jeans and Timberlands-wearing men and girls that looked like copies of Karmen.

As they danced with a couple of guys, Mecca quickly grew uninterested in dancing and went to the bar to have a shot of Belvedere. Karmen joined her and quickly made the night much more interesting. Shot after shot of various drinks were bought by men trying to leave the club with her, and she drank each one of them. Mecca even warned her about how much she was drinking.

"Karmen, you're overdosing on the liquor. Slow down, before you pass out."

"I can hold my liquor. Don't be such a party pooper. Enjoy yourself," Karmen responded in a drunken slur, which made Mecca want to slap her. Instead, Mecca shrugged and watched her dance with a bunch of different men, letting them grope on her. She took out her phone and put in a text message.

Minutes later she watched Karmen being led into the men's bathroom by two men. Mecca followed. Once inside, the two athletically built men led her to one of the stalls. Karmen lifted her dress up, and while one guy sat on the toilet, she took him in her mouth, while the other went in her from behind. No more than ten minutes into their X-rated action, the stall door flew open. Karmen was too drunk to even hear it. She kept on performing orally on one guy.

"Karmen, what the fuck!" Karmen stumbled to face the voice that had called out her name. She wiped the saliva from her mouth and smiled. Mecca stood behind him, shaking her head.

"Miguel, you came to join us?"

"C'mon, Karmen. You going home," Mecca said as she grabbed her by the hand and pulled her out of the stall.

After dropping her off, Miguel and Mecca drove to his apartment.

"Damn, I didn't know she was that type of girl, Mecca," Miguel said while driving Mecca's truck.

"Me neither," she lied.

"Well, at least I don't have to worry about breaking her heart any longer. I was definitely about to cut her off," Miguel said, shaking his head.

"And why were you going to do that?" Mecca asked to see if he would answer truthfully.

Miguel looked at her and smiled his sexy smile. "Because my heart belongs to someone else, and I'm about to show her how much of my heart, mind, and body she has."

"Wow, she must be a hell of a woman." Mecca continued to act as if she didn't know who he was talking about.

"You sure are one hell of a woman."

Mecca thought about the two hundred dollars she had paid to those two guys to take Karmen into the club bathroom and smiled before adding, "Yeah, I sure am a hell of a woman."

Karmen woke up the next day, in the afternoon, feeling like someone had run over her head with an eighteen-wheeler truck. Her mouth was dry as sand, and her jaw was sore, as well as her pussy. Lying on her stomach, she realized she was still dressed. When she lifted her head, she could see the vomit stain on her black satin sheets.

"Karmen, why are you still in bed? Ruby's been calling you all day, and you ain't answer the phone. She is pissed."

Her sister's loud voice made the pounding in her head worse. Karmen had to pee bad, so she got up and dragged herself to the bathroom, walking past her sister.

"We opened the store, anyway, so don't worry, but it sounds like you got more to worry about with Miguel. Tell me it ain't true!"

Karmen sat on the toilet with the door open and groggily asked, "Tell you what ain't true?"

Her sister appeared at the door of the bathroom. "He came over here and got his clothes, and he left. He told me it was over between you and him because you were at Speed last night, getting doubled by two dudes in the bathroom!"

"What?" Karmen barked. Though she tried hard, she realized she could barely remember last night. She did remember going to the club with Mecca, but she didn't remember seeing or going with Miguel.

"That's what he said," her sister continued.

She hoped she hadn't blacked out and done anything stupid. It began to make sense why her pussy and jaw were sore.

"Karmen, how did Miguel know you were at the club last night? Who did you go with?"

"I went with Mecca," she responded while getting off of the toilet and looking at her face in the mirror. She looked a wreck.

"That's strange, because she's the one that drove him here to get his clothes."

"Oh no, that bitch didn't!" Karmen's eyes opened wide with a sudden jolt of sobriety. She realized at that moment that she had been played, and payback was definitely coming in the near future.

***

"The guns, the weed, everything. Nobody knows who did it," Mo Blood explained to Ruby while they sat on a park bench in Brownsville as a basketball tournament was under way. The roar of the crowd and the whistles of referees blocked out their conversation from any possible ear hustlers. While Mo explained what had happened when masked gunmen entered the spot, Ruby sipped on a strawberry shake from McDonald's. Her clothes were unusually feminine, a pair of black capri pants, a white halter top, and a pair of Jimmy Choo pumps. Ruby nodded as he ran down the details that were given to him by one of the workers.

"Mo," she said abruptly, "take a ride with me downtown."

Mo couldn't read the tone in her voice. It was flat, and he couldn't tell what type of mood she was in. That made him nervous.

"Downtown? For what?" he asked. Sensing his nervousness, Ruby tried to make him more comfortable.

"Listen, two other spots of mines got robbed, and I think I know who it is. I want you and your team to handle it for me. I'm going to show you who it is."

Mo shrugged his shoulders. He knew she wouldn't try anything crazy in busy downtown, or so he hoped. Plus, he was holding heat, so if anything got funny, he wouldn't hesitate. He was sure she had no idea that he was involved in the shooting of her niece and Shamel. The only names that came up in that in the streets were Tah Gunz and them. The "them" could be anybody. Mo coughed violently as he walked to Ruby's car.

"You need to check that cough. It sounds crazy," Ruby warned.

Mo waived it off, continuing to cough. In between, he murmured, "Too much of that weed, that's all."

Mo never saw the girl Tasha from the strip club again after that night he went up in her raw. Nor did he go get himself checked out. Tasha quit working at the club once she got the results of her HIV test. She just left without notice to anyone.

At first, she'd wanted to confront Mo about her status, because he was the last person she had unprotected sex with since her last HIV test. She couldn't believe that she let him hit it without a condom. She realized that confronting him wouldn't change her status, and it probably would cause him to blame her if he was positive, and she knew Mo and the guys he ran with were a bunch of cowboys. She would let the disease take revenge for her.

Ruby and Mo drove downtown to the sounds of "Wanksta" cranking out of the car's sound system.

After a minute or so Ruby turned the sound down and said, "Let me ask you something, Mo."

"What's up?" he replied from the reclined passenger seat.

"You grew up in Brownsville projects?"

Pushing his blue Yankee fitted cap up from over his forehead, he replied, "Yeah, lived there all my life."

Ruby nodded, with a thoughtful expression on her face. "Do you remember a dude they called Wise that used to work out there? This was in the eighties."

Mo tried to recollect. "Yeah, that name rings a bell." A moment passed. Then his memory cleared, and he continued, "Matter of fact, yeah, I remember now. He used to live in Langston Hughes. Yeah, I remember dude."

"Do you know any of his family?"

Again Mo tried to recollect. "I know he had sisters, but they didn't live in the PJs. I heard they lived somewhere far out in Brooklyn."

Ruby nodded her head, then turned the music back up. While the *Get Rich or Die Tryin'* CD played, Mo wondered why she was questioning him about a dead old-school gangster and his family. Figuring Ruby out was like trying to answer a calculus problem in Chinese.

Ready for something to eat, she pulled over at a pizza shop on Fulton Street. "You want anything?" she asked before exiting.

Mo began reaching into his pockets. "Yeah, let me get a slice with extra cheese."

He held out money to her, but she simply opened the door and said, "It's on me."

Mo shrugged, putting the money back into his pocket. While she walked away, he stared at her backside, and just imagining getting a piece of that bubble made him hard. Then his thoughts shifted back to the questioning about Wise.

Mo remembered the rumors of who Wise was killed by and why. The rumor mill had it that Ruby and her dead lesbian lover killed Wise in a Langston Hughes project hallway after Wise helped her set up a local hustler named Darnell. Darnell was allegedly responsible for killing Ruby's sister and her sister's boyfriend, Bobby Blast.

Mo knew those were Mecca's parents. Maybe, he thought, Ruby figured someone related to

Wise was responsible for the robbery of his spot. If that was the case, Mo would have to do some homework and put his ear to the street, because someone had to pay for the loss that he took.

Ruby got back in the car and handed Mo his pizza. "I got you some grape juice with it," Ruby said, placing their juices in the cup holders between their seats. Mo immediately devoured his pizza due to him having the munchies from all the weed he'd smoked earlier. After eating, he reclined his seat back as Ruby changed the CD to the radio. Jaheim's voice leaked out of the speakers.

The last thing Mo remembered before falling off into a deep sleep was Ruby looking over at him, smiling. He could no longer fight the heaviness in his eyes. He barely heard her voice. "You think I don't know. . . ." he thought he heard Ruby say, and then everything went black.

Mo felt something cold on his face when he came to. He coughed and blinked his eyes, trying to clear whatever fluid had been thrown in his face. He couldn't move his arms and realized they were bound behind his back, as were his feet. He knew he was seated in a chair, though, and when his vision cleared, he didn't know where he was. The first thing he saw was Ruby's grinning face.

"Glad you can join us, Mo," Ruby snorted.

"Ruby, what's the deal? What's going on?" he asked with fear in his voice. The dim room appeared to be a basement. The concrete walls, with boxes stacked against them, and the floor gave him that impression.

"I'm sure you know what's going on," Ruby said, walking behind Mo and turning him in the chair toward her. The sound of the wooden chair scraping against the cement reverberated through the basement. Mo was shocked when he was now facing a bound and gagged figure in a wheelchair. He focused his eyes on Tah Gunz.

"Allow me to introduce you to the infamous Tah Gunz. Tah, this is Mo Blood. Does he look familiar?" Ruby smiled and grunted tauntingly. Tah's voice was muffled from the gag. Mo immediately began sweating and pleading.

"Ruby, I swear on everything I love, it wasn't me who did your niece."

"Damn, Tah, this is the type of dude you had in your crew?" Ruby asked in a chuckle.

Ruby had found out about Mo's involvement when she visited the East New York neighborhood of Sutter Gardens, where Mecca had once lived. It was Shamel's old neighborhood. She was a legend in that part of the borough also. Everyone knew that Shamel ran the area, selling drugs that he got from her.

When she got out of her Benz in front of one of the buildings, a group of guys playing dice all stopped what they were doing to gaze at the car and the thick, stylish woman getting out of it. Most of them were too young to know who she was. They figured she was coming to see relatives that she had in the Gardens. One of them, the oldest in the crowd, smiled when he recognized his former boss.

"Oh, shit! I know that ain't the boss lady herself," the chubby, Rocawear-jean-suit-wearing guy barked as he walked toward Ruby.

Ruby recognized him even though he had put on weight. "Breeze, what's up, baby boy?" she asked excitedly.

They embraced in a warm hug. "When you get home, Ruby? I thought they threw the book at you, Ma!"

"You ain't know I got that overturned last year? I've been home almost a year now. We need to talk," Ruby told him.

Breeze told his crew that he would be back after Ruby asked him to take a ride with her. During the ride, Breeze updated her on what had been going on in East New York since she'd been absent. They talked about how the September 11 attacks put a serious dent in the crack game, but weed became the new crack.

"It's like it was in eighty-eight, Ruby, but with weed."

When the subject turned to the murder of Shamel and Mecca's shooting, Breeze became sullen as he told her, "I miss my nigga, Ruby. I'm sorry about your niece. How she doing?" Ruby told him about Mecca being back to her old self, which made Breeze smile. Afterward, he told her about what he'd heard about the incident, and the names responsible.

"A lot of my homies are Blood. They let me know that some Bloods out of the Ville did it. Some dude named Tah Gunz and his flunky Mo Blood. They from Brownsville Houses."

Ruby couldn't believe what she was hearing. She almost broke the steering wheel, she squeezed it so hard. She was actually helping a guy get rich who had something to do with her friend and niece being shot. She looked at Breeze's brown, pudgy face and said, "I know who they are. You want some payback?"

Breeze smiled. Mo Blood stared at Breeze as he leaned against the stack of boxes for recognition. When Mo realized he didn't recognize who Breeze was, he looked back at Ruby. He wouldn't look at Tah, because he couldn't stand to look at the guy who had got him caught up in this position. Mo remembered advising Tah that he should forget about Mecca.

"Dog, she ain't all that to be going all the way out to Long Island for," he'd warned through a smoke-filled haze as he sat back in Tah's car, but Tah was adamant about making her and Shamel pay for trying to make him look bad in the eyes of everybody in Brownsville. "Nobody takes nothing from Tah," was his motto. Not even women.

"Breeze, which one you want?" Ruby asked as he straightened up off of the boxes while rubbing his palms together. Breeze poked Tah Gunz with his index finger, making his head move backward.

"This nigga here," he growled.

"Hold up, Breeze. I wanna play a game," Ruby said with childlike excitement. Pointing to a wooden staircase that led up to a door, she continued, "Untie Tah, and if he can make it up those stairs to that door in thirty seconds, we won't kill him. If he can't, he has to kill Mo here, then kill himself."

Breeze laughed at Ruby's proposal. He knew there was no way a paralyzed Tah would be able to crawl ten feet to the stairs and then pull himself up to that door in thirty seconds. But if Ruby wanted to play . . . so be it.

Breeze pulled a thick wad of cash out of his pocket and began counting some. "I got five hundred he doesn't make it."

Ruby pulled out her wad of cash from her jeans pocket. "I got five on it."

Breeze untied Tah, looked at his Oyster Perpetual Rolex, and barked, "Your time starts now!"

Tah leaped out of the chair by pushing himself to the floor. He began crawling frantically toward the staircase. With money in their hands, both Ruby and Breeze roared as if they were at a horse race.

"Go, boy! *Go!*" Ruby screamed.

"Ten, eleven, twelve . . . ," Breeze counted.

Tah's mouth was still gagged with a red bandanna, which was Breeze's idea of a sign of Tah's affiliation with the Bloods, yet he still mumbled inaudible words. Sweat dripped from his face; his black Akademiks jeans were stained with dirt. He stopped a few times to catch his breath and looked longingly at the door.

"That's five hundred for Breeze, baby!"

Ruby howled, "C'mon, Tah! Do it for Brownsville, baby!"

"Thirty . . . Time's up!" Breeze barked.

Ruby removed the clip from her silver and black .40-caliber Smith & Wesson after cocking it and placing one in the chamber. Then they dragged Tah Gunz back into his wheelchair, while Mo Blood shit his pants, pleading with them.

"Word to Blood, Ruby. I didn't do anything to your peeps. I had to come with him. He is the general. If I didn't go, they would have put the green light on me!"

Ruby looked at Breeze, who shrugged his shoulders.

"You damned if you do and damned if you don't. You caught a bad break, Mo," said Ruby. Mo sighed as Ruby removed the gag from Tah's mouth.

"Ruby, listen. I'll work for you for free if you let me ride," he wailed.

"I can't believe these are the niggas that had everybody shook. Yo, y'all niggas, man up!" Ruby barked as she handed Tah the gun. "You got one shot in there. Now, you can get stupid and shoot me or Breeze, but you can't shoot both of us."

Breeze cocked his Desert Eagle .357. "All you gotta do is shoot Mo. It should be easy for you because he gave you up immediately. This boy would definitely snitch on you."

Breeze pushed the wheelchair directly in front of Mo Blood. He and Tah looked at each other, their eyes filled with tears. Mo was taking deep breaths as his life replayed in his mind. He thought about his mother getting herself together in rehab. He remembered how proud he was of her when she checked herself in the rehab, realizing that she had hit rock bottom when she sold almost every piece of furniture in their apartment. He thought of his twelve-year-old sister, now living in Manhattan with their aunt, and how happy she would be when their mother got out and got her own apartment. Then he thought about seeing his dead homies once he was dead. Tupac's words played in his head as he wondered if his homies had saved him a place in Thugs Mansion.

Boom!

"Whoo! Now, that was some shit!" Breeze roared after Tah pulled the trigger, hitting Mo in the forehead. The back of Mo's head exploded, and blood and brains spilled down his shirt.

Tah sat there with the gun in his hand, his arms down on both of the wheelchair's armrests. He stared at the lifeless body of his dead homie. His thoughts were blank. Then Ruby took the gun from his hand, put the clip in, and cocked it. One thought surfaced.

"I'd rather you kill me, instead of doing it myself or this dude." Tah nodded toward Breeze.

"What difference does it make if it's me or him?" Ruby asked.

"'Cause you're from Brownsville," Tah replied.

Breeze chuckled. "Any other dying wish?"

Tah kept looking at Ruby. "You're a Brownsville legend. That's why I want it to be you. Another thing . . . Can you place my body on Rockaway Ave.?"

Ruby smiled at Tah. "Yeah, sure." She nodded to Breeze. "Go 'head."

Breeze put the Desert Eagle to Tah's temple and squeezed the trigger.

Afterward, they crept out of the abandoned warehouse in East New York and walked to Ruby's car. The block was empty except for the rats rummaging through the vacant lots and streets. There were no other buildings on the block, so more than likely Tah's and Mo's bodies would be devoured by vermin before they were ever discovered. And by that time, they would need dental records to identify them.

"Don't forget my five hundred." Breeze held his hand out as he sat in the passenger seat of Ruby's car.

"You don't forget nothing, huh?" Ruby grinned as she pulled the five hundred dollars out of her pocket and handed it to him.

"Never that. You see, I never forgot your pretty face," Breeze flirted. Ruby took the remark for what it was and simply shook her head.

"I guess your memory ain't that good, 'cause you would have remembered I like pussy."

They both laughed as she turned up the car's system and Donell Jones began to sing.

The breeze blowing through the open sliding glass door cooled Mecca's and Miguel's sweating bodies as they lay entwined on the ocean blue satin sheets, listening to Mary J. Blige's voice serenade their lovemaking. The ocean waves could be heard crashing against the shore just outside of the beach house that Miguel rented during his off-season.

Mecca squeezed Miguel's tight ass while pushing him deeper within her gash. Just as she moaned, she heard footsteps enter through the glass door. Immediately, they turned to see a distraught Karmen standing there with a gun in her hands.

"I thought you loved me, Miguel. I thought I was your Puerto Rican princess," Karmen cried, pointing the gun toward them.

Miguel jumped up, while Mecca covered herself with the sheets. Karmen had the gun pointed at Miguel, who stood in front of her, with his manhood wet and dangling between his thighs. Sobbing, Karmen looked down at his pole, then back at him.

"Why, Miguel?"

"Karmen, put the gun down and let's talk. You don't have to . . ." Miguel was suddenly cut off as something hit him in his chest. He fell backward, landing on the plush white carpet. Mecca jumped out of bed immediately.

"Miguel! Oh God, Karmen! What did you do?"

"He's my man, Mecca! Just like Shamel was my man before he met you!" Karmen growled. Miguel was trying to catch his breath as blood seeped though a small hole on his chest. Mecca could see the carpet under him begin to turn red.

"Is that what this is all about? Shamel and me? Why didn't you tell me that you and him were dealing with each other?" Mecca asked, rubbing her fingers through Miguel's hair.

"I love you, Mecca," Miguel whispered.

Karmen snapped out. "Fuck you, Mecca!" Then shots went off.

Mecca's dream switched to her sitting in Lou's office, with him folding his arms across his chest, looking at her as if he were waiting for an explanation.

"I'll be honest with you, Lou. My intentions at first were to get even with her, but as I get to know him, I'm falling hard for him every day."

"Will you be honest with him and tell him the same thing?" Lou asked.

Mecca was taken aback by the question. "For what? Why do that? All that matters now is how I feel about him at this present moment."

"I guess it's all fair in love and war, huh?" Lou shook his head in disbelief. Standing up from behind the desk, Lou walked around to Mecca. "Can I show you something I didn't show you before, when you were in your coma?"

"How much worse could it get? You gonna show me, anyway, Lou, so get on with it," Mecca sighed.

Nervous at what Lou would show her, she told herself that it could not get any worse than it already was. He'd already shown her how her aunt had set her parents up to be murdered, so if he'd held it back from her, it had to be deep. Lou placed his hand on her head, and the vision began.

Flashback, 1974

"Ever since you got pregnant, you act like having sex with me is a terrible thing," Bobby

Sykes yelled at the woman everyone in Brownsville called Big Mecca once she gave birth to her
daughter.

"Bobby, it's not like I don't want to, but, baby,
I'm eight and a half months pregnant. My back
hurts, and sex isn't helping," she told him in a
low voice, trying to conceal the argument from
the rest of the projects.

"I got needs, Mecca, and you're supposed to
fulfill them, like I do yours," Bobby growled.

"You make it sound like you're my pimp or
something. Bobby, go on with the bullshit."

Angered, Bobby simply shook his head. He
grabbed his suede jacket and keys off the kitchen
table.

"So you're just going to leave? Every time we
get into an argument, you quick to run outside.
What you going to see another woman?" Big
Mecca screamed.

"I don't have time for the bullshit. I'll be back,"
Bobby replied, walking out of the door. A por-
celain ashtray crashed into the door, shattering
into dozens of pieces.

"Don't come back, you bastard!"

Bobby made his way out of the building, and
when he got to Rockaway Ave., he spotted a
friend of Ruby's. She was a fine sister who always
gave Bobby a flirtatious look. It was no secret

that all the girls in Brownsville found Bobby "Blast" Sykes to be the finest brother in the neighborhood, and he did not hesitate to cash in on his sex symbol status.

"Hi, Bobby," said a voluptuous, thick woman wearing her hair in two Afro puffs. Her tight blue jeans revealed how thick her thighs were. The three-quarter black leather jacket tied at the waist with a belt hid the plumpness of her bottom, but Bobby knew from seeing her in the summer what she was hiding under the jacket and clothes.

"Hey, baby. How's it holding?" Bobby flirted. He was already sexually frustrated after two months of getting no sex from his girl. It was time he made his move.

"I'm fine. Not as fine as you, though," the woman replied seductively.

That was all Bobby needed to hear. Minutes later, after some liquor and some lines of cocaine, Bobby and the girl were sucking and fucking savagely in a seedy motel on Pennsylvania Avenue. After four hours of sweat-drenched fucking, it was time to check out. As they both dressed, Bobby turned and looked at the girl.

"Damn, baby, I forgot your name. I always see you with Ruby, but I forgot."

The girl rolled her eyes at Bobby as she put on her clothing. "Bobby, you know my name is Monique."

A month later Bobby ran into Monique on Mother Gaston Boulevard, at a grocery store. He nodded to her as he paid for a pack of cigarettes. She had a sad look on her face as she said, "I need to talk to you outside."

Bobby stepped outside while removing a cigarette from the pack and lit it. He deeply inhaled the smoke while Monique blurted that she was pregnant, causing Bobby to choke.

"What? What you telling me for?"

Monique placed her hands on her hips, sucked her teeth, and rolled her eyes. "I'm no whore, Bobby! You're the last person I fucked. It's yours."

"You know I got a newborn baby girl and I love my woman. I don't need no controversy now. If you're gonna have the kid, I'll help you out, but please keep this between us," Bobby sighed.

"I want this baby, Bobby. I just wanted to let you know. Don't worry. It's between us."

When Monique gave birth to a healthy, seven-pound-two-ounce baby girl, she put the baby's name on the certificate and listed the father as unknown. A nurse placed the baby in Monique's arms and asked what her name would be.

"Her name is Dawn." Monique smiled.

The baby looked just like Blast. Not too long after she got out of the hospital, Monique moved out of Brownsville and relocated to Coney Island. Still, the word spread through Brownsville of who the father was. When the vision was over, Lou sat back at his desk while Mecca cried.

"Is it fair that Monique and your father told no one?" he asked while Mecca's mind flashed back to the time she sat on the park bench with Dawn and shot her in the head.

"Baby! It's okay! It was just a dream!" Miguel said, holding Mecca in his arms. He could feel her heart thud against her chest as they lay naked in his bed. After she calmed down a bit, he got up to use the bathroom and get a facecloth to wipe the sweat off of her. When he came back in, Mecca was getting dressed.

"Where are you going? I thought we were having breakfast together," Miguel said, confused.

"I have to go home," Mecca said while dressing quickly.

"I'll drive you, but why do you have to go?"

"You don't have to drive me. I'll catch a cab," Mecca said, fully dressed and grabbing the phone from his bedside table.

"What's wrong? Did I do something?"

"No, Miguel. I just need some time alone, that's all," she replied as she listened to the phone ring. She responded to the operator's question once her call was answered. "Yes, I need a cab. I'm at . . ."

Chapter Eight

Can it be that it was all so simple then?
—Raekwon and Ghostface

Junior McLeod sat on a white plastic chair in his lush garden, chopping a pineapple he had just picked from a tree. His long dreadlocks with sprinkles of gray hung loosely down the side of his face, down to his stomach. His light brown skin was smooth and flawless, belying his sixty years. The strict vegetarian diet he maintained kept him fit and lean. His gray eyes were blood-shot from the weed he smoked daily. Small beads of sweat coated his shirtless body as he chopped the fruit while holding a conversation with Daphne, who sat in a similar plastic chair across from him.

"So many years have passed since my son's murder, yet you still hold on to the pain. This is the life chosen by so many youths, and the consequences are known," Junior said in a heavy Jamaican accent. His voice was a raspy sort of whisper. Every time Daphne looked at him, she thought of how Donovan would have looked if he hadn't been murdered by the police.

Marley, as he was called, had looked just like his father. Junior McLeod left the streets of New York after making millions, returning to his native Jamaica and living a simple, but comfortable life in the mountains of the island. He had had a large house built that was straight out of a *House Beautiful* magazine. The mini mansion overlooked lush green hills. Daphne loved the peaceful surroundings. It was a relief from the concrete chaos of New York City.

After his son was murdered by FBI agents, Junior sought to find out who was responsible for snitching on him. If the person had been hidden by the government, he wanted their family dead. There was no room for mistakes, and plenty of people paid with their lives. When word got out on who the snitches were, the murder rate in New York City reached unbelievable numbers. The city was under siege.

Members of the Shower Posse and their rivals were being slaughtered. It was nothing for a kid playing in a vacant lot to stumble upon a corpse with some of its limbs missing. Junior was finally convinced by his wife that enough was enough. If things continued the way they were, Junior would be dead or would be sent to prison—with so many numbers, his sentence would sound like a Social Security number. When Daphne was convicted, Junior went to Jamaica.

Before leaving, he made sure that Daphne wouldn't spend a day in jail wanting for anything. He loved her like she was his own flesh and blood. She was one of the most loyal people he had ever met, and he knew she loved his son to death. To this day, he could see the pain in her eyes from the loss.

"It was a piece of my life that made up half of my soul. The other half was Donovan," Daphne said in a measured tone as she stared off into the valley. She watched the wind gently blow through the trees from behind her D&G shades.

"Your other issue is trust, I assume?" Junior asked while cutting pieces of pineapple with a small knife and popping the juicy fruit into his mouth. "Has she shown signs of mistrust?"

Daphne folded one leg over the other and straightened the wrinkles in her linen capri pants. Her matching sandals revealed peach painted toenails to match her halter top.

"Not exactly, but something in her niece's eyes when she looks at her tells me there is something I don't know about her. Something evil."

Junior was a very wise man, well learned in all aspects of life, the streets, and politics. It was well known that the Shower Posse, being an organization that was a political force that opposed the Jamaican government and its treatment of the poor natives of the island, at one time influenced many of his ideas and gave him a broader look upon the world. This, together with his dedication to the Rastafarian religion, gave a mystical aura to Junior's person.

Thinking deeply, he responded, "And you have grown close to this niece of hers?"

"Close, yes," Daphne answered in a tone that spoke of the lingering doubt deep within. "But not close enough for her to reveal what's really the core reason I sense her resentment toward her aunt."

"You Yankees are so paranoid of each other. Trust is so hard to come by in the States, especially among our black people." Junior chuckled, and then he asked, "Are you sure yet about your brother's murder? And if not, will you trust your instincts?"

Junior's words were a sad reality. Daphne couldn't even count on two hands how many people she had trusted throughout her life. She couldn't trust her mother, because she was easily influenced by an abusive man that made their family's life miserable. She and her sister were close, but not as close as she was with her brother. She had total trust in her brother. Then there was Donovan. She had trusted him with all her heart. She knew that he would never cross her, that he was a loyal man, and that this was in his blood. That was why Junior was another person she trusted. She knew that she had to earn his trust, and she did that by not snitching when she got locked up. It was clear that if Junior had had the slightest inkling that she was going to cooperate, he could have had her erased, even in jail.

"The answers will come soon, Daphne. What's on the inside of a person will eventually come to the surface. It's a guarantee," Junior said while standing up. "Until then, take a trip with me into town. I have some people for you to meet."

Daphne stood and stretched. "And I have someone I want you to meet," she said with a smile.

Before Daphne and Junior drove into town to meet the people he spoke about, they stopped at the airport in an onyx-colored, chauffeur-driven Rolls-Royce Phantom with tinted windows. Daphne ran into the terminal and minutes later walked back, carrying a Louis Vuitton duffel bag, accompanied by Mecca.

"Junior, I want you to meet my good friend Mecca," Daphne said as they entered the backseat of the car.

"It's a pleasure to meet you." Junior extended a soft, slightly wrinkled hand.

Mecca smiled. "It's nice to meet you."

Gazing into her eyes, he immediately saw the pain in them. It was a deep pain that, if not diffused, would eventually explode to the surface and cause a lot of damage to others as well as to herself. Immediately, she could feel his gaze and knew that he wasn't just looking at her physically; he was studying her. It didn't make her uncomfortable, because she would do the same whenever she met a person. She could also tell that he was a man of deep wisdom. In an odd way, he reminded her of Lou.

"So, you're from Brownsville?" Junior asked, cutting the air of silence in the car.

Mecca looked directly into his gray eyes. *What is it with these eyes?* she wondered. "Yes, I am."

Junior smiled and shook his head. "When I lived in Flatbush, I remember people were very skeptical about going into Brownsville. It was a dangerous place in the late seventies, early eighties. I never had a problem there. I was always welcomed."

Mecca nodded her head while looking out the window as they passed a shantytown where small children played around shacks and adults stood in groups, staring at the Phantom. Realizing they were in the slums, she finally understood what poverty really was.

Eventually, the graveled road turned into well-paved streets, and the slum faded away, replaced by a South Beach replica. The Phantom came to a stop in front of a luxury hotel, where a uniformed valet approached. The driver of the Phantom waived him off as he got out, opening the rear doors for his passengers.

"Greetings, Mr. McLeod," the doorman said warmly.

Junior simply nodded and smiled as he led Daphne and Mecca into the hotel's foyer. It was easy to tell that it was a five-star establishment simply by looking at it. The foyer itself reminded Mecca of the Waldorf Astoria or Le Parker Meridien in New York, and there were a lot of American and European tourists present.

While Daphne and Junior went up to the luxury suite to have a meeting, Mecca was treated to a full day of pampering in the hotel's spa. She enjoyed a full-body massage by a handsome masseur, a facial that made her skin look expensive, and both a pedicure and manicure, courtesy of Junior. Afterward, she felt totally relaxed. The tension built up in her from her dream about Dawn being her sister, Miguel, and from all that had transpired in the past few months, since coming out of the coma, lifted off of her, making her feel rejuvenated and refueled.

She felt bad about how she treated Miguel, though. Since the Dawn dream, she'd been avoiding him. She told herself that she needed the space from everything, and when Daphne asked her to accompany her to Jamaica, she quickly accepted. Now she wished Miguel was with her, enjoying the island.

As bad as she didn't want to fall in love with him, she found herself falling hard. She didn't want to repeat what she found out about Shamel, so while she soaked her feet, she made a long-distance call to him.

The phone rang a couple of times; then Miguel's warm voice answered, which made her smile. Yes, she realized, she was in love. Again.

While Mecca and Daphne soaked up the sun in Jamaica, Ruby was roughing out a cold New York winter, hanging out in clubs and bars and collecting money from the grocery store Karmen ran and from Breeze, who was now pushing weed in his Sutter Gardens neighborhood.

Even though Ruby was still trying to find out who was responsible for the robberies of her spots and Daphne's restaurant, there hadn't been any other robberies committed, and there was still no word about them on the streets. Ruby found that strange and suspicious.

Did those involved hear that both Ruby and Daphne were on the hunt and wanted them dead? Maybe that scared them off. Or were they waiting for another opportunity to strike? It stressed her out trying to figure out their angle.

Things were flowing smoothly, except for Karmen's attitude. Ruby figured she was suffering from a broken heart, because she didn't see Miguel around anymore, but Karmen was letting her emotions get in the way of making money. She opened the store late a lot, and she let the product run out before calling for more, resulting in lost sales when customers wouldn't wait around for the next supply of weed. When Ruby spoke to her about it, she would apologize and say it wouldn't happen again, but it did. When Ruby asked one of Karmen's sisters what Karmen's problem was, she told her that Miguel had broken up with her. He'd caught her in the club with another guy.

Neither Karmen nor her sisters dared to tell Ruby that they suspected Mecca of stealing

Miguel. They knew how she felt about her niece, and if Ruby thought that Karmen had ill feelings toward Mecca, that could spell trouble for Karmen. So Karmen did the "scorned woman" thing and slashed Miguel's tires and left notes on his door.

When Miguel walked in the store, angered by the tire slashing and notes, Karmen was glad she had got his attention. Her plan was to confront him, then apologize, hoping he would take her back. Her plan backfired.

"If I had known you were this immature, I would have introduced you to one of my little cousins. They're some horny twelve-year-olds." Miguel threw the notes on the floor and stormed out of the store.

Karmen stood there, embarrassed and humiliated. It was then that Karmen started thinking of ways to pay Mecca back for taking her man. She had already realized that it could only have been Mecca who called him to the club, and she remembered how Mecca would stare at him. For a moment, she'd been blind to the facts, but no longer. They both would pay.

However, Karmen underestimated Ruby's ties to the streets. So when she hollered at a guy she knew from Bed-Stuy, where the store was located, about robbing it, word quickly got back to Ruby.

"Do the job," Ruby told the guy that Karmen was conspiring with. "That will be part of the pay for getting rid of her. Wait till after Christmas, though."

"Why after Christmas?" he asked.

"I like her sisters. I don't want to spoil their holiday."

They both burst out laughing.

"Nah, seriously. Wait."

Back in Jamaica, Junior brought Daphne and Mecca to the shantytown they had passed on their way to the hotel. The area was dark and loud, with reggae music blasting from some of the shacks. The pungent odor of dead animals filled the air. Mecca followed them inside a small shack where a skinny old man sat at a wooden table, wearing African garb, including a beaded necklace made of wood, with what looked like the teeth of some animal connected to each bead.

The small house was decorated with wooden African sculptures, various potted plants, and a small bookshelf, which held books on healing, African black magic, and medicines. In the middle of the house, in a makeshift living room, sat a table covered with what looked like lamb's wool. Surrounding that were candles on shaded lamps that made shadows dance across the cement walls.

"Ladies, I'd like you to meet Doc Benjamin," Junior said as the old man stood up and bowed slightly.

Doc Benjamin smiled, showing his missing teeth and soon to be missing ones. He twisted his gray chin hairs, which grew from his lined, dull black skin. Mecca had noticed that the majority of the people she met in Jamaica had bloodshot eyes. Doc Benjamin was no exception.

"I am honored," Doc Benjamin responded in an accent that wasn't broken like that of the native Jamaicans. He spoke clear English. His words were pronounced as if he were an English professor at a prestigious college.

When Doc offered his company tea, Mecca knew it was customary to accept the offer. When you were a guest in someone's home, turning down the offer was a sign of disrespect, so she reluctantly accepted.

They sat at the table while Doc poured tea into small glass cups out of an old teakettle. He gazed into Mecca's eyes as he poured her tea, and unlike the gaze she had received from Junior, Doc's gaze made her nervous.

"What are your names?" he asked.

They told him their names, and Mecca noticed that Doc kept looking at her strangely.
Sometimes it appeared as though he was looking
around her head, as if something was on it or
floating over it. Nervously, she found herself
looking up and around. Doc gave her the creeps.

Turning to look to see if Daphne felt the same
way, she was puzzled that she did not seem to be
affected by the strange old man. Junior talked to
Doc about what he'd been up to living up on the
mountains and about mutual friends that they
had not seen in a while. Doc then turned and
studied Mecca again.

"Don't hold on to the grudge. They will have
their day."

Mecca looked behind her, then at everyone in
the room, only to find they were all looking at her
as if she was onstage, ready to perform.

"What . . . what do you mean?" she asked nervously. How was he able to read her thoughts?
How did he know the words Lou told her in her
dreams?

"I mean, you are angry at people who can't
cause you any more harm than they're doing to
themselves," Doc said.

As he spoke, Mecca became dizzy. Her head
felt hot, and the room seemed like it began to
spin. All she heard was Doc's voice as she felt her

body being lifted, and she was floating in the air until her body touched something soft and flat. Her vision blurred, and she felt as if she were sinking into the soft surface she was lying on.

"Let it go. You don't need him no more," Doc's voice echoed as her blurred vision went dark. "You are stronger than it."

Then Mecca saw him. He was drowning in a vast ocean, while she stood on the deck of a yacht. He held out his hand from the strong black current.

"Mecca! Help me! Don't listen to him!"

Mecca cried as she looked for a life jacket. She found one and threw it to him. "Lou, grab the jacket," she yelled.

"You can make your own decision, Mecca. God has given you a choice," Doc's voice echoed somewhere in her mind.

"Mecca, please don't leave me. I love you. All I want is what's best for you!"

Mecca held out her hand to grab Lou's. "Hold my hand!"

Lou grabbed on, but the current was strong. He struggled to pull himself up on the deck, but Mecca was losing her grip.

"Lou! Hold on!"

"Don't drink any more tea!" Lou yelled.

"What?"

Lou increased his grip on Mecca's arm and pulled himself up on the deck. Mecca immediately hugged him.

"Lou, go hide in the boat. People are trying to get rid of you. Go!" Mecca ordered.

Lou did what he was told.

"He is gone. I don't need him anymore!" She yelled into the darkness.

Her vision went black; then it blurred, and she was able to see the shapes of people. When it cleared, she looked up into the smiling faces of Doc Benjamin and Junior. Junior held out his hand to lift her off of the table.

"What happened?" she asked, confused. She could not remember how she ended up lying on the table. She felt light-headed. She sat up and saw Daphne walking toward her.

"You fainted, Mecca. Doc said it's probably the humidity in the air. Plus, you're not used to that kind of tea. It's marijuana tea mixed with spices," Daphne said, pulling Mecca off the table.

"We're ready to leave now," Junior said, shaking Doc Benjamin's hand.

Doc then shook Daphne's and Mecca's hand. He looked into Mecca's eyes and in a soft voice said, "No one can show you what you don't want to see."

Inside Junior's Phantom it was silent as they rode back to his home. Mecca stared out the window as the slum villages turned into postcard countryside. She still couldn't believe she'd fainted. She felt so embarrassed, despite Daphne telling her that it had happened to her also on her first trip to the island.

"I passed out longer than you did. I had a big cup of the same tea," Daphne had told her while walking out of Doc's home to the car.

Mecca remembered feeling hot from drinking the tea, but not to the point where she felt a fainting spell coming on. It had happened so quickly, though, and that Doc guy was a strange man. She didn't even get that creepy feeling from Lou that she got from Doc Benjamin. One thing for sure, she thought, she never wanted to see the likes of him again.

Her thoughts switched to Miguel, and she smiled thinking about their talk on the phone. She was glad that he wasn't offended to the point where he didn't want to see her again.

"I understand if you don't wanna be involved with me. I just want you to know that I'm sorry for the way I acted," Mecca had told him.

"Mecca, I want to be involved in every aspect of your life. Talk to me. That's what I'm here for. You can tell me anything. I won't judge you or look at you differently. I promise."

Miguel knew how to make someone feel at
ease. His voice was soothing, and to Mecca it
was an aphrodisiac. His voice made her wet and
horny. She wanted to pull his lips through the
phone just to taste them.

"There is so much to talk about Miguel. It's
hard to explain."

Mecca knew that she would have to share
personal things with Miguel, but what she would
tell him was something she found hard to figure
out. She couldn't tell anyone about Lou. No one
would understand. Telling him about Ruby and
Karmen wouldn't change anything. The hurt
from Ruby's betrayal would still be there, and as
far as Karmen was concerned, she couldn't tell
him that she was with him initially as a get back
for her having an affair with Shamel. She would
have to figure it out someway, somehow. Then
she wondered if Lou might have the answer. She
couldn't wait to go to sleep that night.

Flashback, 1976

"Look at you. You're a big girl now, huh?" Big
Mecca announced while standing at the open
bathroom door, smiling at her daughter on the
white potty. Little Mecca simply looked up at her
mother and smiled.

"Bobby, come look at your daughter. She's using the potty!"

Bobby Blast appeared at the door, also smiling. "That's Daddy's girl. She can do things on her own. She's just like her daddy!"

Mecca's dream fast-forwarded to six years later, with her coming out from under the bed after witnessing her parents' murders. She ran to the telephone and dialed her aunt's house. A half hour later police arrived at the apartment. Mecca was left with her aunt's friend down the hall.

"What's her name?" the female detective asked Ruby's friend as she bent down to her.

"She can speak," the neighbor answered. Tears ran down her face.

"Mecca."

"Can you tell me what happened here?" the detective asked.

"My mommy and daddy are dead. I won't see them again until I'm dead," Mecca responded.

When the detective tried to elicit more information, Mecca fell silent. She began to look around for the man with the neat Afro. She did not see him and was confused. Then Ruby walked in.

The vision disappeared, and Mecca found herself sitting in Lou's office. He faced away from her in his large swivel chair, and though she could not see him, she heard his voice.

"You didn't need help making those decisions, Mecca. You used the potty all by yourself. You knew without anyone telling you that you wouldn't see your parents again. You can and will decide your own destiny. Making mistakes is all part of being human. You're not perfect, and no one should expect you to be perfect."

Though the voice sounded like Lou's, Mecca wasn't sure. What he was saying was something Mecca knew Lou would not say. It was like Lou expected her to walk a straight line, or he would be angry. This voice she was now hearing was a voice of reason, pleading with her almost. Then the chair turned, and Mecca's eyes widened at the sight of Doc Benjamin.

Mecca awoke out of her sleep in the guest room inside Junior's home. The room was dark, and you could hear the sound of crickets and other night creatures talking to one another. The canopy bed she lay on had a netted covering to keep out mosquitoes or any other creeping night creatures. As she struggled to control her labored breathing and bring it back to normal, she mumbled to herself.

"I've had enough of Jamaica." With or without Daphne, she would be on the next flight back to New York, as far away from Doc Benjamin as possible.

Chapter Nine

Do not trust in a friend; do not put your confidence in a companion.

—Micah 7:5

Daphne's and Mecca's flight arrived at Newark International Airport. Once there the women separated. Mecca was picked up by Miguel, and Daphne's BMW was in long-term parking. Daphne drove out to an eatery on Long Island called Jillian's to meet Ruby. During that drive, Junior's take on Mecca kept repeating in her mind.

"She has been betrayed, and it was a betrayal that left a deep wound. She is loyal. That's why she clings to you. But whatever pains this woman, it's a pain that's been there for a long time."

Daphne needed to know what it was, and if she couldn't get it from Mecca, she had no choice but to confront Ruby. When she'd called her after landing, Ruby had quickly warned Daphne to call her from a public phone and gave her the number to one on Long Island. When she finally called her from a phone, Ruby sounded excited.

"Daphne, where's my niece?"

"She's at a duty-free shop. Why? What's up?"

"Tell her Tah Gunz and his homie are washed up," Ruby answered, as if she was telling Daphne she had just won a lottery jackpot.

"I'll tell her," Daphne said. "But I need to see you now. We have to talk."

"What's up, Daphne? Something happen?" Ruby asked, not liking the tone of Daphne's voice.

"No. I just have to discuss some business with you. We haven't talked in a while," she lied. She did not want to put Ruby on the defensive. She wanted to catch Ruby unaware so that she would not make up answers about Mecca's situation. That way, she would be able to detect the lie.

Without question, she knew that when it came to Ruby, she would have to use all of her cunning to illicit the answer from her. Ruby was no one's fool, and she knew her well enough to know you couldn't game her. Being friends with her in prison had allowed Daphne to see how easily Ruby could talk another inmate into believing that they were the best of friends or lovers, only to have Ruby con her out of money and drugs.

"Meet me at Jillian's," Ruby told Daphne.

Jillian's had been a favorite of Ruby's since she'd been home. They served traditional American cuisine, and you could also enjoy bowling and shoot pool. Ruby loved to eat and then bet on a game of pool.

When Daphne arrived, Ruby was already deep in a game of pool against a tall, handsome man who looked like a young athlete. On closer inspection, Daphne recognized the NBA star. He looked like he was embarrassed as he watched both Ruby's plump bottom and her shot on the pool table. Almost every man in the place looked at her tight, low-cut jeans with the strap of her thong showing. Ruby loved the attention she received from men, and doubly enjoyed telling them after they hit on her that she was into women.

When she saw Daphne, she smiled and refocused back on her shot. There was only the black eight ball on the table, so obviously this was the end of the game. Ruby tapped the table with the pool stick, then pointed the stick at one of the corner pockets. She hit the eight ball and watched as it slowly made its way to its destination. When it dropped in the hole, the NBA guy sighed and reached into his pocket to remove a small stack of cash to hand to her.

"Don't be stingy with that NBA money. Pay up," Ruby teased as she counted the money. She smiled at the guy. "Stick to basketball. This ain't you."

The basketball star laughed while eyeing Daphne. Those eyes of hers could really make a man weak on resisting. He had noticed her when she walked in like every other guy in the place. Her confident swagger, blended with the beautiful face and sexy physique, was a sight for sore eyes. These men just didn't know that their chances of scoring with her were slimmer than a young boy's chances of not being violated in a room full of Catholic priests.

"You gonna let me try and win my money back or introduce me to your friend?" His voice was Kobe Bryant deep as he approached the table Daphne and Ruby had taken to talk.

"I'm not here to socialize with strangers. If you could be so kind and leave me and my friend to talk, that would be appreciated," Daphne blurted, placing her Hermès bag on the table and not even looking at him. The basketball star shook his head and walked off.

"Damn, girl, that man is fine," Ruby said, laughing, before turning her attention to Daphne. "Are you okay?"

"I'm no one's groupie, and I don't have time for headaches," Daphne shot back. Ruby looked at her for a moment and could tell by her tone and body language that something was on her mind. Something that seemed to be eating at her.

"So what's up, Daphne? What's good? Tell me about Jamaica."

"It was a good trip for me, but I'm not sure it was for Mecca," she responded, looking directly into Ruby's eyes. She always noticed that the mention of Mecca's name made Ruby's facial expression change. Mecca was a sensitive topic for her. The guilt was still an issue for Ruby because she had not stopped blaming herself for what happened to her.

"Why do you say that? Did something go wrong?" Ruby asked in a low voice.

For a moment Daphne looked into her eyes and knew that she did not want to hear sad news about Mecca. Ruby was tired of blaming herself for Mecca's downfall.

"Nothing went wrong. Something is wrong. Very wrong," Daphne stated.

Ruby stiffened, ready to go on the defensive. "What do you mean?"

"Something is eating at her, Ruby. What do you think it is?"

"The girl just came out of a coma—"

"She's been out of the coma for a year now. That's not it," Daphne said, cutting her off.

"Why are you asking me, Daphne? Ask her!" Ruby shot back as she began to feel the anger rise within. Daphne seemed to be cross-examining her, as if Mecca's attitude was somehow Ruby's fault.

Daphne was tempted to tell her that she did question Mecca about the look she gave Ruby and Karmen, but Mecca's answer about both women sleeping with her boyfriend didn't convince her that that was the root of the problem.

"I asked you because you're her aunt. You know her better than anyone else. Talk to her, Ruby. It's like you've been around her, and maybe that's the problem. Y'all were close before you went to jail. Maybe she feels your time away made y'all grow apart."

Ruby looked away, as if her attention was diverted to something else in the restaurant. She wouldn't tell anyone that the guilt she felt was deeper than just Mecca being shot. That was just the surface of the matter. Ruby felt that if she hadn't set Bobby Blast up to be robbed and both of them hadn't got killed, Mecca would have grown up living with her parents, who would not have allowed her to run the streets and get knee-deep into the game.

Ruby's time in jail had made her reflect on the mistake that she'd made raising Mecca the way she did. What kind of person would do that to her own flesh and blood? She told herself she had to accept who she was, but not what she'd made out of Mecca. She wouldn't allow her to be involved in street life ever again. It would be over her dead body. Ruby sighed.

"You're right, Daphne. I'll have a talk with her. Where did she go?"

"She's with Miguel."

"With who?" Ruby's eyes widened. Daphne looked dumbfounded. She'd forgot that Ruby wasn't aware of Mecca and Miguel. She'd let the cat out of the bag, so she decided that she would tell all.

"You didn't know they were messing with one another?"

"No, I didn't know that. And when was I going to find out?" Ruby grumbled.

Daphne took a sip of her chocolate milkshake and shrugged.

"That's why this bitch Karmen been acting up lately," Ruby said, shaking her head. Now Daphne was confused.

"Acting up? What did she do?"

After Ruby explained about Karmen's plot to have the store robbed, Daphne growled in anger.

"I'm not too enthused about all the killings, but on this one, do what you see fit."

Four days after Christmas, the snow blanketed the streets. Christmas lights blinked on and off in houses and storefronts, lighting up the dark streets. Yet something contrary to the holiday spirit was being plotted. Three men in dark apparel sat in a black Lincoln Town car on the side block that Ruby's store cornered.

"All y'all gotta do is climb the fence and go through the back. The door is open," the leader of the three-man gang said to his comrades. The leader, who was the one Karmen had conspired with to rob the store, never told his crew that it was more than a robbery, that it was a hit. He didn't feel it necessary to tell them, because he didn't plan to split all the spoils.

"I'ma walk in like a regular customer. They about to close, so it won't be anyone in there," he said while taking a look at his watch. "Let's move."

"I want you to cum in my mouth, *Papi,*" Tina moaned as she took her new friend, whom she'd just met earlier, in her mouth while he sat on a crate in the back room of the store.

The young Spanish guy held her head as her neck moved up and down and she bent between his knees. His eyes were closed, and Tina never saw the two masked men enter the room. They became aware of their presence when they heard the sound of the gun being cocked.

"Hey, *Papi,* fun time is over." A masked man pointed the shotgun in his face.

"Don't shoot please!" The Spanish guy's face went pale with fear.

The other gunman pointed his Heckler & Koch MP5 at Tina. "Put homeboy dick back in his pants and lay down on the ground."

Out front, where Karmen and Maria sat on crates, watching a small color TV, a customer walked into the store. The dark-skinned, medium-high man with a black ski hat on his head, covering his cornrows, which touched the bottom of his shoulders, looked around.

"I forgot to lock the door," Maria said, looking at the face of the guy, whom she recognized from Bed-Stuy. "We're closed, *Papi!*"

"Nah, bitch, I'm just opening up for business." He smiled at Maria, then quickly brandished a nickel-plated .50-caliber Desert Eagle from the inside of his black leather trench coat. Maria froze in her tracks. Her heart pounded in her chest as she raised her hands.

"Lay on the floor." He pointed the gun at Maria and then looked at Karmen, who was slowly walking toward Maria. "You do the same, sexy."

Karmen and Maria did as they were told. At the same time, Karmen was wondering why he was showing his face. *My sisters aren't supposed to see him! He must be drunk! Dumb-ass nigga!*

Two shots rang out from the back of the store. Maria let out a short scream, and Karmen looked up at the man with the gun.

"What the fuck was that? Why are they shooting?" Karmen yelled frantically. She knew it was a setup, but had the plans changed?

"Shut your ass up, bitch! It's warning shots," the man spat back sharply. The two masked men came from the back of the store, holding trash bags.

"It's done," one of them said to the leader.

"What's done? Don, what the fuck is going on?" Karmen yelled again, confused as to when the plans had been switched up.

The two masked men looked at Don, confused. How did she know his name? Then they realized he wasn't wearing a mask. Maria looked at her sister, confused, too. How did she know this man?

"Oh, you remember me?" Don asked, trying to play dumb in front of his partners.

"Don, don't get all—" Karmen's words were cut short when he pointed the Desert Eagle at the top of her head and squeezed. Blood and brain matter squirted all over Maria's face upon impact, but before she could scream, Don put a bullet in her skull, shutting her up forever.

"Yo, son, what the fuck you doing?" one of his partners asked.

"C'mon, we going out the back," Don replied as he started off, with his crimeys in tow.

When they got in the back, Don saw Tina and her new lover, still alive and tied up, with tape around their mouths.

"Meet me in the car," Don told his partners. They looked at him as if he were losing his damn mind. "Fuck y'all waiting for? Go ahead!"

Once they did as they were told, Don went to the stash spot Ruby had told him about. It was a small door underneath the small refrigerator. He opened it and removed four pounds of weed inside of a shopping bag. Tina had tears running down her face and held a fearful expression, which got Don off a little bit.

Both of them were mumbling inaudible words right before Don put bullets in their foreheads.

He bent down to pick up the shell casings, like he did when he killed Karmen and Maria, and then exited the store. When he got to the car, where his partners waited, he popped the trunk and placed the shopping bag in it.

"What's in the bag, Don?" one of his crimeys asked as he got in the passenger seat.

"I got my mom some groceries," Don lied. He started the car, and the hard beat and lyrics of Beanie Sigel filled the interior as Don sped off.

Mecca tried to open the office door, but it was locked. Confused, she decided to knock instead.

"Lou, you in there? Why is the door locked?"

As she put her ear to the door, she heard movement inside. It sounded like a scuffle was going on and someone was choking.

"Lou, what's going on? Open up!" Mecca grabbed the doorknob while banging her shoulder against the door.

"Mecca, go away. I will deal with him myself," answered Doc Benjamin's voice.

Mecca was infuriated. "No!" she screamed, and then, with two hard kicks, the door flew open and Mecca watched as Doc Benjamin had Lou down on the desk, choking him. Mecca reached into her Louis Vuitton purse and removed a nickel-plated, pearl-handled .380 automatic. She pointed the gun at Doc Benjamin's back and grunted, "You let him go, or I'll kill your ass."

"Mecca, those days are over. Plus, you don't love this man." Doc Benjamin howled a throaty laugh. He squeezed harder, and Lou's eyes rolled in his head.

"Let him go!" she yelled as she squeezed the trigger, emptying her gun in Doc's back.

"It's okay, baby. No one's here. You had a nightmare," Miguel said, holding Mecca's head against his bare chest as they lay naked in his bed. Miguel could hear her heart beat. He figured her nightmares were from her being shot and going into a coma. However, recurring nightmares of being shot by Tah Gunz weren't even close to what Mecca was experiencing. Mecca knew that Miguel wouldn't understand. Nobody would.

Chapter Ten

A whisper separates the best of friends.
                                        —Proverbs 16:28

Club Opium was jam-packed with people from all walks of life as the Las Vegas club hosted a "welcome home" celebration sponsored by the famous *Don Diva* magazine. A who's who of the famous and infamous was in attendance, from athletes and entertainers to politicians and gangsters. With this high-profile gathering, law enforcement from government and local agencies were also strategically roaming the premises, eyeing targets of criminal investigations and their associates, potential targets themselves. Against Daphne's advice, Ruby attended the event, because she was invited to welcome home her former cell mate, friend, and lover after a ten-year stint.

"Why don't you and her celebrate it privately? That place gonna be crawling with Feds," Daphne had warned, only to have her words fall on deaf ears.

There was no way Ruby was going to miss it. She would not just see her lover, but she didn't tell Daphne that the people from *Don Diva* wanted to do a story on Ruby's life in the eighties, up until her arrest and conviction. When Ruby had shared that news with Mecca in an attempt to reach out to her and rekindle the bond they had had prior to her imprisonment, Mecca simply stated that she didn't think that would be wise. In fact, she thought it was plain stupid.

"I know what and what not to say. Plus, double jeopardy is against the law," Ruby had replied, taken aback by Mecca's tone. Mecca shrugged while she read an *Essence* magazine while sitting in Ruby's kitchen.

"It's your life."

Thinking to herself, Ruby realized that she didn't have time to keep trying to be nice to someone who got an attitude for God knows what. *If that's the way Mecca wants it, then fuck it.* Truth be told, Ruby was saddened by the way Mecca treated her, but she sucked it up.

"I love my niece," she'd explained to Daphne, "but I'm no ass kisser."

To Ruby, it was a good thing Daphne had helped Mecca find an apartment of her own, because Ruby hated feeling like she was living with a stranger. Ruby believed in her heart that Mecca needed her own space. In the meantime, Ruby had got a call from her friend Tashera from Harlem, stating that she was coming home and that her father was throwing a celebration in Vegas, sponsored by *Don Diva,* who did a story on Tashera "Tashy" Williams.

Ruby stepped out of her rented baby blue X5, handed her keys to the valet, and walked the red carpet into the club. She was definitely a head turner when she appeared wearing a skin-gripping white catsuit under a waist-length chinchilla and a pair of Jimmy Choo heels. The short Halle Berry haircut made it easy to spot the sparkling Harry Winston diamond earrings that adorned her earlobes, and above her bulging cleavage sat a diamond choker to match. Ruby walked and looked like money. Before entering the party, she gave her name to a man standing at the podium, checking a list. The party was exclusively invites only. The man checked the list and smiled at her.

"Ms. Davidson, Ms. Williams told me when you came to call her so that she could walk you in herself."

The man dialed a number on his cell phone and spoke when a person answered, informing them that Ruby was there. He looked at Ruby with a smile that was becoming annoying to her. Ruby hated a kiss ass. No more than a minute later, a short, deliciously dark-skinned female ran toward Ruby excitedly. Ruby opened her arms to embrace her friend. Both women were overly excited to see one another; it was a much-awaited reunion for both of them.

"Tashy, what's good, Ma?" Ruby asked while hugging Tashy, then releasing her to look into her eyes. They weren't used to seeing each other in clothing that wasn't prison issue.

Tashy knew from Ruby's letters that she was doing well in the world. She didn't send Tashy pictures, because they weren't allowed to correspond with former inmates in the prison, so they stayed writing every month.

"Damn, Ruby, you look good, baby," Tashy said, grabbing Ruby's arm and walking her into the club.

"All this is for you, Tashy? Your father loves his baby," Ruby responded as she scanned the club, which was decorated with "welcome home" banners, noting the live entertainment from the hottest hip-hop and R & B stars, the free food, and drinks of the most expensive kind.

"Daddy's little girl, even at the age of thirty-seven," Tashy giggled.

They met before Ruby was transferred out of the women's federal detention center in Virginia. Tashy came to the prison in 1992, after being convicted of money laundering and federal tax evasion. The initial investigation was directed at her father, a one-time member of a heroin-dealing organization headed by the notorious kingpin Frank Matthews, who had disappeared from sight after posting a two-million-dollar bail.

Tashy's father, Tommy "Scooter" Williams, was allegedly a lieutenant in the Matthews organization, but the government couldn't prove it. Tashy owned a hair salon in Harlem, which Scooter had bought her and which he used to wash his money. When Tashy started living a lifestyle that owning a hair salon couldn't provide, the government was watching. Informants told the government that dope was sold out of the place, so the Feds felt that arresting Tashy would put Scooter in a bind. They figured he would give himself up to save his only daughter. They knew how close they were and figured they had Scooter at last. They were wrong.

They had no idea how much of a trooper Tashy was and how far she would go for her father. Even against Scooter's wishes, Tashy fought the case. She knew they had no solid proof that heroin was being sold from the salon. Her customers were longtime friends from the neighborhood and wouldn't dare snitch on her.

Everyone loved Tashy in Harlem. She was the most charismatic person and was always in a jovial mood, making everyone around her feel happy even when it wasn't called for. And she was humble, graceful, and the warmest woman in the neighborhood. Whenever a girlfriend was feeling down, they would go see Tashy, just to talk. She always knew what to say or do to make a person feel good. Tashy would either give the person a free hairdo and makeover or take the sad soul to a movie or out to a club. That was Tashy.

The government could not prove that heroin was being sold, so they convicted her of other charges. Since she was a first-time offender, the judge gave her ten years, instead of the twenty she could have received. The loyalty and honor she showed made her loved even more in Harlem. She did her time with the same attitude she had on the streets.

Her fellow convicts loved her just as much as people on the streets. Inmates that were without family and friends to come visit them or send money would receive some of her joy. Tashy would have someone send them money, and during family outings she'd invite the inmate to sit with her family. Tashy became good with the law and helped others with their cases without charging, unlike your average jailhouse lawyer. Many hated her for that but wouldn't dare let it be known. Despite her efforts to help, a hater or three always lurked in the background. There practically wasn't an inmate in the jail that wouldn't attack you for even saying a bad word about Tashy. Especially Ruby.

"C'mon, Ruby, there's some people that I want you to meet. The two most important people in my life," Tashy said, pulling her by her hands and passing tables with white coverings and candles placed there for the event. Seated all around were people old and young. Most of them were friends and associates of Scooter and were there to celebrate the release of his daughter, whom some had known since she was a child, and some had never met her but had heard about her. Because it was Scooter's daughter, they came from far and wide.

Ruby was rushed to the VIP section by an overexcited Tashy, to a table that seated two people, a tall older man, unmistakably her father, and a young, pretty woman who looked like Tashy's twin. A woman that Ruby had seen in pictures and had heard so much about during her time in prison.

"Daddy, Simone, I would like you to meet Ruby," Tashy announced, standing aside so her father could stand and shake Ruby's hand. Ruby noticed how handsome Scooter was up close. His skin had a copper tone and a rich glow. Scooter, now in his early sixties, was a well-respected old-school hustler with deep pockets. For a man in his sixties, Scooter held on to a well-built physique due to his daily workout of jogging and exercise and a strict no-red-meat diet. The only signs of age on his tall frame were the graying short Afro and matching mustache.

"Wow, you're beautiful, just like your mother," Ruby complimented.

"Thank you," Simone said to Ruby after embracing her and sitting back down.

Ruby remembered the days when they shared a cell and Tashy would stare for hours at pictures of her now twenty-two-year-old daughter. She was twelve then, but Tashy had pictures of every special event in Simone's life. Scooter made sure of that. Birthdays, graduations, proms, and all. Scooter taped and photographed everything for her. Every month Scooter would have someone bring Simone to the prison to see her mother. Tashy cried for long hours after every visit.

When Ruby asked about Simone's father, it was the only time Tashy's jovial aura would become dark and somber. Ruby figured the topic was a sensitive issue. Still, Tashy explained it to her.

"I was sixteen, and he was twenty at the time. I really liked him, Ruby. His name was Shane, and he was from Washington Heights. It wasn't meant for me to get pregnant, but it happened, and when my father found out, he blew a lid something crazy. He found out about Shane, whose father was a Dominican hustler my father knew. A week later I find out Shane was sent to the Dominican Republic forever. He was told to never speak to me again. Last I heard, he's married with kids."

"I've heard so much about you, Ruby. It's good to finally meet you." Scooter spoke in a deep bass voice.

Ruby wondered if Tashy had told her father that they were lovers who had spent nights in a small cell, having lesbian sex, using lotion bottles as dildos and melting commissary candy bars to lick chocolate off of each other.

Scooter cut his eye to Tashy with a smirk. "I wish Tashy would have told me you've been home. I would have made arrangements to meet you. So what have you been up to?"

Even though Ruby knew Scooter was an old gangster, she didn't think telling him that she was getting rich off of selling exotic weed in Brooklyn was a good idea. She didn't think he wanted Tashy around the criminal element anymore.

"I've opened up a business in Brooklyn. A grocery store. I'm about to open a restaurant," she answered, straight-faced.

Scooter nodded. "That's wonderful. I was hoping Tashy would get back into the spirit of running a business."

A maître d' brought over two chairs so Ruby and Tashy could sit at the table with Simone and Scooter. Ruby noticed Simone had a serious look on her face. She didn't inherit the constant jolly mood of her mother. Her face was oval shaped, like Tashy's, and surrounded by shoulder-length, dark, shiny hair and a bang that was slicked back, revealing a long forehead. Her eyes were elongated and a flat brown. Ruby figured she was a deep thinker.

"Can I enjoy my freedom first, Daddy, before you start on me about running a business?" Tashy spat with a playful grin.

A photographer from *Don Diva* approached the table. "Excuse me, Ms. Williams?" the photographer said humbly. "May I get a picture of you and your family?"

Tashy smiled. "Of course." She grabbed Ruby's hand and tried to pull her from the table to join her in the photo.

Ruby grunted between clenched teeth, "Tashy, she said family!"

"You are family. Now get up." Tashy smiled to the photographer. "This is my friend Ruby."

The photographer raised her eyebrows. "Are you Ruby Davidson from Brooklyn?"

"In the flesh," Tashy answered excitedly. "C'mon, take the flick. You can holler at her later on!"

Scooter, in his three-piece silk black Armani suit, red silk tie over a white shirt of exquisite quality, and a pair of Italian-made shoes in glove-soft leather, stood between his daughter and granddaughter, with Ruby next to Tashy, and posed for the picture.

Afterward Tashy, Ruby, and Simone danced, ate, and talked, while Scooter rubbed shoulders with the black politicians in attendance. Among them were New York City councilmen, a state representative, and a few members of the Congressional Black Caucus, who believed that Scooter was not the gangster that the government had made him out to be, but a black businessman from Harlem who had struggled though poverty by initially being involved in the numbers racket. Starting legit businesses, such as barbershops, hair salons, and a bar, and hiring local residents legally servicing the Harlem community were on his list of good deeds.

A lot of politicians had grown up in Harlem and had known Scooter coming up. They never forgot their friends when they made it in politics. So when the government began targeting him, they stood by him, and when Tashy was convicted, they rallied for her freedom. Though their cries went unheard, Scooter's name was cleared of drug dealing when the government couldn't prove the heroin was being sold out of Tashy's hair salon.

"How's your niece, Ruby?" Tashy asked while catching her breath after dancing with a famous R & B singer. Tashy knew everything about Mecca from Ruby's correspondence with her after she was transferred to the prison in West Virginia. Two years later Tashy was transferred to the same prison, and she and Ruby wasted no time becoming cell mates again.

"She's good," Ruby answered, avoiding eye contact. While Ruby had no problem sharing her personal issues with Tashy, this wasn't the proper place to talk about her concerns about Mecca. Even though they were lovers, they acted like sisters. They had sat up plenty of nights in the cell, sharing their life stories. They had bonded because they had a lot in common. When Tashy had told Ruby that she never had a mother, because she died giving birth to her, Ruby shed a tear.

When Tashy saw that, she knew that Ruby was her friend. Ruby hardly showed her feelings or emotions. The only time she showed any was when she was beating someone up. That was the first time she saw Ruby cry, and the second and last was when Ruby found out about her niece.

"When do I get to meet her?" Tashy asked with a wide smile.

"Whenever. Right now she's in New York, hanging with Daphne," Ruby said, knowing that simply mentioning Daphne's name would get her to change the subject.

Everyone in the West Virginia prison had known the two women had it in for each other. Though Daphne didn't need to hustle in jail, hustling was in her blood, so with her knowledge of the law, she became a jailhouse lawyer. Tashy was transferred to the prison, and word got out that she was also good with the law and she wouldn't charge an inmate for help.

It didn't upset Daphne that Tashy was helping inmates free of charge; what got under her skin was Tashy supposedly told inmates that Daphne didn't know what she was doing. So a confrontation between the two women was inevitable. Daphne didn't appreciate anyone talking behind her back, assassinating her character.

One sunny afternoon in the rec yard, while Ruby and Tashy sat on a bench, playing cards, Daphne walked up and sat next to Ruby, turning to stare at Tashy. Tashy was no punk, but she wasn't a fighter, either. She had grown up spoiled and protected by her father and her neighborhood. She never had to lift a finger at anyone.

That couldn't be said about Daphne. She'd grown up on the rough streets of two of Brooklyn's roughest neighborhoods: Bed-Stuy and Brownsville. She'd had to fight either in school, when girls would pick fights with her, out of jealousy mostly, and in the Tompkins projects. Tashy was no match for her.

"I hear you got a sweet tooth, Tashy." Daphne scowled while cracking her knuckles. Ruby looked at both women, confused.

"Daphne, what's up?"

"What are you talking about, Daphne? What is that supposed to mean?" Tashy snapped.

"It means you have my name in your mouth when it shouldn't be."

Tashy rolled her eyes and sucked her teeth. It was the first time that anyone ever saw her come out of character.

"Ruby, get this bitch before I—"

Daphne reached across the table and tried to choke Tashy, but Ruby grabbed her behind her waist. "Daphne, chill! Leave it alone!" Ruby ordered.

Tashy was on her feet, ready to rumble. "Let her go. I'll fight her. She don't scare me."

"Tashy, shut up. Nobody's fighting. Y'all both my peoples, so off the strength of me, squash this bullshit."

Both women knew that if they didn't respect Ruby's wish, they would have to face off with her, and neither one of them wanted that. Ruby was a ferocious fighter and wouldn't hesitate to use any weapon she could get her hands on. So both women went their separate ways. From that day forth, they disliked each other with a passion.

Tashy rolled her eyes. "You got your niece hanging around Miss High-and-Mighty, huh?"

"Tashy, you're a grown-ass woman," Ruby replied as she watched Simone, who sat quietly next to her mother. "Your grown mom's had a petty beef with this girl in jail over nothing, and she acting like a teenager. That is over. That is all behind us, Tashy."

Tashy waived Ruby off. "Yeah, whatever. Just don't have that bitch around me."

Ruby simply shook her head. "Grow up." When Simone got up to go to the restroom, Ruby inquired, "She seems uptight. What's up?"

Taking a sip of Dom Pérignon, Tashy replied, "I can't call it, Ruby. These young chicks these days are spoiled. Plus, she isn't the party type." She looked around and lowered her voice as she changed the subject. "I'm glad you came when you did. My father tried to hook me up with one of his politician friends' son. Girl, this man is so ugly, it looked like his face hurts when he smiles."

Ruby giggled. "How rich is he?"

"Who cares? A billion dollars couldn't make him cute," Tashy spat.

After the celebration, and after everyone emptied the club to do things in Vegas that stay in Vegas, Tashy snuck off to Ruby's suite in the Palms for a long-awaited episode of sucking and touching. Once they entered the luxurious suite, the women wasted no time coming out of their clothes.

As they kissed, passionately exploring each other's bodies with roaming hands, Ruby asked in a husky whisper, "Does your family know about us?"

Tashy moaned in her ear, "Don't ruin the moment," and pushed Ruby on the bed.

With a seductive grin, she parted Ruby's thick thighs and placed a warm, long tongue against her erect nipples. Ruby groaned and closed her eyes. To her, Tashy was the best lover she'd ever had. Tashy knew how to please her in ways Ruby couldn't resist.

She knew exactly where to touch Ruby, making her go nuts. When Tashy placed her tongue between her thighs, Ruby arched her back while holding on to Tashy's ponytailed head. The silk sheets felt smooth under Ruby's skin as they changed positions to eat each other out in the sixty-nine position, as well as using the doggy style and missionary. Their faces were wet with each other's juices, while their dark, voluptuous bodies glistened with sweat. When they were done, they both leaned up against the headboard, smoking a joint of potent Mexican bud.

"So does your family know?" Ruby asked, blowing smoke circles toward a ceiling fan.

"No, and it's none of their business." Ruby knew that wasn't Tashy's real reason for not telling them about her lifestyle. She knew how much Tashy tried to please her father, and hearing that she was a lesbian might not sit right with him or Simone.

"Don't you think they'll start to question and wonder why you're not with a man?"

"Shit," Tashy grumbled while passing Ruby the joint. "I'm a grown-ass woman. I don't have to explain my lifestyle to no one. I just did ten years for my father, so I'll be damned if he judges me. Simone, I think she'll understand. I mean, a lot of women are into it."

Putting the joint out in an ashtray on the bedside table, Ruby changed the subject. "So, what's your plan?"

Always the hustler, Tashy chimed right in. "I hear that weed is really popping. I know where to get it real cheap. I got a Cali connect, and you don't have to do a lot of traveling. I got a hookup at this FedEx joint back home."

"So you wanna sell strictly weight?"

"No doubt. You can get it from me cheaper than what you're getting it for. One hand washes the other." Tashy grinned.

Ruby knew that Tashy loved the idea of cutting Daphne's throat. Daphne's connect in Texas had good prices, and when she brought him other customers, he looked out for her by giving her a pound for free. She knew that if she stopped coppin' from the connect, he'd lose a customer and Daphne's commission would get shorter. She figured that Daphne would be angry if Ruby

decided to switch connects, and hearing that
Tashy was the reason would probably piss her
off even more. Yet Ruby was about money, and
no one got in the way of her making money. She
owed no one an explanation. So the decision was
easy for her.

"Give me a hundred pounds next week."

"It's a done deal." Tashy smiled.

Grabbing Tashy's face between her hands,
Ruby smiled. "I'm so glad you're home, baby."

For another two hours, the women made love.
Tashy left a sleeping Ruby to return to the hotel
room she shared with Simone. As Tashy tiptoed
through the hotel room so that she would not
wake Simone, she couldn't remove the smile on
her face. After a shower, Tashy climbed under
the Versace quilt on the king-size bed. In the
dark, she did not notice Simone sitting halfway
up, leaning her head on a large down pillow.

"So are you and Ruby lesbians?"

For the past few months, veteran detective
Thomas Caldwell had been vigorously investigating the triple murders of Karmen and her
sisters. Tall, athletically built, with a stubbled
chin, hooded blue eyes, and a weathered face, he
resembled Brett Favre, except for his jet-black

hair. Frustrated, he knew that he desperately needed to solve this case. It would be the biggest case of his career and could mean a promotion to captain with a conviction.

Sitting behind his desk cluttered with paperwork, family photos, and a mug of coffee, Caldwell read interview after interview of witness statements, trying to see if he had missed anything of value. Tapping a pencil on his desk, he scanned the office that he shared with four other homicide detectives. Being thirty-eight, he was the youngest of them all. His thoughts were interrupted by the ringing of his desk phone.

"Am I speaking to Detective Caldwell?" the voice on the line asked, with a vintage New York accent.

"Yes, this is he. Who's speaking?"

"This is Detective Mike Levy. I'm down at the Seven-Three. I'm working a double over here in East New York, and I think there might be a possible link to your triple."

The news made Caldwell sit up in his chair, as the hairs stood on his neck. "Fill me in."

"The owner of the bodega where your bodies were is a resurrected problem out of prison, after putting in a little over a decade. Been home for a few years now, and bodies start dropping where the circumstances surrounding the murders make her a possible suspect."

"You said her?" Caldwell asked with a bit of surprise in his voice.

Levy sighed. "You heard right. Her name is Ruby Davidson out of Brownsville. This ain't your average mademoiselle we're talking about here, pal. She makes some of these male thugs look like the pope himself. Real evil broad, buddy."

"So where's the link?" Caldwell asked, anxious to hear the promising lead that would crack the case wide open.

"My double over here were guys rumored to have an involvement in the shooting of her niece, who recently came out of a coma, and the murder of her boyfriend. Her boyfriend's cousins, who were also murdered, one of them was romantically linked to one of your corpses. I think her name was Karmen," Levy said.

"Yeah, that's one of mine."

"She was questioned about the murder of her boyfriend and his brother due to suspicion that she was involved. I interviewed the detective working on that case, and he said after talking to her, he felt she knew more than she was letting on. What I'm saying is, all these murders some-way, somehow, could be the result of dealing with Davidson and her niece."

Though not overly excited anymore over the lead Levy had given him, Caldwell tapped his pencil on the table a few times before responding. "What's the intel on her niece?" he asked.

"From what I heard, she ran Davidson's organization while Davidson did time. Now she's out of the game. I guess the coma was a wake-up call that she answered when she woke up."

Caldwell thanked Levy and promised to follow up and share intel relating to Ruby and Mecca. Hanging up the phone, he tapped his pencil against the desk, in deep thought. He leaned back in his chair and thought out loud. "If it was a robbery homicide, why would Davidson rob her own store and have the workers killed?"

Shaking his head, he rose from his seat and put the tan cotton blazer on over his stark white dress shirt. "Police work," he mumbled. Checking his police-issue Glock .40, he made a mental note to find Ruby Davidson for an interview.

More and more, his thoughts drifted back to the pretty Spanish girls murdered in cold blood. He felt a sadness for their family and friends. So young they were, with their whole lives ahead of them. He had nieces their age, who were full of life and promise. Their lives were cut too short for material things that could easily be replaced. Now all that was left of them was memories and faces painted on the metal gate of the store, saying, IN LOVING MEMORY OF KARMEN, MARIA, AND TINA.

"I'm not a baby. I'm a grown woman who can figure things out." Tashy avoided eye contact with Simone after she turned on the light to face her mother.

"Please, Mom, don't lie to me. I'm tired of living a lie."

Tashy looked over at her daughter, the spitting image of her, with traces of her father in her complexion, and sighed.

"It's true. Please don't be disappointed in me, Simone. I just don't want to embarrass you. I want to be the perfect mother and make up for all the lost time."

Simone's eyes filled with tears. "I'm not disappointed in you, Mom. I'm proud that you're my mom. I'm so happy that you told me the truth. It's okay with me, because I understand."

"Oh, Simone, come here, honey." Tashy cried as she embraced her daughter.

Afterward she wiped the tears off of her daughter's face and asked, "Why did you say you were tired of living a lie? What did you have to lie about?"

"I have a girlfriend, too." Simone shook her head, looking down at her hands.

Tashy's eyebrows rose. "Get out of here! You kidding, right?"

Simone gave her the "do I look like I'm kidding" look.

"Your grandfather know?"

"Yeah. That's why I wound up going to school out on corny Long Island, living in a corny neighborhood, surrounded by corny people, and having to lie to my friends about liking boys and playing girlfriend to this corny guy Scooter practically made me date."

Simone called her grandfather by his nickname at his request. He thought "grandpa" made him feel too old. Facing her daughter, Tashy folded her legs under her and sat upright in the lotus position. Simone did the same. Feeling like a teenage girl all over again, Tashy started the girl talk.

"What's her name? Tell me about her."

"Her name is Mona. She lives on Twenty-ninth and Frederick Douglas. . . ."

They sat up all night, catching up on each other's lives. Tashy listened attentively, learning what Simone's life had been like after her incarceration. Sometimes, Tashy teared up, feeling that she had missed some of the important moments that Simone told her about. Secretly, she vowed never to miss these moments in her daughter's life again.

At the same time Simone couldn't be happier. She felt free from the burdens that she carried, talking to her mother. Scooter had sheltered her and locked her away from the real world. He had plans for her to be married to the son of a football star, whom she was currently dating, to live in a big house and produce great-grandkids he could spoil like he did her. She never talked to any of her friends like she did to Mona and now to her mother, and it felt good. Scooter had forbidden her to go to Harlem to see Mona, and she knew that he had lots of people on watch for her. All she could do was call Mona on her cell phone and talk for hours. Otherwise, she dug deep into her schoolwork and classes at LIU.

"When was the last time you and Mona were together?" Tashy asked.

"It's been two months now."

"Guess what? You're coming to live with me in the city as soon as we get back." Tashy grabbed her daughter's hand and held it tight. Simone's face lit up with excitement.

"What about Scooter?"

"What about him? You're my daughter. He can't tell me what to do with my child. Girl, please! And guess where my crib is at?"

"Harlem?" Simone cooed.

"You know it. Right on One Hundred Fortieth and Lenox."

"Ruby seems like a tough chick. Tell me about her. She must be somebody if *Don Diva* wants to do a story on her."

With a grin and a sigh, Tashy rolled her eyes. "Girl, I don't know where to begin. Ruby is more than a magazine article. She's a book."

Simone giggled. "What would you call the book?"

After briefly thinking on the title, Tashy smiled. "*Hell's Diva*."

Chapter Eleven

When I lie down, I say, "When shall I arise,
and the night be ended? And I am full of tossings
to and fro unto the dawning of the day."

—Job 7:4

Tears rolled down ten-year-old Mecca's face
as she made her way from her bedroom, down
the carpeted hallway of her aunt's Coney Island
duplex. The pain in her head made her attempt
to sleep fruitless.

Making it to the closed, locked door of Ruby's
bedroom, she heard Luther Vandross's voice and
smelled the strong odor of weed coming from the
other side of the door.

"Auntie!" she squealed as she banged on the
door.

After a few more tries, the door flew open and
a naked Ruby, with bloodshot eyes, stood before
her. Mecca looked in at the bed, where Monique

sat, leaning on the brass headboard, smoking a joint.

"What's wrong, baby?" Ruby asked.

"My head hurts bad."

Monique quickly grabbed a pink terry-cloth robe and held Mecca by the hand as they made their way up the stairs to the kitchen.

"I'll give you something for the headache. You want some warm milk and cookies?"

Mecca nodded. Monique crushed an aspirin with a little water on a spoon. While the milk and cookies made Mecca forget all about the headache, Monique slipped her the spoon. Afterward, she wiped the milk off of her lips and took her to her room to tuck her in.

She kissed Mecca on her forehead once and whispered, "I'll see you tomorrow, okay, honey?"

Mecca smiled and nodded. Without question, Monique was one of Mecca's favorite people in the world, only after her mother and father and, of course, Aunt Ruby. In a way, Monique reminded her of her mother. Nothing seemed to bother her. With all the things Mecca saw living in Brooklyn, she wondered how Monique could be that way.

Sometimes, she wondered if it was seeing them making love on the couch one day that had made her that way. Then she realized that she would probably never know. Monique was probably just a happy person, because to Mecca, whatever it was they were doing on the couch, it bothered her, almost made her feel sick. Either way, Monique was happy. In the middle of the night Mecca awoke, crying, because of the throbbing pain in her head.

"Shhh . . ." she heard from the darkness. "Sleep comfortably, Mecca."

She recognized the voice of her friend and smiled, happy that he was present again. She thought he didn't care for her anymore, because he'd been gone for so long. Now he was back, and she could feel his touch on her head, which made the headache go away. Then she fell asleep. As soon as Mecca walked into the office, Lou wasted no time snorting.

"You think 'cause you saved my life that I'm supposed to ignore what you're up to?"

"You welcome. I'm fine. Nice to finally have you back," Mecca said sarcastically as she stood with her hands on her hips, eyeing Lou. Lou leaned back in his chair and folded his arms across the desk.

"You lied to me, Mecca. Why?"

"I have no idea what you're talking about, Lou," she replied, confused.

Lou shook his head. "You're better than I thought. Pulled one over on me. Could you believe that? Me!"

"Are you okay, Lou? Did that Doc guy give you some of his tea?"

"Cut the crap," he snapped. "I know you're plotting to start a war between Daphne and your aunt. I'm no fool!"

Mecca shook her head in disbelief. "You're kidding, right? Do we have to change positions? I'll be the one to enter your dreams and attempt to get you to see the reality of things, because you're tripping, Lou, for real!"

Lou rose from behind the desk and walked up to her. Though she took a nervous step back, Lou was face-to-face with her and grabbed her cheeks with his large, warm hands.

"Lou!"

"Shhh . . ." He cut her off, and then he softly kissed her forehead.

In a flash, the office and Lou disappeared, and Mecca stared at a vision of herself getting out of her Range Rover at Sutter and Hendrix in Sutter Gardens at night. Looking both ways, she entered the hallway of a building, with her face and head covered by a large black and gray North Face hood.

"What's up, Ma?" Breeze mumbled, standing in the hall, with his tan Woolrich hood over his head.

"Wassup, nigga? What's poppin'?" Mecca blew into her hands, warming them.

Breeze pulled out a brown paper bag that was stuffed and handed it to her. "That's from the Jamaican restaurant. I got the loot from the Brownsville spot in my crib. I ain't wanna be out here with all that change on me," he replied.

Mecca looked in the bag and fingered the thick wad of cash. It was her half of the money Breeze passed off for putting him onto robbing Daphne's restaurant and Ruby's spot in Brownsville run by Mo Blood. Breeze and Mecca were the best of friends from when Mecca and Shamel were an item. Breeze and Shamel had been friends since they were kids, and when Shamel introduced him to Mecca, he immediately dug her style. To him, they were the perfect match. Mecca was a classy hood chick who had more heart and drive than most dudes Breeze knew. So, he didn't hesitate to act when she came to him, asking him to rob the spots. He did wonder, *Why her aunt's spots, though?*

"She's a snake, Breeze. I can't go into details now, but you know me, and you know how I operate. I'm loyal to the bone, but if you cross me, it's on," Mecca had simply growled.

He'd nodded. "I can dig it. You know I'll ride with you anytime."

"What you doing? Let's go get something to eat," Mecca suggested, stuffing the brown paper bag in her coat. Breeze put his arm around her and smiled.

"Your treat?" he asked as they walked toward her Range Rover.

"You know, you've always been a stingy nigga."

As they drove away, they concocted the idea that Breeze would move weed for Ruby and devised another scheme to make her business in East New York crumble like the Brownsville one.

"You tryin'a start a war with your aunt and homegirl?" Breeze inquired as he reclined in the Range Rover's plush leather seat. "I thought you liked Shorty?"

"I do. She good people. Plus, there's no way my aunt will come out on top if they go to war. Daphne's connected to the Shower Posse. My aunt has no army."

Breeze shook his head. "You'd be a hell of a chess player."

What Mecca didn't realize was that Ruby would partner up with Tashy, and Tashy's connections through her father were just as dangerous and powerful, if not more so, as the Shower Posse's. Sometimes, things didn't always go according to plan.

Mecca drove, smiling to herself. Revenge was definitely sweet. She thought of the pictures she had of Ruby conversing with Mo Blood outside a building in Brownsville Houses. When she gave them to Daphne and explained that those were the guys who shot her and robbed the restaurant, Daphne would realize why Mecca held something against her aunt and why Daphne should also. Wicked.

Mecca was awakened by a blond, bulimic stewardess with a nasal voice. "You'll have to fasten your seat belt. The plane is about to land."

Excited about her trip to Italy to spend a weekend with Miguel, who had returned overseas to start a new season with his basketball team, Mecca half smiled and fastened her seat belt.

The thought of seeing him made her horny and moist. When her thoughts drifted back to the dream in which Lou showed her the plot on her aunt, she shrugged and smiled. *Deal with it, Lou.*

A week after they returned from Vegas, Tashy could see why Simone was infatuated with

Mona. She was New York sexy. Her eyes were big, brown, and full of life. She had a smooth bronze complexion that complemented her catwalk-lean body on long, toned legs. She walked with a confidence that oozed seduction, which many women just did not have. She was charismatic, street-smart, and worldly. These were the things that Tashy noticed the day she met her.

During the time Simone was in Mona's presence, the skin-stretching smile never left her face. Tashy knew they were truly in love and was a little envious of their relationship. Hers wasn't an emotional, spiritual intimacy; it was pure lust. She wished Ruby felt the same way she felt about her, but Ruby was a strong, independent woman who knew how to take care of herself. She didn't sit around looking for handouts; she was a go-getter. And she knew how to please a woman.

Still, Tashy knew that Ruby was the type that didn't become emotionally attached. Sure, she was a friend you could count on, but Ruby treated relationships like clothes. Wear them, and when it was time to buy new ones, put the others in the closet until you wanted to wear them again. Ruby's only loves were money and power.

Mona and Simone made a cute couple. While Simone was the listener, Mona was a talker. She wasn't a boring talker; she had lots of interesting stories and gossip. Living in Harlem made it possible for her to hear stories and gossip that would put the tabloids out of business. When Tashy noticed a scar on Mona's jawline, she inquired about it.

"That scar makes you favor Sanaa Lathan. How you get it?"

"I'll take the Sanaa Lathan comparison as a compliment," Mona replied while rubbing it. "I take it that Simone didn't tell you, but this scar is the reason we met."

Tashy folded her arms on the table and raised her eyebrows, waiting to hear the story. "Simone never told me exactly how you met. . . ."

Mona burst off into a fast-talking, excited narrative, which had become her trademark. It was after a house party thrown at a brownstone two blocks from Mona's house, where a group of neighborhood girls with too much liquor and weed in their system decided to cause some trouble. They were jealous of Mona's fashionable appearance and happy-go-lucky attitude. However, unknown to them, that was only a facade. Mona suffered internally. She was a hurt soul from losing both her parents in a fatal bus accident years ago, and she was never able to come to terms with the loss.

But the girls weren't aware of that, and they decided to pick a fight with her outside of the party. At the same time, Simone, who was there, after lying to Scooter that she was going into the city to buy some expensive-looking bag for her collection of books in college, partied it up. The downside to the lie was that Scooter had Wayne, Simone's fake boyfriend, escort her to the city. When she told him about the party, he gave Simone the corny speech she expected from him.

"Do you think it's wise of you to disobey your grandfather, then try and have me condone it?"

Simone sighed, wondering how this dude could be so lame. "Listen, Wayne," she began. "Loosen up a little. Live your own life, not the life your parents want you to live. Get your thumb out of your ass. Now, I'm going to this party, and you're coming, too, and if you keep your mouth shut, I might give you some tonight."

While they were dating, Wayne had begun to sense that she wasn't really interested in him. He figured that with his charm, she would come around; however, six months had already passed. Now his eyes widened. "Since you put it that way, I guess we can live it up a bit."

Wayne actually enjoyed himself. Simone tried to dance with him, but he looked like a stiff white boy. He reminded her of the character Carlton from the show *The Fresh Prince of Bel-Air*. After a while, she left Wayne to chat with friends she grew up with to catch up on what was going on in the old neighborhood.

A few blunts later and loads of gossip, Simone was ready to leave. She found Wayne dancing with a round girl in tight clothes that made her look like an overstuffed suitcase. It would figure that the two people in the party no one wanted to be seen with dancing would find each other. And Simone had to be with one of them. When her friends asked who the weirdo was who'd come in with her, she quickly answered, "My father sent him to bodyguard me."

When they got outside, Simone spotted a crowd of girls stomping and kicking someone on the ground. She knew it was another girl they were jumping when she heard the girl cry out.

These were the same girls that she'd noticed staring at her in the party and whispering to one another. She knew they were jealous of her clothes and real diamonds, because they looked raggedy as all hell, but she didn't really care. Now they were jumping some helpless female. She knew they did not like her, and she didn't really care for them, but they knew their place and would not try anything, because they knew who her father was. She walked toward the crowd.

"Simone, that is none of your business. We have to get back to Long Island!" Wayne squeaked.

"Shut up, Wayne!" Simone parted the crowd. "That's enough. Y'all get off of her!"

"Simone, mind your business. This ain't got nothing to do with you!" one of them grumbled.

"Don't ya'll see she's had enough? Damn, it shouldn't take all of y'all to beat on one girl. Real women fight their own battles!"

Simone helped the girl off the ground. Blood leaked from a gash on her face. Her blouse and Italian-made pants were ripped and dirty, and her hair was out wild. She looked wrecked. Even with everything out of place, Simone could tell that the girl was beautiful, and the way she was dressed with her Manolos let her know she was fashionable and on point. These bitches were probably jealous. When Simone held the girl up, they both walked away toward busy Lenox Avenue. She could hear the girls mumbling under their breath, but they said nothing. Wayne followed.

"Where do you live?"

"Two blocks up. Thank you so much," Mona said, limping.

"Why were they jumping you?" she asked.

"I got too much attention from their boyfriends, and I'm new around here. Crazy thing about it"—Mona chuckled while holding a bloody hand on her open wound—"I don't like boys."

Mona then passed out. When she came to, she was lying in a bed in a Harlem hospital with twelve stitches on her swollen face and Simone holding her hand.

"Where am I?" Mona asked groggily.

"The hospital. You passed out."

Mona remembered the girls jumping her after the party, but she couldn't remember anything after that.

"My name's Mona. What's yours?"

Simone visited Mona in Harlem every weekend afterward. They had the same taste in fashion, TV shows, books, and the same feelings for the same sex. They were inseparable until Scooter found out that Simone was still seeing Mona against his wishes.

"That's it. That's the start of our relationship. Every time I see this scar in the mirror, it no longer makes me sad. I think of my honey, and the scar becomes like my lucky charm." Mona smiled at Simone.

Tashy had to hold back the tears. Afterward, Mona became a regular at Tashy's apartment now that Simone was back in New York City. At first Scooter protested, but when Tashy demanded that she be able to get reacquainted with her daughter, Scooter surrendered. Then, one day, Mona was introduced to Ruby.

At the first sight of each other, Ruby and Mona were attracted to each other. Mona was the type who liked to live life on the edge, the wild side . . . and to her Ruby seemed like the one who could provide that life.

For Ruby, Mona's aura was a seductive elixir that stirred the pure lust within her. Mona knew the more time she spent around Ruby, the more the temptation would grow, but she didn't want to hurt Simone. She loved her with all her heart, but love and lust were two different things. As far as Ruby was concerned, she had no commitments to anyone and she barely knew Simone. Tashy knew better than to try and lock Ruby down, because she had already tried in prison and couldn't do it there. So in the free world, that would be impossible. Still, Mona avoided being in Ruby's presence at all cost. If she saw her car outside Tashy's brownstone, she wouldn't stop by. She would call Simone and ask her to come to her apartment.

One thing Mona was sure of was that if she crossed Simone, it could be bad for her health. And from what she'd learned about Ruby, there would definitely be hell up in Harlem if a confrontation started between them. What she did not know about her was that when Ruby wanted something, she usually got it.

One night Mona answered a knock at her door, believing it was Simone coming over, and received a big surprise. Ruby stood in her doorway with a horny expression written on her face. No words were exchanged, but they both understood their silent communications and wasted no time devouring each other in a long night of passion. Mona had never experienced such pleasure before with a woman. It was as if everywhere Ruby touched or licked was a trigger for sending orgasms throughout her body.

In return, Mona explored every part of Ruby's curvaceous torso. The firmness of her body excited Mona. But to Ruby, Mona was okay in bed, but not as good as she'd expected and nowhere as good as Tashy. She decided that it was nothing worth repeating. But Mona was hooked.

After they concluded their lust making and Ruby left, Mona awoke in the morning with a huge smile, picturing the next time she and Ruby could sneak off and get into it again. She would soon find out that Ruby had no intentions of ever getting in bed with her again. The lust was gone.

Chapter Twelve

Your secrets are safe with me. . . .
                                    —Alicia Keys

Mecca leaned on the terrace of her hotel bedroom overlooking the streets of Rome, holding a glass of champagne. She inhaled the Italian air, smiling to herself and thinking about how well her plans were playing out. The manila envelope sitting on the king-size bed reminded her that the final part of her plan would soon be put into motion. Life was good.

While she awaited Miguel's return from a game, she toured Rome in her rental, using the navigation system to find places in the city. Thoughts raced through her mind as she took in the sights. The city was beautiful in an old, but rich way. It looked nothing like the buildings in Brooklyn and made her feel like she was in another world.

She was happy that she was financially comfortable to enjoy such pleasures and travel the world with the man she loved, who loved her back. Yet not all her thoughts were joyous. Occasionally, she would drop down into a depression as she remembered the things she'd seen on the mean streets. Streets where poor kids didn't have the opportunity to experience what she was experiencing right now. It was on those same streets that children saw their mothers, fathers, sisters, and brothers addicted to drugs, selling drugs, selling their own bodies, and murdered by gun-toting thugs or the police. They also saw their friends murdered. On these streets it was dangerous for them to play, and it was so easy for them to find themselves in the wrong place at the wrong time.

It saddened her because she knew she was part of the cycle of death that hovered over the city. Of course, it was all she knew, but that did not make it right. Even now she was using what she knew to pay back those who had wronged her when all she was trying to be was loyal. She thought about Daphne, those eyes, why she was in her dreams, and everything they had experienced since meeting. She hoped that her plan would make Daphne come out on top, because she really liked her. However, personal feelings had to be set aside in order for her plan to be successful. Too much was at risk.

When she stepped out on the town, she adhered to the saying, "When in Rome, do as the Romans do," and dressed in the finest Italian clothing and made sure Miguel did, too. They dined at outdoor restaurants, and they even played a game of boccie with a group of older Italian men and took in an opera.

Mecca hated the opera. For Miguel, Mecca's declarations of love weren't etched in stone until one morning, when he awoke and went to the bathroom. There he found her sitting on the toilet, defecating, with the door wide open. She smiled at him and wiped. That was when he knew they were in love.

For Mecca, Miguel's love was proven when she finally decided to tell him about her vision while in a coma and Lou. Once she began, everything came out like a flood, and she could do nothing to stop it. She cried when she told him about the murder of her parents and her aunt's involvement and how Lou had exposed all the lies in her life told by people around her.

Miguel simply listened, and when it was all over, he hugged her. "It was a vision, Mecca. How can you be so sure they are true?"

"A lot of the circumstances made it obvious," she replied.

Miguel didn't know how to take her revelations. All he knew was that he loved her and he wanted to spend the rest of his life with her. So he left it at that. The coma was behind them, and life was moving on. Realizing she'd been through a lot, he was determined to fill the rest of her life with happiness.

While they toured the ruins of the Colosseum, Miguel removed a small box from his silk white slacks and got on one knee. Mecca lost her breath when he opened the box, which held a four-carat diamond in a platinum setting.

"Mecca Sykes, one day isn't worth living if you're not my wife. Marry me."

"Yes!" Mecca yelled before he could even finish.

"Damn, what a brother gotta do to be more than just a fuck?"

"Don't ask to be more than just a fuck is what he gotta do," Daphne answered with a smile as she rushed one of her casual sex partners out of her apartment. Men practically begged for her to be their woman. She received so many flowers at her restaurant so often, people were

starting to think it was a florist/restaurant. She
didn't even read the cards. Andrea would amuse
herself reading them to her, but she never paid
any attention.

Daphne used men that she met on occasion
like men used women. Purely physical. She
wanted no attachments to any of them. To her,
no man could replace Donovan. Everyone tried
telling her to let go and open her heart, even
Junior, who advised, "You will never be happy if
you don't love again. What is life if you have no
legacy to leave behind? You will achieve happiness from raising a family." While she listened
and nodded, her heart said otherwise. There
were big shoes to fill to receive her heart, and so
far all the men she dealt with had come up short.

Shutting the door of her brownstone after the
inadequate plumber left, she had a moment to
think. Wrapped in a black silk robe that reached
her toned thighs, she grabbed the manila envelope that had a bunch of stamps on it, had been
postmarked in Italy, and had no return address,
and opened it.

Daphne smiled as she saw photos of Mecca
and Miguel posing in front of various European landmarks. The Eiffel Tower, Westminster
Abbey, the Louvre, Buckingham Palace, the
Leaning Tower of Pisa, and the Colosseum.

The smile vanished as she eyed the photos of Ruby smiling with Mo Blood, with Tah Gunz in the background. There was even a photo of Ruby and Breeze in front of his Sutter Gardens building. Daphne was confused. She had no idea who these people in the pictures with Ruby were, or why Mecca had sent them. She looked back in the manila envelope and took out a letter from Mecca.

> *Daphne,*
> *First, let me say, I took your advice and traveled the world. What makes it more exciting is that I'm doing it with the man I truly love and trust. (You should give love another chance. You deserve it!) And guess what? I'm engaged! There are pictures of me there with the four-carat rock on my finger. Can you say bling-bling? I'm happy now, Daphne, and it feels good having people around you that care about your happiness. That brings me to the pictures of Ruby and those men.*
>
> *I told you once before that at one time my aunt was my idol. She was everything I wanted to be. She is courageous, independent, self-sufficient, and business minded. At the same time she is a ruthless, self-cen-*

tered, "it's all about her" snake! She is the reason why my mother and father got killed. Her greed made her help set up my father to be robbed. She did it because she was strung out on dick. A man's good dick is her weakness. That's why she lives a gay lifestyle, so she can remain in control. She killed the men responsible for the murders so they wouldn't expose her.

She let me fall in love with a man who she was having sex with behind my back. He worked for her, but in reality, he called the shots because she was weak for the dick. Those men in the photos (the one in the wheelchair and the one with him) are the guys who shot me, putting me in a coma. She had them selling weed for her in Brownsville.

They are dead now. She killed them for the same reason she killed the men who killed my parents. Not to be exposed. She uses people for what she needs, and when she's done, she kills them. She's a black widow. The other man in the picture with just him and her, his name is Breeze. He is the guy who robbed your restaurant, and she staged the robbery of her store.

I'm telling you these things because she doesn't deserve to have the opportunity to do what she does to another person who has been loyal to her. What you do with this info is all on you, but I assume you will move wisely. I don't think I'm coming back to New York. As much as I love it, my heart belongs to my man now. Hopefully, we will see each other again. We gotta do Paris and Italy together. I met Donatella Versace!

Take care, Daphne. Oh, did you like my tearful act at Karmen's funeral?

Peace

Mecca

Daphne put the letter down, infuriated. Donovan's words played in her head as she contemplated her next move. "The longer someone stays in the game, the more likely they will slip up and show their hand. And most people bluff, as if they have a good hand, until the cards are shown."

Looking at Mecca's picture, Daphne mouthed, "Thank you, Mecca. We are definitely the last of a dying breed."

Daphne reached for her multicolored Louis Vuitton pocketbook and pulled out her Nokia cell phone. When the person she called answered, she spoke.

"Junior, I'm going to need an umbrella. A storm is brewing."

"Can you come out of the rain without getting wet?" Junior inquired.

"No. I was locked out of the house," Daphne sighed.

The line went dead. In their coded language, Daphne made it clear that a war was inevitable. There was no other way of dealing with Ruby that would leave her on top, and she would have to deal with the storm head-on. Junior wanted to know if it could be avoided, and from what Daphne said, it couldn't. Ruby had to die.

"Happiness is short lived when you enjoy making others unhappy."

"And what is that supposed to mean? Are you about to give me another of your speeches? Because I got better things to do," Mecca announced to Lou, who sat on a bench, reading a newspaper, with his legs folded.

In this dream they were both dressed in eighties apparel, sitting on a bench in the Langston Hughes projects, which she'd grown up in. The streets were empty, and a cold breeze flowed through the dark night. Mecca pulled the earflaps of her gray sheepskin hat over her ears, shivering at the cutting cold. As she looked up, she could see movement in the lighted apartments above.

"What do you have to do that's more important than being here with me?" Lou asked jealously. Mecca held her hand in front of her, showing her engagement ring off.

"I'm engaged, so what I have to do is be a good fiancée." Mecca smiled. "And travel the world."

"Just don't forget where you came from," Lou murmured.

"How can I?" she asked as she gestured at her surroundings with her hands. Afterward, she folded her arms across her chest and said, "You never told me why, out of all places and all people, you chose Brownsville and me."

Lou smiled. He smiled because he loved showing Mecca answers instead of telling her. He snapped his fingers, and suddenly the neighborhood came alive with sunshine and people. They watched as a group of children stood over a syringe that sat on the ground, among the litter of broken glass, crack vials, soiled Pampers, and the other filth that ghetto streets are adorned with.

One boy, about nine years old, picked up the syringe to show the rest of his group that he was brave. At the same time, Lou said, "You're not the only one experiencing the likes of me, Mecca. There are Meccas and Brownsvilles everywhere, so there are Lous everywhere."

Mecca watched the boy with the syringe and wondered if he knew what it was. The boy acted like he was about to shoot dope, an action that he'd probably seen someone do before, because he knew exactly how to hold the needle. He grinned and spoke to the other kids, but Mecca could not hear him. Then he plunged the needle into his arm.

"*No! No!* Don't!" Mecca jumped up and ran toward him.

Mecca awoke out of another dream, feeling cold from the open hotel windows. The white curtains blew in gently, giving the room an eerie feel. She knew she didn't scream, because Miguel was still sound asleep next to her. Slowly, she got up and closed the double windows. She crawled back into the bed and cuddled up next to Miguel, who had his back to her. Feeling warmer, she wrapped her arms around him and held on a little tighter.

She watched as the colors of the sky began to change slightly as dawn approached. As Miguel turned, he tugged on the blanket in a way that exposed his nudity. Mecca felt his hardness and smiled. The sun wasn't the only thing rising up this morning.

Chapter Thirteen

If you cause opponents to be unaware of the place and time of battle, you can always win.
—Sun Tzu, *The Art of War*

Ruby was nervously puzzled. For a week straight, she had had no idea where Daphne was. It was as if she'd ceased to exist. The Crown Heights restaurant had been shut down, and when she went to Daphne's house, a strange woman with a Haitian accent and bad skin, wearing a crooked wig, a cheap floral-print dress, and house slippers that revealed to the world her ashy and crusty feet, answered the door.

"I know no Daphne. I bought this house last week from a real estate agent representing the owner," the woman yelled over the sound of music that Ruby could not recognize. When she tried her cell phone number, the robotic voice told her that the number was disconnected.

She wanted to explain to Daphne that she'd got a better deal with another weed connect. She hoped that Daphne would understand and believed she deserved at least an explanation. Ruby had a lot of respect for Daphne, but business was business. Plus, she was hoping she could squash the animosity between Daphne and Tashy. Having the animosity exist between her two friends made her feel uncomfortable, and Ruby hated being uncomfortable.

In prison, she'd tried to bring the women together, but it wouldn't work. On the streets, she needed it to work, because such animosity could be bad for business, and she still planned on being in business with Daphne. Everybody was useful. That same week when she drove to Brooklyn, she received news that she was in no mood to hear.

"They raided the joint and took everything," Breeze told her while they walked up and down a rainy, empty block in Sutter Gardens.

Ruby stood under a large black umbrella, while Breeze wore a black rain suit. She didn't care about getting wet, but she found that her paranoia grew each day, and that prevented her from speaking in cars or houses about anything illegal.

"Everything?" Ruby asked, surprised.

"The safe and all. Luckily, my dudes ran out in time. Nobody got knocked." Breeze nodded.

"Why was everything in one crib?" she inquired, suspicious of the circumstances.

"We were just about to switch cribs because the other spot was hot. Some cat tried to rob the joint, and my man Kap had to clap him."

Ruby and Breeze stood silently watching as a black Caravan drove by slowly. The two white faces made it obvious that they were cops. The stocky cop in a flannel shirt on the passenger side smiled at Ruby and Breeze as they kept on driving. That smile made Ruby nervous.

"Come check me tomorrow, Breeze," Ruby said, walking toward her Benz.

"Where you gonna be at?" he asked as he began backpedaling into the building.

"I'll call you," Ruby roared as she jumped into her car.

She didn't like the way things were turning out. She was having a bad week, and she knew the police could make it more than a bad week. They could make it bad years. Brooklyn was becoming bad for business, with too many setbacks occurring. First, the robberies of her and Daphne's spots, then Karmen plotting against her, now the raid on the Sutter Gardens spot. A spot that was bringing in good money. In fact, all the money Ruby was making was coming from Sutter Gardens. She had closed the store after Karmen and her sisters were murdered. She had considered keeping it open to let Mecca run it, but Mecca was in her own world. She wouldn't sell weed out of it if she let her run it, because she did not want to put her at risk again. She finally decided to keep it closed when the cops came snooping around, until she could sell the place.

Breeze pulled his hood off his head after he came out of the rain. He grinned, thinking to himself that she fell for it. The cops had never raided the spot; it was still up and running. It was his and Mecca's now.

When Mecca had offered him the deal, he couldn't refuse. She'd told him that once Ruby was out of the way, she could get him weed and coke cheaper than he'd ever seen and that they could split it down fifty-fifty. He'd agreed, but he really had no intentions of doing business with her. He knew she was washed up and wanted to make money, but she didn't realize that she was cutting her own legs from under her by separating from her aunt. Mecca had no power without her aunt. It was a win-win situation for Breeze.

What he did not know was that Mecca had no intentions of partnering with him, either. He was Shamel's best friend, and Shamel had betrayed

her. She knew Breeze was down with what was
going on and said nothing. So he was on the list
for payback, too. Plus, he proved that he couldn't
be trusted by plotting against Ruby. They were
supposed to be tight. It was another reminder to
Mecca that no one in the game was your friend.

Breeze lit up a blunt before walking up the
steps of the building. Taking his time, he stepped
to the side as a tall, dark-skinned female with
long dreadlocks down her back in a ponytail
descended. He gave her a quick glance, thinking
that she was coming from a friend's apartment,
being that he never saw her before, and chuckled
to himself after noting the strange clothing she
wore. Her black-and-white Chuck Taylor sneakers looked weird with yellow spandex under a
tan cotton trench coat. He shook his head as she
passed.

"Excuse me, sir, can I get a light?" the woman
said with a deep Jamaican accent.

Breeze turned to look down at her. She held a
beedi cigarette in her hand, made of small brown
paper. Taking a lighter out of his pocket, he
walked back to her and lit it. He didn't notice her
slide a machete down her sleeve and drop it into
her hand. In one swift movement, she swung.

His eyes widened in fear just as the sharp
blade connected with his neck, severing his

head. When his headless body fell to the bottom of the staircase, his head landed beside it, etched with his stunned expression.

The war was on and popping.

"That's the Davidson broad," Detective Mike Levy mumbled from the passenger seat of the black Caravan he cruised the street in. Levy smiled as they drove past Breeze and Ruby, recognizing that they now saw them. He already knew who Breeze was from the neighborhood and his clashes with police and had decided to torment him a bit by keeping an eye on him.

Feeling this was his lucky day, he turned to his partner when Ruby got into her car. "She's taking off. Let's tail her."

The Caravan pulled over behind a parked car, waiting for Ruby to pass. Inside it was silent, except for the sound of the windshield wipers and cars passing over the wet streets.

Ruby noticed the Caravan as she drove by. When they began tailing her, she became nervous. "What is these crackas up to?" she mumbled to herself, nervously looking in her rearview mirror.

She drove slowly down Sutter Avenue with them on her tail, and her heart almost jumped out of her chest when she saw the light flash from the Caravan's dashboard. Then a voice over a loudspeaker roared, "Pull the car over to the right!"

Ruby sat still while she waited for the cops to get out of the Caravan with their hands on their side holsters. They approached the car from both sides, with bright flashlights beaming through the windows and right in Ruby's face.

"Turn the car off, and roll the windows down," Levy said after tapping the driver-side window. Ruby calmly did what she was told, well aware of trigger-happy cops in the city.

"What's the problem, Officer?" Ruby asked, trying to remember if she had run a stop sign or red light.

"I'll ask the questions, Davidson."

Him saying her last name without her giving him identification sent red flags up. She knew this wasn't a routine stop. Playing the confused role, she looked at Levy with a surprised expression.

"You know my name, so I guess there is no need to show my license, huh?"

"I don't think you're foolish enough to drive around without papers and a license, so we'll skip that. I need to ask you some questions about some particular murders out here in East

New York. Would you be willing to come in for
questioning, or are you going to play hardball?"

"Am I under arrest?" Ruby asked with a serious face. Rain dripped off the bill of Levy's
Giants cap and splashed Ruby's cheek. She
resisted the urge to wipe it off.

"No, you're not. Just some questions is all I
want, and hopefully some answers."

"Give me your card. I'll come to the precinct
with my lawyer. Until then, I'm on my way
home. So, if you'll excuse me, I'll be pulling off."
Ruby rolled her window up and turned the music
in her car up to the max so that the cops could
hear 50 Cent's voice sing, "Many men wish death
upon me." The Benz's tires screeched, leaving
Levy frustrated in the rain.

Ruby could not believe it. Murders . . . How
the hell did her name come up in that conversation? She knew it could only be Tah Gunz's and
Mo Blood's murders that the cops were talking
about. The only person that knew anything
about them besides her was Breeze. Could he be
talking? she wondered. One thing for sure, she
wouldn't risk her freedom by not tying up loose
ends. Her freedom far outweighed a friendship
or business association. Breeze had to go.

Detective Levy was unaware that he would be
Ruby's alibi witness when Breeze's murder came

to light. Just as he and his partner were driving off after pulling Ruby over, the call came in over the radio.

"All available units report to Sutter and Hendrix. Report of a homicide by decapitation."

Levy looked at his partner, wide-eyed. "Let's roll!"

When they arrived on the scene, there was only a marked squad car there. They were patrolling the area, and as they passed the building, a young woman wearing a robe, with her head wrapped in a scarf, and under an umbrella waved them over. The uniformed cops were apparently rookies, Levy noticed. Their young faces were ghost white as one of them patted the other on the back while he vomited on the sidewalk.

"You fellas okay? What we got?" Levy asked.

"Someone chopped a guy's head off in there. It's the most gross thing I ever saw," the cop doing the patting said.

"This is Brooklyn. Believe me, fellas, you'll see worse." Levy smiled back at his partner, who just shrugged. They walked into the hallway, and Levy shook his head at the bloody scene and headless body. Then he recognized the face.

"Ain't this a bitch?" Levy grunted.

"Holy shit! That's the guy the Davidson broad was just with," his partner grunted as he looked at the face.

"Fucking A right it is. Can't say she committed it, either," Levy sighed.

"Death just surrounds her. What a broad," Levy's partner replied while shaking his head. "I guess I'll call my old lady. Won't be home for dinner tonight."

Once in the comfort of her own home, Ruby decided to take a hot bath. Whenever she was on her period, she soaked in a bubble bath. It was her way of cleaning the pussy hairs of dried blood and relieving the tension of a grumpy mood. She had heard all the bad things about menopause, but she would rather deal with that than the cramps and the bleeding. She had even once thought about having a baby so for at least nine months, she wouldn't have to deal with it. But when she witnessed her sister give birth to Mecca, she told herself, she'd rather have blood come out than a human being.

After the bath, Ruby went into her kitchen, wearing nothing but her own skin, to fix a meal. She was one of those people who could eat breakfast all times of the day and night. So she fixed a cheese omelet and toasted some Eggo waffles. Her cell phone rang as she was flipping the omelet over. Reading the caller ID, she knew it was Tashy.

"Tashy, what's up? Please gimme some good news, because it's been a terrible day." Ruby told her about the spot being raided in Sutter Gardens, then about the cops pulling her over and asking about some murders.

"Murders?" Tashy barked. "God, Ruby, you just got to lay low, Ma. You got too much to lose."

"Don't I know it? I got things covered, though."

Tashy sighed. "I hope so. Anyway, Simone is really getting on my nerves."

"How? Already? She just moved in!"

"This Mona chick got her stressed out. She thinks Mona's cheating on her."

"Why she thinking that?" Ruby asked, picturing the rendezvous they'd had. Though Mona's performance wasn't memorable, it was nothing to be strung out over. Simone must be new to the lesbian experience. What Simone needed was a woman to rock her world, and she'd forget about Mona.

"She say's Mona's been acting different. Mona's been avoiding her. I try to tell her not to get all bent out of shape over her. If she's acting funny, let her go. Just now she went out, looking for her. She using that GPS they got on these cell phones to find her. Girl, the technology they got these days," Tashy rambled as Ruby's doorbell rang.

"Someone's ringing my door. I hope it ain't no damn cops," Ruby said, putting on her whorehouse kimono and walking to the door.

She unlocked the door leading to the brownstone's vestibule; then she looked through the curtain of the building's front doors and couldn't believe who was standing there, soaking wet from the rain. Mona. Ruby sighed. How the hell did this child know where I live?

To Tashy, Ruby said, "Tashy, I'll call you back."

"Who is it?" she asked.

"One of my peoples I got on the job," Ruby lied, ending the call and opening the door, frustrated.

"Mona, what the hell are you doing here, and how do you know where I live?" Ruby snapped.

Mona stood there with a sad look on her face as drops of water fell from her soaked hair. "I need to talk to you, Ruby. Can I come in?"

Reluctantly, she let her in. "Take those sneakers and those clothes off. I'll get you some dry ones. Why don't you have an umbrella?"

"When I got on the train uptown, it wasn't raining," Mona said, quickly stripping out of the wet Baby Phat sweat suit and Nike Air Max sneakers.

"Simone is looking for you as we speak. She knows you're in Brooklyn with that GPS stuff on your phone," Ruby said flatly.

"How do you know that?" Mona asked, staring at her. Ruby turned to walk into the bedroom while Mona stood in the living room in a pair of lace panties and matching bra.

"I just got off the phone with Tashy. How else would I know?"

"I don't care. I just wanna be here with you," Mona replied with a shrug. Ruby came out of her room with a robe for Mona. She placed her hands on her hips and looked at Mona with pity on her face.

"Mona, we're not going to be together, so get that out of your head now. Put the robe on. I'm gonna put your clothes in the dryer and when they're dry, you're gonna get a cab uptown to be with Simone."

"I don't want Simone. I'm in love with you. You should have never made love to me, Ruby. I didn't want to hurt Simone, and I tried to avoid you, but no. You had to come and make me feel better than I've ever felt in my life. "

"Listen, Mona, I don't want to hurt your—"

"Then don't . . ." Mona cut Ruby off. Leaving her robe open, she walked toward Ruby with a horny look on her face.

Ruby looked at her pussy through her panties and at her tight stomach, which served only to highlight her perky breasts, and almost entertained the thought of having one more session of mediocre sex with her. Maybe she could teach her something to use on Simone later on. Then she thought better of it, knowing she would never be able to get rid of her after that. Moving closer to Ruby, Mona was stopped by an outstretched hand that took a firm grip on her arm.

"You're young, Mona, and you got a lot to learn. If Simone ain't the one for you, you'll find someone that is. That person ain't me."

Mona's eyes began to tear up. Ruby wanted to snap, but the doorbell rang. Ruby threw her hands up in disbelief, wondering who the hell it could be now. She had just hung up with Tashy, so she didn't think it was Simone that fast. She also hadn't inquired about what time Simone left, but at that point she was already at the door.

"If you don't want to be bothered, I'll answer it. I'll tell whoever it is you're not here," Mona said while wiping the tears from her face.

"Good idea. In fact, tell them a Ruby doesn't live here. Tell them you own the place now," Ruby directed. While she went to put Mona's clothes in the dryer, she wondered what had happened to Daphne. Did the Feds get her? Loud screaming broke her thoughts, and Ruby paused to see what was going on.

"Who the fuck lives here, Mona? Is this your secret lover's house? Move! Let me in this bitch!"

Ruby didn't immediately recognize the voice but knew it could be only Simone. That damn GPS! When Simone finally saw Ruby standing in her living room, in a robe, like Mona, she figured she'd walked in on a lovemaking session in progress or one that had just finished.

"Ruby?" Simone said, not believing her eyes. "How could y'all do this to me? How could you do this to my mom?"

"Hold on, Simone. There's nothing . . ."

"Don't fuckin' lie to me. You know what? Fuck this and fuck y'all. I hate y'all scandalous bitches."

Simone rushed out of the house, not giving either of the women a chance to speak. Ruby was vexed. She walked into her bedroom and returned with one of her own sweat suits. She couldn't believe how this shit was going down.

"Put this on, and get the fuck out now!" Ruby threw the sweat suit at Mona, who was about to say something, but Ruby cut her off. "Mona, don't make me beat your young ass up. I said go!"

Mona dressed quickly and left. Ruby didn't even give her cab fare. Exhausted, she plopped down on her couch and looked at a portrait of her sister. *I miss you, sis,* she thought as her eyes watered. She really needed someone she could talk to about her life. If only she were here. The portrait over the brick chimney and mantel was next to a picture of Mecca and Monique from 1984, standing in a Coney Island project hallway. Ruby smiled. She reached for her cell phone and dialed Mecca's number. Ruby's smile vanished when she heard the mechanical voice announce that the number was no longer in service.

Meanwhile, at a Jamaican restaurant in the Tremont section of the Bronx, Daphne sipped an Irish Moss out of a plastic container with a straw while sitting in a small office in the back. Engrossed in a card game with a young, light-skinned Jamaican guy who looked like a double for Spragga Benz, she checked her cards and smiled. The room was filled with marijuana smoke, which made her eyes water a bit. Then a dreadlocked woman walked in.

Daphne looked up and saw the huge mole on her nose that looked like a raisin sitting on a chocolate bar. Her dark skin was smooth and shiny. Her face was long and sculpted like that of an Ethiopian beauty queen. The woman smiled at Daphne and the Spragga Benz twin and then made a cutthroat gesture, which Daphne understood.

As the dreadlocked woman was walking away, Daphne murmured, "Just him?"

The woman shook her head and closed her eyes for a moment before opening them and saying, "The man's family, too." And then she walked out.

Daphne stared at Spragga's twin for a few seconds, imagining the carnage left behind. She didn't want innocent people getting caught up in the war she was bringing to Ruby and her associates, and hearing that the woman had killed Breeze's family was something that she didn't want. Especially considering that the woman did not like using a gun.

"Daphne, you all right?" the Spragga twin asked in a heavy Jamaican accent.

She snapped out of her thoughts. "Yeah, I'm good. I was just thinking." She knew she would have to accept the fact that innocent people would get caught in the middle. It was called collateral damage, she reminded herself. *Charge it to the game.*

***

A pool of blood flowed from under the door of apartment 2A in the Sutter Gardens building. Neighbors peered and came out of their apartments after hearing a woman scream in the hallway. A few minutes afterward, a ten-year-old boy wearing an oversize G-Unit T-shirt pointed to the floor in front of apartment 2A.

"Mommy, look at the blood," the boy called out as noisy neighbors gathered in the hall. The revelation caused other neighbors to look. A middle-aged man, home only an hour from work at a construction site, looked at the blood and walked to the top of the staircase to called down to police.

"Officer!"

"Yeah, how can I help you?" A balding, short man in a suit and long raincoat looked up the stairs. The man pointed to 2A.

"There's a whole lot of blood coming from that apartment!"

"Levy!" the cop yelled toward the front of the building.

Detective Levy entered the hall. "What's up, Joe?"

"Guy says there's blood coming from the deceased's apartment. Let's have a look."

Levy and the suited Joe Pesci look-alike walked up the flight of steps to Breeze's door.

Once there they looked at the pool of blood and shook their heads. Calling back to another cop, Levy waited until he brought him a pair of latex gloves, put them on, and then tried the doorknob to the apartment. It opened. What they saw was a scene out of a horror film. There was blood everywhere. It even dripped from the ceiling fan. The decapitated and mutilated bodies of Breeze's seventy-eight-year-old grandmother, his twenty-two-year-old sister, whose eighteen-month-old baby's headless corpse lay beside her, along with his five-year-old son, were all inside.

"Holy shit!" the Joe Pesci look-alike wailed. Levy shook his head as his partner walked up next to him, looking at the gruesome scene. "Fucking animal, whoever did this shit!"

Levy looked at his partner. "This is bigger than the Davidson broad."

"Yeah, this is the work of foreign organized criminals, Colombians, Chinese, or some Caribbean gang," his partner commented.

"Hate to say it, but we may have to rub shoulders with the government dicks." Levy shrugged.

He walked out of the building, welcoming the drizzling rain on his face. It made him feel like God was looking out for him and washing away the sight and smell of death.

Reluctantly, he removed his phone and made the call. When a voice answered, he simply asked, "May I speak to Agent Doyle?"

Levy was put on hold. Putting his hand in his tight blue 501 Levi's, he grunted, "Fucking Feds."

Chapter Fourteen

If everything in a dream were realistic, it would have no power over us. . . .
— Robert Greene, *The Art of Seduction*

"So this was your plan? Lie to me, cause trouble between all the people you hate, and watch them kill each other off, while you live happily ever after away from the mess you've created?" Lou asked as he and Mecca sat on a worn couch in what she recognized as a project apartment Ruby once lived in with an ex-boyfriend.

"Smarter than you thought I was, huh, Lou?" Mecca responded, then swung her small legs back and forth without them touching the floor. Mecca was shocked at the sound of her own voice. It was the voice of a young child, about nine years old. It was the first time she realized she was in the body of a small girl.

"I never denied your intelligence, Mecca. I felt that you didn't know how to use your smarts. You could have been anything you wanted, besides a contributor to the death and destruction of your community. You could have—"

"Blah, blah, blah. Damn, Lou! You can't show me any kind of appreciation for saving your life, can you?" she interjected.

"You haven't shown me appreciation for saving yours," Lou replied.

Mecca fell silent. Lou's comment made her feel a tinge of guilt. He was right. Lou did save her life. She could have died in that coma, but it was Lou who wanted her to live. Yet all he expected in return was for her to fly straight. Nobody in her life besides her parents had wanted that for her. Then she thought about Monique. She wanted Mecca to do good, but Monique had lied to her.

She could have gotten any man she wanted, but she chose Bobby Sykes to sleep with and disrespected Mecca's mother by not telling her everything. Lou never lied to her. All he did was tell and reveal the truth.

"Lou, I am sorry for lying to you. Please understand I'm human. Everything I've ever loved wasn't real. It was all a sham. The people, the life I lived, were all nothing. It wasn't my fault, Lou." Tears dripped down her face.

Removing a silk handkerchief from the breast pocket of his white linen blazer, he wiped away her tears and then hugged her around the shoulders. "Do you remember me telling you that you didn't have to do anything to the people who betrayed you, because the laws of nature would deal with them?"

Mecca nodded.

"Mecca, even the most coldhearted people have a conscience. They hide it from others, but they can't hide it from themselves."

"What do you mean?" Mecca asked, hating that he was beating around the bush.

"Come with me." Lou grabbed her hand and walked to the bathroom door.

"I want you to open the door, walk in there, and close the door behind you," he said.

Mecca was confused.

"Trust me, Mecca. You will see what I mean."

Mecca opened the door slowly and stepped into the small beige tiled bathroom. She looked back at him before closing the door and saw that he was smiling and nodding his head reassuringly. When she closed the door and turned around, she saw her aunt Ruby sitting on the toilet, crying, with a razor blade in her hand, holding it to her wrist.

"Auntie, what are you doing?" she screamed, but Ruby could not hear her. Mecca looked to the floor and saw a folded piece of paper with writing on it. When she picked it up and read it, she realized it was Ruby's suicide note. Tears fell as she began to read.

My dearest niece,

Baby, I'm so sorry for the pain I caused in your life. I wish I could rewind the clock and go back to the day you were born. The family has never been happier than the day you were brought into the world. Me and your mother's lives have been extremely hard and stressful, but you eased that stress and made life worth living. I never meant for your life to turn out this way. I hate myself for things I've done. I'm no good for you, and if I can't be good for you, then life ain't worth living. I left enough money with Monique for you to live comfortably until you get a job and straighten your life out.

The game ain't where it's at. I played it because it was my way of surviving without parents to hold me and your mother down. I hate the life, though. Understand, Mecca, it's all I know. I love you so much, and I'll carry that love with me to the hereafter.

Loving you till death . . .

Auntie

Just as Ruby put the blade to her wrist, a knock came at the door.

"Ruby, what's taking you so long? We got to go!"

Mecca recognized Monique's voice. Thinking for a moment, Ruby placed the razor blade back into the medicine cabinet and ran cold water on her face.

"I'm coming. Hold on. I'm peeing. Don't rush me!"

After drying her face, Ruby examined herself in the mirror, making sure there were no signs of the depressed state she was in.

Mecca threw the note on the floor and opened the door. Lou stood there with a blank look on his face. She turned her head to see if Ruby was still standing there and saw nothing. Feeling her eyes water, she wiped away the first of the forming tears. She never would have guessed how deeply affected Ruby was by her sister's death and how it would affect Mecca's life. She couldn't imagine her going out like that. She figured Ruby would rather go out in a hail of bullets.

***

"You seem nervous, Miss Davidson. I assure you that you have nothing to be nervous about. I understand that your situation, coupled with the stresses of prison life, can sometimes become unbearably stressful. And we sometimes need someone with a good ear and open mind to vent those stresses to. That's what I'm here for. I assume you've never talked to a psychiatrist before."

Ruby shook her head no.

"Okay, well, I will explain some things about psychiatry and let you know my opinion, then give you options on how to deal with them. I can make recommendations, but it's all up to you. What's said in this room is strictly confidential. Only me and you will know," Dr. Clark said reassuringly.

After explaining psychiatry and her job at the prison, Dr. Clark asked, "Can you tell me about Ruby? Not Ruby, the convicted felon, but the Ruby that no one knows about but you."

For the first time in her life, Ruby totally opened up about how depressed she was about her life. As she spoke, she surprised herself at the things she revealed to this strange white lady. Mecca listened to her aunt say things she never would have imagined her saying to anyone.

"I'm a lesbian by choice, but the reality is that I hate being one. I want to have a family, get married to a good man, but I hate to show weakness," Ruby announced as she began to cry. Dr. Clark handed her a Kleenex tissue.

"So men are your weakness?"

"That's why I stay away from them." Ruby nodded.

"Why do men make you weak? What is it about them that makes you succumb to their power?"

"When they fuck me good, I can't control myself," Ruby responded through her tears.

Dr. Clark's eyes grew wide. When the doctor changed the subject to Ruby's relationship with her family, she noticed Ruby's facial expression change. The doctor knew from the look that it would be a topic she would have to approach lightly.

"You told me about your parents and how you and your sister had to go through life without them. Your sister's death affected you more than any other death in your life, I assume."

Ruby looked away from the doctor and toward a framed portrait of the doctor with a tall, medium-built, silver-haired man in a tuxedo. The doctor wore a long black dinner gown. Tears ran down Ruby's face.

"I miss my sister so much, it's killing me. Now my niece is out there on her own. She was unable to protect herself and got shot. She's in a coma!"

Dr. Clark came around the desk and rubbed her back. "It helps to talk about the pain. Don't hold that in, because you'll go crazy and do something irrational. You don't want to do that. You don't want to carry all that pain and anger around. You want to release it. It will take time, though. Time will heal the wounds." Handing Ruby more Kleenex, Dr. Clark sat back down behind her desk. "Did they find the people who shot your niece?"

Ruby shook her head. "No. I don't really know all the details."

"How does that make you feel?"

Ruby gave the doctor a gaze that bordered pure menace. It was one that made Dr. Clark nervous. She had seen the look before in the blank glares of sociopaths and psychotic killers. She would make a note of it in Ruby's files, she told herself.

"Like getting revenge on anybody responsible."

"Come now, Mecca. I think you saw enough." Lou opened the door, bringing the vision to a close. The office turned back into the bedroom, without Ruby or the doctor. Lou grabbed her hand and led her back to the couch while she sobbed.

"Why, Lou? Why didn't you show me this before?"

"What would have been different, Mecca? Do you honestly think that your aunt was happy about your mother's and father's murders? Do you think that she enjoyed hearing you were in a coma? You know your aunt, and you knew she would seek revenge. She didn't have sex with Shamel to hurt you. She was having sex with him because she's weak. He was just a symbol of her weakness. Your aunt doesn't know love, because she doesn't know what love feels like." Lou's words made Mecca sob harder while she held her face in her hands.

"What did I do, Lou?"

"What you did is take things into your own hands. What you did is start a war for revenge. But what you did not know . . ." Lou lifted Mecca's face to his by holding her chin up and continued, "The war was going to happen regardless."

Mecca awoke to the bright sun shining on her face. She squinted her eyes, looking at Miguel placing a tray of food on the table on the terrace. The food smelled lovely to her, and her stomach growled its agreement. She could pick out the various aromas of scrambled eggs and cinnamon French toast.

"Good morning, pretty girl," Miguel said while walking bare chested, with just a pair of black boxer briefs on. "I made you breakfast. I want to eat on the terrace with you before I leave."

Mecca got up and made her way to the large bathroom. She looked in the mirror and saw remnants of the dream. She wondered what Lou meant when he said that the war would happen regardless. One thing was for sure, she knew she had to get back to the States and try to stop what she'd started. Ruby deserved a second chance. She just wanted to be loved, and Mecca loved her aunt. She wanted Ruby to know that. When she sat down to eat with Miguel, he noticed the sad look on her face.

"You wake up to your man cooking you breakfast in Rome and you got a sad look on your face? What's up?" he asked while helping her sit in her chair. "Did I do something to depress you?"

"No, Miguel. It isn't you at all." She placed her hand over his to reassure him. "I have a lot on my mind, that's all."

"Talk to me, Mecca. What's bothering you?"

Mecca sighed. "It's my aunt. I have to get back home to see her."

It rained for two days straight in New York, and like the weather, Ruby's head had a black cloud over it that wouldn't go away. The episode with Simone and Mona had put her in a bad mood. It lasted even into the next morning, when she awoke, and then throughout the day. She cursed the rain as she jumped into her Range Rover and drove to a diner in the Sheepshead Bay section of Brooklyn to meet Breeze to discuss her next move. The raid Breeze had mentioned had put a big dent in her business, and she planned on using the money he was to give her to buy a hundred more pounds of weed to set up shop in a spot in Harlem that Tashy had established for her. The spot was in the perfect place to make lots of cash.

A young Dominican guy would sell the weed on consignment out of a car-repair shop. Ruby was paying fifteen hundred a pound from Tashy's connect and selling the pound in New York for four thousand. Her deal with the Dominican she dealt with in New Jersey was for him to give her thirty-five hundred for each pound to make it appear as if he was getting a great deal.

To calm her nerves during the drive, Ruby listened to her Anthony Hamilton CD. Yet, for some reason, even his soul-soothing voice couldn't calm her restless nerves, which were jumpier than a fleet of Chevy Impalas with hydraulics at a Cali lowrider contest.

To make matters worse, when she got to the diner, Breeze's black Charger on double deuces was nowhere in sight. She looked through the rain-soaked windows of her truck for any sign of him as she pulled into the diner's parking lot. It was packed with morning diners grabbing a bite on their way to work, those coming from a club, and those on their way to a motel to get freaky.

"Where the fuck is this nigga?" Ruby grumbled as she fit the truck in between a beat-up, multicolored station wagon and a dull white minivan. Putting her hood on, Ruby jogged into the diner, which smelled of a mix of culinary odors, cigarettes, perfume, and wet hair. Ruby made her way to a booth far in the back that gave her a window view. A young, thin white girl with an apron on over faded jeans and a black T-shirt placed a menu on the table.

"Are you ready to order?" she asked, popping gum in her raggedy-tooth mouth. Ruby removed her wet leather bomber and placed it on the leather-cushioned seat.

"Yeah, let me get some scrambled eggs with cheese, home fries, and bacon, with a toasted cinnamon raisin bagel."

"Anything to drink with that?" The anorexic wrote down the order, still popping her gum.

"Orange juice, fresh squeezed," Ruby ordered.

The girl grabbed the menu and walked with a strut, trying to show off a body that just wasn't there. Looking out from her window, Ruby saw no sign of Breeze or his car. Once again, she pulled out her cell phone and dialed his number. The house phone just rang. Ruby spotted the pay phone by the diner's bathroom and went to use it. She dialed Breeze's cell phone; on the second ring she heard a voice answer.

"Who dis?"

"Who dis?" Ruby asked with attitude.

"You looking for Breeze?"

"Give Breeze the phone, whoever this is," Ruby commanded.

"Sorry. Can't do that. Maybe you can come down to the Seventy-third Precinct and . . ."

Ruby quickly ended the call. If the police had Breeze's phone, she knew Breeze was locked up. Damn!

"Is there a problem?" the long-faced, skinny, greasy-haired waitress asked, holding a cup of orange juice in her hand.

Ruby shook her head and glared at her. "Nothing you can help me with except getting my order."

The girl placed the cup down in front of her, rolling her eyes. She wanted to cuss Ruby out but thought the better of it. Ruby looked like one of those ghetto girls who could fight and probably carried a box cutter in her purse. She walked away without saying a word.

Ruby dialed Tashy's number. When Tashy answered, Ruby said, "Girl, I got problems."

"Yeah, I heard," Tashy responded.

Ruby paused, hearing attitude in her voice. "What did you hear?"

"Simone came in here last night, calling you every name a mother doesn't want to hear coming out of her child's mouth."

Ruby sighed, rubbing her forehead. "It was a misunderstanding. She didn't give me a chance to explain why Mona was at my house."

"And the reason was?" Tashy spat in disgust.

"Hold on, Tashy. Don't give me attitude. I don't know how that girl got my address, first off. She shows up at my door, soaking wet from the rain, after I got out of the shower. I give her a change of clothes, while I was going to wash her wet ones. Then your daughter pops up and throws a tantrum."

"Did you do something with Mona, Ruby?"

"Tashy, please with the bullshit. The girl is obsessed, and I don't know why. I got a lot of shit going on in Brooklyn. I got no time for no little girl. Tell Simone to get rid of the crazy little bitch."

"Mona says y'all did something and she's in love," Tashy said flatly.

"Fuck, Mona." Ruby grimaced. "I need to get some stuff. Brooklyn is shut down. I'm moving uptown. I'll be there in an hour."

Ruby ended the call. When the waitress brought Ruby her food, she suddenly no longer had an appetite. She pulled out a wad of cash from her coat and counted out two hundred-dollar bills, throwing them on the table.

"I'm not eating. Here's two bills for your trouble." Ruby snatched her coat, put it on, and jogged to the Range Rover. She drove uptown in a rage. Things had to be put back in order. She had to find Daphne. When she turned the car on, Anthony Hamilton sang, "Sometimes I get lonely coming from where I'm from. . . ." That was exactly how Ruby felt.

Chapter Fifteen

So it is said that victory can be made.
—Sun Tzu, *The Art of War*

Detective Levy's eight-hour shift had turned into a twenty-hour one by the time the last body was taken out of the apartment. The crowd and media representatives, with their vans and equipment, dispersed, leaving the rainy East New York block eerily silent, with the exception of the sound of passing cars.

With a faintly stubbled chin and bags under his eyes, Levy came alive sitting in his unmarked car as Breeze's cell phone rang. It was like he'd just won the lottery.

"That was definitely Davidson's voice," he announced when the call ended.

"Sure of it? I haven't heard it in years," replied FBI agent Phillip Doyle from the backseat. Agent Doyle had agreed to drive from his Long Island

home to Brooklyn after hearing about the open
investigation on a woman he'd helped put away,
supposedly for the rest of her life. That was until
her conviction was overturned.

Doyle was a twenty-eight-year vet of the FBI's
New York office. A native himself, he had seen it
all. He'd been part of some of the city's biggest
investigations, from the La Cosa Nostra indict-
ments of the five biggest families to the Russian
mafia, Colombian cartels, Black, Jamaican, West
Indian, and Latin drug gangs, and even the little
hoods that suddenly got some big score.

He became part of the investigation into the
"Davidson Organization" when she shot and
killed a Dominican drug dealer the FBI had
targeted. He'd learned from other agents' investigations about a drug ring in the Brownsville
section of Brooklyn of which Davidson was the
boss. The word was, she was one bad bitch.

Doyle was a year away from retiring from law
enforcement. He looked every bit of his fifty-five
years. A head full of gray hair, which he wore like
a politician, weathered olive-tone skin, sagging
blue eyes, a tough Irish scowl, which became his
natural expression, highlighted the crow's-feet
at the corners of his eyes. Though he was five
foot eleven, with stooped shoulders, his potbelly
made him seem stockier than he was. With

his outward appearance, coupled with a deep smoker's voice from cheap cigars, he gave off the stereotypical image of a drunken Irishman. Which, in fact, he was. Yet, throughout it all, he was known as a cop's cop.

He was far from a shallow bureaucrat who looked down on the locals. Doyle had no problem sharing intel with city or state cops that stumbled upon a federal investigation or vice versa. He was the agent, or G-man, the NYPD top brass reached out to before trying to convince the director or city officials to coordinate an investigation. That was why it was no surprise that he rushed to Brooklyn at four in the morning on a miserable, rainy day to meet with Levy.

"I just finished talking to this broad right before the corpses pop up," Levy said.

"So, you're saying she has an alibi?" Doyle asked, reaching in his tan camel-hair trench for a lighter. When he spoke, his double chin shook.

"She was definitely at the scene, but when she left, the headless guy was alive."

Levy's young partner, who favored Johnny Depp, interjected, "I assume the guy's family was alive also. Most likely got it right before he was caught on the staircase."

"Police work doesn't call for assumptions, young man. We need facts," Doyle sermonized. He did everything by the book.

"So what do you think?" Levy cut in before Doyle gave one of his "how to be a good cop" speeches.

"It's definitely not her style. Did you contact the cop investigating the triple over in Bedford-Stuyvesant?" Doyle asked.

Levy sighed. "Yeah, I did. The guy is hard pressed for more details than I have. He said her owning the store where the murders took place ain't enough to go chasing her around."

"And he's right," Doyle barked, lighting up the cigar. "You mind?" He cut an eye at Levy.

"No. Go ahead," Levy said, immediately regretting his decision once Doyle lit up the foul-smelling cigar. Doyle spoke while smoke came out of his mouth.

"No sense in chasing ghosts. I think maybe Davidson has aligned herself with some real cowboys. Probably met some connections in prison and planned a takeover, once they got out. Looks like the work of some Middle Eastern syndicate, which I doubt would go into business with an American black girl from the ghetto. Has to do with trust issues, or the work of the Jamaican posses or other islanders, like Haitians, Trinidadians, that sort."

Levy rolled his window down, then looked at Doyle through the rearview. "So where do we start?"

"We can start by grabbing some breakfast," Doyle murmured, rubbing his rounded gut. "Then we go to the prison Davidson was housed at for thirteen years and find out who she was affiliated with. Plenty of rats in the federal joints that will gladly share information with us."

Levy nodded his head as he began to start the car. Doyle opened the back door to get out and get in his black eighties-model Lincoln Town Car. He pulled the collar of his trench coat around his neck, ducked his head back in the car, and growled, "Where do you Jewish guys grab a bite at this time of the morning?"

"I forgot Brooklyn has never been a place for the micks," Levy joked. "Just follow me, pal."

Doyle chuckled. "Brooklyn humor. Brutal as the streets."

The cool air that blew in from the Miami River was a welcomed act of nature for Daphne after temperatures reached ninety degrees in the shade during the day. Daphne, wearing a peach tank top, white capri pants, and white open-toe sandals, removed her Chloé shades while sitting on the porch of her beach home to read an article in *Don Diva* magazine her sister had referred her to.

Miami was Daphne's second best getaway spot, after Jamaica. To Daphne, Miami had the pace of New York, with its trendy boutiques and "party till the sun burns out" nightlife, and the tropical feel of Jamaica, with its lovely beaches and resorts and kind, courteous natives, while a mean, ruthless, murderous drug-culture underworld was in its belly.

When Daphne was relaxing at her white stucco, wood-framed, one-story beach home with two bedrooms, she felt at home. The master suite had glass sliding doors with an ocean view, while the whole place was decorated in an African motif, with carved wooden stakes imported from the Ivory Coast, bamboo woven chairs, African pottery, and portraits of the African grasslands. Miami was definitely one of Daphne's favorite places because it so often reminded her of Donovan. It was he who had shown her the city, which, he'd once said, "America didn't deserve."

When her sister brought the *Don Diva* magazine to her, she'd opened it up to the article and handed it to her. "Your homegirl done got herself famous."

Daphne stared at a picture, obviously taken in the eighties, of a younger Ruby sitting on a large straw-cushioned chair with a background picture of New York City. She was dressed in a brown and gold Dapper Dan leather Louis Vuitton coat, a white silk shirt, a large rope chain connected to a Nefertiti medallion, Vidal Sassoon blue jeans, and black snakeskin boots. On each of her hands she wore a two- and four-finger ring that spelled out *Ruby* in diamonds.

The title of the article caught Daphne's attention. In big, bold black and gold letters it read, "Brooklyn's Bosstress."

She stared at Ruby's picture for a few seconds, looking into her eyes. She could see the sadness there and realized that she was the type of person that made it appear as if everything was cool on the outside, but on the inside were confusion, pain, sadness, and a desire to cry out for help. She was one of those people on a search for answers to their problems, knowing that no one had the answers but themselves. Daphne continued on.

"For those who thought that New York City's eighties crack era was ruled by ruthless, violent drug gangs led by black or Hispanic men, think again. The tough streets of Brownsville, Brooklyn, have a secret. A true story of a Don Diva who was just as ruthless as, if not more ruthless than, some of her male counterparts.

After serving thirteen years of a federal life sentence, it was overturned in 2001. The government alleged that Ruby Davidson of Brownsville, Brooklyn, murdered a Dominican drug dealer in broad daylight on a busy Manhattan street. She is believed to have ran a criminal enterprise out of several Brownsville housing projects, grossing two hundred thousand a day in crack sales. Ruby Davidson is now a free woman, giving *Don Diva* an exclusive first-time interview from Club Opium in Las Vegas, where she and others are celebrating the release of one of Ruby's prison homies, Tashera "Tashy" Williams of Harlem infamy."

Daphne looked at a few pictures of Ruby posing with Tashy and what appeared to be Tashy's family. The words under the pictures confirmed who the people were. Daphne looked at Simone and saw the unmistakable resemblance between mother and daughter. Daphne had heard about Scooter Williams, Tashy's father, from the streets, prison, and the *Don Diva* story, but now everything seemed to fall in place.

She turned the page and saw small pictures of Ruby in eighties fashion standing next to a black 300 Benz. Another picture was of her standing next to a Sterling and some chick named Kima in beige prison clothes. Kima was one of Ruby's cell mates and lesbian lovers from the South Side of Chicago. There was even a map and pictures of the dilapidated Brownsville streets. The article continued.

"Ruby was sometimes called "the Black Widow" due to the rumors around Brownsville that she was responsible for the murders of two men she was allegedly romantically involved with. The two men were members of the Five Percent Nation and went by the names of Darnell (a Brownsville hustler and stickup kid) and Wise (another Brownsville hustler, who served time for murder and was allegedly the man who introduced Ruby to the game)." Daphne swallowed hard before reading on.

"After allegedly ridding herself of these men, it is said, and was confirmed by Ruby, that she became a full-time lesbian. Word on the street was that Ruby's lesbian lover, a girl named Monique, was gunned down on a Brownsville street as revenge for the murder of Darnell. There was no retaliation for Wise's murder, and Ruby denied any involvement in both."

When Daphne turned the page, she was shocked when she saw a picture of Ruby, Monique, and Mecca sitting on a couch in someone's apartment. Mecca appeared to be around thirteen years old. She wore her hair in a bang and ponytail, had on a pair of large door-knocker earrings with *Mecca* encrusted in diamonds, and a white sweatshirt. Daphne could see the same pain in her eyes that she'd seen just recently. The article continued with questions.

DD: Ruby, how does it feel to be free after thirteen years?

RD: I can't even put the feelings into words, but it feels good.

DD: I bet. So you grew up in Brownsville?

RD: No doubt. Langston Hughes projects.

DD: What was it like growing up in Brownsville?

RD: Growing up in the Ville, you learn how to mind your business, to fight and never be scared to lose. Just fight . . . and you learn to duck and stay low when the guns blast.

DD: The things you've heard, the rumors about things you did, which ones are false and true?

RD: I won't answer that on the grounds that I won't incriminate myself or others.

DD: Answered like a true G. People say that once you were locked down, your niece took over your dealings and that eventually got her shot and out of the game.

That would make ya'll some very unusual women. Y'all would be like the Candaces of Brooklyn. (Reporter's note: Ruby's face turns serious.)

RD: None of that is true. My niece had nothing to do with the game.

Daphne could imagine the look on her face. Mecca was still a sensitive issue with Ruby. Daphne looked up when Andrea walked onto the porch, wearing a long, flowing, one-piece cream cotton dress with a plunging neckline. Her thong-toed flat slippers clapped against the back of her heels as her dreads swung freely by her lower back. Donovan's father had strong genes, because all his children looked alike. Andrea just didn't have hazel eyes like him. Her eyes were black and mysterious. She always stared off into the distance, in deep thought. Andrea laughed when Daphne told her that she always reminded Daphne of Lauryn Hill. A deep soul.

Andrea carried two glasses of sweet carrot juice in her hands and placed them on the small, white, round table Daphne sat next to. She was a strict vegetarian.

"Why not bring this thing between you and her straight to her? Why prolong it?" Andrea asked, sitting across from Daphne and looking her in the eyes. To her, Daphne was a unique object, because the sun always made her eyes appear to be different hues.

"She isn't even aware that I'm after her," Daphne said as she broke eye contact and looked away at the distant river. "I want her to suffer the loss of close friends like I suffered the loss of my best friend and heart."

"You said she is a selfish woman who only thinks of herself. I assume it is unlikely she will be affected by the loss of a business partner and his family."

Daphne turned back to Andrea. "She loves money. If she can't make money, she becomes miserable. This is why I made sure she had money when she came home. I wanted her to get comfortable and then snatch it all away. Then I'll kill her."

It was Andrea's turn to look out over the blue water. "Are you having doubts that she is responsible for your brother's death? You know it's just rumors, she never spoke about it to you, and you said she was pretty open with you about her business in the streets."

"Yes, she is pretty open about street stuff, but not personal business. From what I hear, her and my brother had something personal going on."

"What about her niece? Isn't she close to her? Wouldn't losing her deeply affect Ruby?"

Daphne sighed. Explaining Mecca and Ruby's relationship was complicated. She wouldn't know where to begin. The fact that she liked Mecca also played a part in leaving her out of the war. Mecca had suffered enough.

Andrea read her expression. "You're fond of her niece, aren't you?"

Daphne avoided Andrea's gaze, causing her to smile.

"That's a good sign that you have not lost the ability to feel compassion. I almost thought you were becoming a monster." Andrea got up and walked into the house but paused before disappearing from the door. "I read the *Daily News*. Two children were in that house. Don't become what you want to destroy. You'll wind up destroying yourself."

As Ruby gripped the sheets and arched her back, a deep moan escaped from her lungs. It was a much-needed multi-orgasmic release from the stresses she had been experiencing lately. The tension just melted away with the flow of juices that creamed Tashy's face.

When she drove to Tashy's apartment, she went there expecting a verbal confrontation from her about Mona. However, when Tashy answered the door, wearing her silk kimono robe with nothing on under it, nipples harder than tire caps, and a seductive, "come fuck me" look on her face, Ruby grinned and gave Tashy what she wanted, and what Ruby needed her damned self.

Afterward, they lay naked on their backs, breathing laboriously, staring at the ceiling. Tashy grabbed one of her overstuffed pillows and hit Ruby on the stomach with it.

Ruby flinched. "Tashy, what the fuck are you doing?"

Smiling, Tashy responded, "I can't believe you tried to turn that young girl out. You got her obsessed."

Ruby grinned. She knew there was no sense lying to Tashy. She knew her better than a lot of people. She knew from experience that Tashy wouldn't be hurt by her habit of testing the playing field.

"You got to admit the chick got it going on," Ruby said, amused. Then she straightened her face out and became serious. "I didn't do it to hurt Simone, though. It was a one-time thing. The girl kept giving me googly eyes."

Tashy nodded. "I will keep it real. She's a cutie, but too young for me, and I won't do that to my daughter. I have seen her giving you the eye."

Ruby got up to go to the bathroom. Her once tight buns were now a bit jiggly. Tashy watched them with great interest as they bounced and realized that Ruby wasn't working out like she used to in jail. Plus, she was getting older now, and time was starting to take its toll. Still, she had a body to die for.

"So, how is Simone doing? Did she get over it?" Ruby asked from the bathroom.

"I hope she did. She's over my father's. I spoke to her yesterday, and she sounded like she was okay."

On her way out, Ruby grabbed a newspaper that sat on top of Tashy's entertainment system. "What about Mona?"

Tashy sighed. "Still wondering if you will give her a chance. The girl is crazy. I saw her on the Ave., and she came to me, apologizing, while at the same time asking if me and her could share your love. Ain't that—"

"Oh, shit."

Tashy was startled at Ruby's sudden outburst. "What?"

Ruby slammed the paper down on the bed and began dressing quickly. Tashy looked down at the headline in big, bold letters on the front page. BROOKLYN BLOODBATH. Underneath it continued, "Three adults, two children, slain by decapitation. Story on page three."

"Ruby, what happened? Do you know about this?" Tashy asked while getting up and putting on her robe.

Fastening the button and zipper on her pants, Ruby answered, "That's my boy Breeze and his family! I was just with him last night. He was telling me how the cops raided the spot I had up in Brooklyn. The article said it happened last night. That had to be right after I left him. I got to see what the hell is going on!"

"You want me to come with you?" Tashy asked.

As Ruby walked toward the door, she turned to face Tashy. "Nah. What I need is for you to get that work for me so I can pop the spot over here. I'm really done with Brooklyn."

"I'm on it. Call me."

Ruby walked out the door.

A young Mecca and Dawn, who Mecca had thought was a friend but who was her sister, stood on the corner of Rockaway Avenue and Dumont, watching a funeral procession of luxurious and average cars following a hearse. The day was bright and sunny. The streets of Brownsville were alive at their usual pace. The corners, Chinese stores, liquor stores, and bodegas hosted the usual street corner congregations. People froze to watch the procession, as if it were the West Indian Day parade going through Brownsville.

It was common to see funeral processions come through the neighborhood. The dead were always driven through the place they lived before being buried. It was a way of letting the deceased and the deceased's neighborhood say good-bye to each other. Unfortunately, Brownsville was a place where death was a common occurrence. Mostly because of drugs, AIDS, and murder.

Mecca watched as a couple of guys on the corner across the street from where she stood poured beers on the ground. Some threw up peace signs with their fingers toward the hearse. Another guy walked up to the corner where Mecca and Dawn stood and placed his fist against his chest, then held up his own peace sign and said, "Peace, Wise."

Mecca looked at the hearse and thought about what the guy had said. She exchanged a glance with Dawn, who wore the same expression on her face. They remembered.

Nothing could erase the memory of Mecca and Dawn mistakenly walking into the scene of a murder. They'd rounded the pissy, graffiti-littered hallway steps after hearing the sound of something tumbling down the steps. They were startled when the body of a man landed in front of them, faceup, with eyes open. For a moment Mecca didn't recognize the man, because she had not seen Ruby's ex-boyfriend in a long time. He had been in jail and had just recently gotten out. When she looked up, she saw Ruby with a gun in her hand, standing next to Monique.

Back on the corner, Mecca looked at all the cars in the procession and admired the Benzes and other European sedans that drove by. She watched as a wood-brown Chevy Nova cruised slowly by.

The car meant nothing to her, but the person in the front seat did. Once again, she stared at those hazel eyes that shined like wet crystals when in the sun's light. It was the same blank stare Mecca had got from the girl in the mall. When Mecca looked closer, she saw the girl was crying. Obviously, Wise was somebody close to her.

"Mecca!" Mecca's attention was broken by a call coming from behind her. When she turned, she saw Ruby walking up the block with Monique. She waved her over. "I got to talk to you. Come here!"

Mecca turned to look at the hazel-eyed girl one more time and was shocked to see the girl out of the car, with a gun in her hand. She was no longer staring at Mecca, but her eyes were focused on Ruby and Monique.

She pointed the gun and started walking toward them while they were distracted by a group of women sitting on a project bench. When Mecca realized Ruby and Monique were the intended target, she yelled, but the sound of the gunshots overpowered her scream.

The scene disappeared. Mecca found herself sitting in Lou's office, on a leather-cushioned chaise lounge. Lou had his feet propped up on his desk, hands folded across his lap, watching her.

"Are you ready for the answer?" Lou asked.

"The answer to what?"

"The girl with the eyes. Aren't you curious as to who she is?"

"You figure?" Mecca said sarcastically.

Lou pointed to the wall, where framed pictures hung. Mecca turned to look at a picture of the same funeral procession. The girl's face in the Chevy Nova was different from the one in her dreams. Her jaw fell into her lap.

Awakened by the shaking of the Alitalia plane during a flight to New York, Mecca looked around, confused. A white woman in a blue business suit sat next to her, rapidly pressing letters on her laptop. Mecca noticed the woman had a *New York Daily News* folded beside her.

"Do you mind if I look at the paper?"

"Sure," the squeaky-voiced woman answered.

The bold letters on the front page immediately screamed out to her. After seeing the "Brooklyn Bloodbath" front page, she turned to page three and read. Her heart fluttered after she realized what she'd started. Guilt set in.

She didn't think mailing those pictures and that letter to Daphne would cause something like that to happen to Breeze's family. Especially those children. Mecca put the paper down beside the lady.

"You can keep it. I'm done with it," the woman said.

"No thank you." Mecca half smiled, then excused herself to go to the bathroom. Once inside the small, disinfectant-smelling bathroom, she vomited in the toilet. She rinsed her mouth out and stared at her reflection in the small mirror. Her skin was darker than usual from her days in Italy.

Leaving the bathroom, she made her way back to her seat and sat down, looking out the window at the New York skyline. She began to regret trading the Roman winter for the brutal New York winter. Was warning her aunt about what she helped put into play between Daphne and her worth leaving behind her wonderful fiancé, traveling, and relaxing in places of romantic bliss? She took a deep breath and rationalized. She would just have to find out.

Chapter Sixteen

For he comes out of prison to be king, although he was born poor in his kingdom.
—Ecclesiastes 4:14

The federal prison in West Virginia looked more like a college campus or retirement community surrounded by a barbed-wire fence than a prison. The clean, cemented pathways cut through manicured grass and led to a red and tan two-story, brick, cottage-like building.

Agent Doyle, accompanied by Detective Levy, paid the prison an official visit. Both men came dressed like underpaid public defenders, with their cheap suits that resembled Salvation Army giveaways. They had spent the previous night in a motel in Ohio, after spending the day at the women's federal prison, interviewing guards, a prison psychiatrist, and inmates who knew and associated with Ruby while she was an inmate.

Doyle knew some of the inmates there either from previous cases or from them being informants. The ones he'd put there that associated with Ruby were happy to tell him to go fuck himself; the informants, on the other hand, had no valuable information, because, as one of them put it, "She was usually a loner, and when she talked, she never got personal."

Doyle felt that they would get lucky at the West Virginia prison. It was a less secure jail than the one in Ohio. The inmates in the West Virginia prison were mostly short timers there for white-collar crimes, and a lot of them were snitches. Ruby had been brought there when her court hearings started, and Daphne had been there when her time was getting short. Another plus for Doyle was that he knew the psychiatrist at the prison on a personal level.

She was a former agent at a New York field office with whom Doyle on occasion cheated on his wife. When she'd become tired of chasing criminals, she'd put her degree in psychology to use and got into the minds of criminals. The FBI used her expertise from time to time, when they needed the profile of a potential suspect, usually a multistate serial killer.

The mention of Ruby's name to certain staff members caused them to sigh, shake their heads, and grimace. Only a few of them smiled. A captain, who was an overweight redneck, said Ruby was a real cocky bitch with a stink New York attitude. Then he added a wink and said, "No offense, fellas."

The interview with the inmates did not go as expected, until a Spanish girl from Washington Heights, who was being held for cocaine distribution, overheard Doyle ask another New York girl about Ruby. She managed to maneuver her way over to Doyle and Levy when they were in the receiving area.

"Can we talk?" Doyle asked the five-foot-two, black-haired, light-brown-skinned girl.

Levy immediately noticed the three parts in one of the girl's eyebrows. Her eyes were chinky and brown, and she had a full set of lips and a pretty oval face. Though she was petite and was covered with baggy prison clothes, he could see the nice legs, plump rear, and tight, flat stomach that were her body. She spoke with a tough, cocky New York accent.

"About Ruby? What's in it for me?"

"What do you expect?" Levy inquired.

The girl rolled her eyes. "Look around. Does this look like a place I want to spend another ten years in?"

"Is the information that valuable?" Doyle asked.

"Depends on what's valuable to you," she spat.

"Who were Ruby's closest associates?" Levy asked.

He didn't want to play games with the girl. He knew these convicts would tell them anything they wanted to hear to get them out of jail. It didn't matter to them if they were lying; it was part of the deal.

It was up to the cops to sift through the tall tales to find the truth. Doyle could tell that the Spanish girl was most likely one of those jailhouse snitches who would sell her own children to get out of her situation. Knowing Ruby, there was no way in hell she would share anything incriminating with this girl.

"She hung with Daphne and Tashy the most," the girl announced.

"You wouldn't be talking about Tashy Williams, would you?" Doyle asked, wide-eyed.

The girl looked around to see if anyone was close enough to hear her, then continued. "Yeah. Tashy from Harlem."

"And who else did you say?" Levy asked.

"Daphne. She's from Brooklyn."

Before going to see the psychiatrist, Doyle had the records of all inmates named Daphne in the jail at the time Ruby was there pulled by the prison administrators. Doyle found out there had been fifteen Daphnes in the jail. Five from New York. There was only one from Brooklyn. Daphne Carter. After reading her file and finding out why she was convicted, Doyle had a big smile on his face.

"Looks like our dear Davidson made some interesting connections here."

"Shower Posse." Levy read the file. After a minute of reading, he looked up at Doyle with the same smile.

"You got it," Doyle blurted.

"Who is this Tashy Williams chick?" Levy asked.

"You've heard of Scooter Williams? Big fish uptown, rubbed shoulders with Frank Matthews back in the day?" Doyle shook his head no when Levy shrugged. "Before your time. Plus, you were confined to Brooklyn. Listen, I'm going to make some copies. I'll explain it on the way back. First, let's see this shrink."

Margaret O'Connely's office looked like the office of a CFO for a Fortune 500 company rather than a prison psychiatrist. On her mahogany desk a gold-plated nameplate stood out amid the neat clutter. Tiffany floor and table lamps, upholstered gold silk sofas and chairs, and other French furniture sat on top of a beige carpet by Edward Fields. Her floor-to-ceiling bookshelf was filled with leather-bound books and occupied a whole wall in the spacious office.

Directly behind her large desk chair was a wood-paneled wall with her many achievements on display. Degrees in psychology, behavioral science; awards as an FBI agent; photos of a younger O'Connely with J. Edgar Hoover and former president Jimmy Carter.

When Doyle and Levy entered the office, they no longer felt like they were in a federal prison. The office was warm and cozy. Margaret O'Connely's light-scented perfume permeated the air. She sat at her desk, in a tan business suit, which Levy immediately noticed. The woman's curly reddish brown hair reached her bony shoulders, and he reasoned that it had to be a wig.

Her penetrating blue eyes caught everything that went on and spoke volumes of confidence under the rimless spectacles. With an erect posture, she gave no illusion of who was in charge. Though her skin was pasty and showed signs of a few face-lifts, Levy figured she'd been one of those classic New York debutantes.

"Miss O'Connely, I would like you to meet—"

"Cut the crap, Phil. You never called me Miss O'Connely in your life. Don't start now," she said with a strong Irish/New York accent.

Doyle cleared his throat. "Marge, this is Detective Levy. Brooklyn Homicide."

Levy reached over the desk and shook her hand. Her pale, vein-filled hand was swallowed in his massive paw. To him, it felt like he was holding four cold French fries in his hand.

"Strange. I swear I had a premonition that you guys would be coming to me, asking about Davidson," she announced, shaking her head. Doyle and Levy exchanged curious glances.

"I don't understand," Levy announced.

Folding her arms and hands across the desk, Margaret spoke frankly. "When Phil called me and said he wanted to speak to me off the record about an inmate named Ruby Davidson, I thought maybe the FBI had a hard-on for this woman. I mean, she threw their conviction right back in their face. That her name came up in some Brooklyn homicides didn't surprise me, and I'll explain why."

Margaret reached in her desk and pulled out a yellow folder with black letters written in Magic Marker and handed it to Levy.

"You know you owe me, Phil. You know this is against the law and unethical. This is privileged information." Margaret took back the file and opened it on her desk. Before reading it, she removed her glasses and looked at Levy.

"Detective, I grew up in Hell's Kitchen when the neighborhood lived up to its moniker. I saw treachery at its worst. I grew up vowing to one day return to that kitchen and clean it up. When I joined them, that's exactly what I did. I put some mean sons of bitches away. I psychologically evaluated some crazy people. Some of them scared the crap out of me. I'm saying this to say, Davidson didn't scare me. She's tough, no doubt about it.

I know what those Brownsville streets can turn a good kid into, or anyone, to say the least. Al Capone grew up on those streets. Davidson is hard on the outside but would melt in your hands on the inside. She is controlled by emotions, and her emotions get the best of her. From what Phil told me, you are investigating some pretty brutal murders. What was it? A beheading and stuff like that?"

"A whole family, children included." Levy nodded.

Margaret bowed her head slightly, shaking it in disbelief. "Do you suspect Davidson is the murderer?"

"No. We suspect she is involved. We know she is not the actual killer," Doyle answered. Margaret sighed. To Levy, it seemed like a sigh of relief.

"Well, if it would help, she once told me that she wanted to get revenge on the people responsible for shooting her niece." Margaret put her glasses back on. "If any of those people were responsible, you may have your motive."

"From what I gathered, there was only a rumor of who was responsible for that. It happened out on the Island," Levy stated.

"Out of your jurisdiction," Margaret said abruptly.

"They never named suspects, anyhow." Levy acknowledged that fact with a nod.

After the meeting, while Doyle and Levy were preparing to leave, Margaret walked them to the door. She grabbed Doyle by the arm and stopped him.

"Why haven't I heard from you? You don't even return my calls."

"My schedule has been hectic and—"

"Don't lie, Phil. I can tell when you're lying. You can't look me in the eye," she growled and waited. When Phil was not forthcoming, she continued, "I understand. You can't afford a scandal before you retire. Just remember, I'm always a phone call away." She grabbed his hand and squeezed. He returned the squeeze and smiled.

During the ride back to New York, Doyle explained to Levy, who was driving, who Scooter and Tashy Williams were.

"This Frank Matthews guy was the largest heroin dealer, well, black one at least, in the country during the sixties. The guy was big. The government busted him for trafficking and other charges related to drug distribution, gives him a quarter-million-dollar bail. It gets posted, and he disappears, never to be seen again."

"A quarter million?"

"Cash," Doyle replied.

"Who brought that type of cash to bail him out?"

"Scooter Williams. Matthews's partner. The partner the government could never touch. The man is well connected at all levels. This guy could run for mayor of New York City with campaign money financed by drug proceeds that everyone knows about and win. They paint this guy as some type of Robin Hood of Harlem. He even let his daughter take the fall in a case of money laundering."

"That's this Tashy Williams?" Levy asked as he swerved as a deer ran across a stretch of the Pennsylvania highway.

"Correct," Doyle answered. "Now, this Daphne Carter. This is interesting." Doyle opened the copy of Daphne's file. "I don't know how dangerous she is, but the people she's involved with are extremely dangerous. I haven't seen this name in years." Doyle pointed.

"Who is that?"

"Junior McLeod."

"Daphne is Wise's little sister."

"What! Wow, do you know that?" Ruby asked Mecca over her cell phone while driving on the FDR Drive on her way to Brooklyn.

Mecca had rented a blue Dodge from the airport and was on her way to Ruby's house.

"I just remembered while I was in Italy. Trust me, it's true. Auntie, you have to be on point. She's after you, and she'll start by attacking anyone or anything close to you. I found out about Breeze and his family. Daphne is behind it," Mecca warned.

"Where are you?" Ruby asked nervously as she was contemplating Mecca's words. She thought about how, out of nowhere, Daphne had just vanished. Then these murders had occurred. Ruby also had a feeling about Daphne's background. Ruby only saw Wise's family in a picture he had in one of his dresser drawers in an apartment she'd once shared with him. That was why she'd asked Mo Blood if he knew Wise's family.

Daphne had told Ruby while they were in prison together that she was originally from

Brownsville but her mom moved to Bed-Stuy when she was young. When Ruby had asked what part of Brownsville, Daphne told her a house off of Rockaway and Newport. Now Ruby remembered Wise mentioning his family living over there. She wondered how Daphne knew Ruby was the one who had killed Wise. No one knew for sure that it was Ruby except Mecca and Dawn, and none of them had known Daphne at the time.

"I'm on the Belt Parkway, on the way to the crib," Mecca answered while exiting off Pennsylvania Avenue.

"Don't go there," Ruby commanded. "Meet me at Prospect Park."

"Auntie?"

"What's up?"

"I love you." Mecca ended the call.

Ruby made a call after Mecca ended hers. Tashy picked up on the first ring.

"Ruby? What's up? You okay?"

"We're going to have to lay low for a while. That bitch Daphne is taking me to war."

"Who? That light-eyed bitch?" Tashy yelled.

"Yeah."

"For what?" Tashy inquired, ready to say "I told you so," but opting not to.

Ruby sucked her teeth. "'I won't discuss that now. Just stay low until I figure out the next move. Put that other thing on hold, too." Ending the call, Ruby tightened her jaw in anger, then banged on the steering wheel. "This bitch don't know."

Simone closed her eyes and leaned her head back on the headrest of Wayne's green Mustang convertible while her legs rested on the dashboard and his head was in between her legs. She imagined that it was Mona's tongue exploring her shaved middle and clit. She had to give it to Wayne when it came to his ability to please her with his tongue talent. It was the only way she was able to cum with him. When it came to his pipe game, he was a dud.

They were parked in a heavily wooded area in a Long Island park where a lot of young lovers came to do things they weren't able to do at their private schools and expensive Hamptons homes. The sun was setting, and the sound of crickets and other insects could be heard, along with Simone's low moans.

"Yeah, eat this pussy. That feels so good, Mona."

Wayne suddenly stopped and looked up at Simone with a glazed face, sporting an angry expression. "Mona?" He got up from off his knees, climbed over Simone, and sat in the driver's seat, wiping his mouth with the back of his hand. "My name is Wayne, Simone."

"What are you talking about? I know your name, boy. Now, finish, because I'm 'bout to cum again. C'mon, baby!" She added a seductive tone while rubbing his crotch, hoping to make him forget. It worked.

His angry expression changed when the blood rushed back to his penis. He grinned. Something moved in the bushes. Startled, they looked around but saw nothing. When they heard nothing, Wayne started to move to reacquire his position between her legs. In a quick motion a gloved hand appeared in the cracked window of the driver's side, holding a gun with a silencer. Before Simone could scream, the window was broken out and another gloved hand was placed over her mouth.

Blood, skull, and brains exploded on her legs as Wayne's body slumped against hers. She felt herself being pulled out of the car as she closed her eyes and tried to scream. When she opened them again, she was being held and pushed from behind.

In front of her was a person in all black. A leather three-quarter coat, black slacks, and boots to match. She saw the back of a van and couldn't tell if it was black or blue. When the man dressed in all black opened the back of the van, she was pushed in the back and landed on a carpeted floor.

"You scream, you die," a masked man said before closing the back door of the van.

Simone recognized the Jamaican accent as her body shook from fear. Why was she being kidnapped by Jamaicans? Ransom? Maybe they wanted Scooter to pay a ransom. He was rich and famous, and everyone new she was his granddaughter. Tears rolled down her face at the thought, even though she knew that he would pay the ransom. She just prayed that a ransom was what it was all about. Her body jerked as the van pulled off.

She could hear voices, but she couldn't see who was driving or who was in the passenger seat. There was a solid black wall dividing the back from the front. The people spoke in deep Jamaican accents, so deep she could barely understand them. Her heart almost burst when she understood one of them when he said, "Me wan feed er to me blood clot pirahna seen."

Then they laughed. Suddenly the ransom idea became questionable.

Scooter was tipsy and exhausted. Sitting in back of his emerald and black chauffeur-driven Rolls Royce Phantom, Scooter had a "love of life" smile on his face. He always felt that way after a sexual encounter at a five-star hotel with a twenty something model/actress who was the daughter or niece of one of his associates and who looked at him as her sugar daddy. Scooter had no problem spending money on women just as long as they filled his voracious sexual appetite.

"How was this one, Scoot?" asked the driver, who was a childhood friend from his old Harlem neighborhood. Scooter smiled at his old pal with the close-cropped beard, speckled with grays, on dark, weathered skin, the puppy dog eyes, and inviting smile. But Charlie "Big Gee" Thomas's humble disposition was contrary to his infamous reputation as a strongman/enforcer from the days of Frank Matthews. Not only was he employed by Scooter as his driver, but he also doubled as his bodyguard, and Scooter trusted him more than anyone he knew . . . even Tashy. The big, cuddly Charlie would literally jump in front of a bullet for Scooter.

"She was a workout, Gee. Young, energetic, and built like a thoroughbred," Scooter said, grinning.

The aspiring model he'd just bedded at the Plaza Hotel flashed in his mind. He wondered what his Ethiopian ambassador friend would think if he found out Scooter was banging his almost twenty-year-old daughter. It really didn't matter what the guy thought, Scooter told himself. He was probably one of those African guys who married his daughter off to some guy she had never met or didn't like who paid a herd of cattle to him for his daughter's hand. What better than to have a handsome, successful black businessman fuck her brains out for a shopping spree at Neiman's, Saks, and Tiffany?

"I need to just lay down in my bed now and recuperate from that episode. That dame almost gave this sixty-two-year-old heart a wipeout," Scooter added, putting his hand to his chest, emulating Redd Foxx on the classic TV show *Sanford and Son*.

"I tried to tell you, Gee, we ain't the same cats we were back on Lenox Avenue. We can't have two dames in one session, then go a few blocks up and bang another broad in one night. Those days are behind us," Big Gee said, glancing at Scooter through the rearview mirror.

Loosening his silk tie from his Italian shirt, Scooter stared out at the Long Island Expressway as he headed home. He realized that he had come a long way from the rough streets of Harlem. He was the son of Collin "Skins" Williams, who was called Skins for his love of shoes with different reptile skins, and Bernice "Bee Bee" Johnson, the niece of the infamous Harlem gangster/ street legend Bumpy Johnson.

For Scooter, growing up was like waking up to a party every day where people gambled, hustled, got high, and lived like there was no tomorrow. Life in the Williams brownstone was just that. Skins was at first a numbers runner for his girlfriend's uncle and made a lot of money working for him. He always told Scooter, "Bumpy was the best black gangster this country ever had. He made sure everybody around him got rich. Nobody could complain with Bumpy."

Scooter wasn't schooled by Bumpy; he learned the street life in another way. In fact, he never caught a glimpse of him and didn't really care. He chose to emulate his father, who was the coolest man that he ever saw. Skins never dressed down; it didn't matter where he was going. He would dress up to run to the supermarket. Then, when Scooter turned ten, Skins taught him about the "policy," as the numbers racket was called.

Skins would drive Scooter around in one of his shiny Cadillacs, collecting policy slips and money and sometimes paying clients who hit the number. Scooter loved driving around Harlem with his father. Skins was a celebrity, and being the son of a celebrity made Scooter feel like one.

People in Harlem definitely treated him like one. The hustlers, pimps, and gangsters acknowledged him with the nickname "Little Skins" whenever they saw him on the street. They would give him money, or they would call him over to one of the corners or pool halls they hung out at and let him shoot pool, dice, or listen to music. One pimp even got one of his prettiest hoes to pleasure Scooter orally in a bathroom.

When the chick was done with Scooter, he practically fell in love with her. Scooter snuck to that pool hall almost every day to see if he could see the chick again. Though he never saw her, he did see her pimp. By that time, he was a numbers runner for Skins, who ran his own operation when Bumpy Johnson was off the scene. While Scooter was collecting a policy slip from the pimp, he asked, "Say, where is that dame you introduced me to a few ticks back?"

The pimp looked at him, puzzled. "Who you talking about, Little Skins?"

"My name's Scooter," he quickly corrected. He had earned the nickname by outrunning a cop who rode on a small scooter, trying to catch him after spotting him with a handful of policy slips.

"Okay, I can dig it," the pimp acknowledged with a smile.

"I'm talking 'bout a dame you was with 'bout a year ago in the pool hall on Lenox. You had her take me in the bathroom."

"Oh, you talking about Leslie," the pimp replied. "Leslie back in Detroit. That's where she was from. I got her from a player's ball when I was out Chicago. The dame chose me and came back to the Apple. Told me she had to go back to see family." The pimp dropped his voice down. "You ain't tell your old man 'bout that, right?"

"No way, I'm no tattletale," Scooter said pompously, which made the pimp smile.

Saddened by the news, he knew one thing for sure: he would never forget her face. She was the most beautiful woman he'd ever seen. Detroit was so far away, and he hated it. He hated it more now because he felt like Motown took a piece of him away. When Skins died of lung cancer, Scooter was fifteen and he was devastated. By that time, he was partnered with his father in the numbers racket and he had a good amount of money to play with. He dressed as sharp as his father and emulated his walk and talk.

At the funeral for Skins it was as if the president of the country had died. The whole of Harlem showed up to pay their respects to one they deemed a gentleman gangster. During the sixties and seventies, the streets of Harlem changed for the worse. Scooter still operated the numbers spots his father left behind, but when a man named Frank Matthews showed up, Scooter's life changed also. Heroin found its way into Harlem during the Vietnam War, but Frank Matthews brought even more with him.

When Scooter saw how rich guys were getting from the sale of "H," or "Boy," as it was called, he quickly cashed in. When he met Matthews, he quickly agreed to move product out of the numbers spots. It was a good cover because the cops turned their heads when it came to numbers. Of course, they were receiving payoffs. In no time, Scooter was rich.

He never forgot the woman who gave him his first head job. In 1965 twenty-one-year-old Scooter traveled to Detroit with Frank Matthews. He was a known gangster all over the country. They attended a dinner party for a notorious Detroit gangster celebrating the release of one of his sons, who was a pimp, from prison. Pimps from all over the Midwest were there, and, of course, they showed up with their stable of women.

There were well-dressed people from all walks of life at the party. The pimps wore colorful suits and shoes with diamond-flooded jewelry. Their women came in full-length fox and mink coats. You definitely had to be somebody to be there.

Though it was a celebration for a pimp returning from prison, Frank Matthews seemed like the focus of everybody's attention. Hands down, he was the richest gangster in the dining hall. He and Scooter were dressed to impress. Both men were in tailor-made suits. Scooter's was bloodred, and Matthews's was a canary yellow. They both wore ostrich shoes and diamond pinkie rings. Just being in the company of Frank Matthews brought Scooter the same attention. Then Scooter saw her face.

It was a face he would never forget. She looked as if she hadn't aged a bit. She had to be at least ten years his senior, but she looked the same as she did in the pool hall in Harlem. She walked in the hall with a full-length white fox, diamond earrings, followed by two other women on both sides of her.

Fortunately for Scooter, the women were seated at a table next to him and Matthews. A table directly in front of a makeshift stage, where A-list entertainers were due to perform. She smiled at Matthews as they were seated. Matthews nodded his head.

"You know her, Frankie?" Scooter asked.

"Who? Leslie? Who doesn't know Leslie? She's one of the biggest pimps in the Midwest!"

Scooter went wide-eyed. "Pimp?"

"Yeah. Why? You wanna meet her?" Matthews asked.

"Sure," Scooter responded. "Yeah, why not?"

The rest was history. When Leslie found out that Scooter was second in command of the Matthews organization, she didn't hesitate to start dating him. Scooter would fly her into New York for weeks at a time, staying in a luxurious suite at the Plaza or Waldorf Astoria Hotel. He would visit her sometimes in Detroit, on business trips. Scooter started lots of businesses across the country under different names of people who were willing to help him go legit.

Leslie was one of those people.

That same year, in the winter, Leslie gave birth to Scooter's daughter at a Harlem hospital. Leslie named her Tashera. Scooter was the happiest man in the world until, hours after giving birth, Leslie died.

By the time Scooter snapped out of his thoughts of the past, the Phantom was entering the driveway of his Long Island home. Pulling into the five-car garage, Scooter noticed Simone's sky blue two-door, drop-top Mercedes

parked next to his caramel brown 1975 Cadillac
Fleetwood. The Benz was Simone's twentieth
birthday present. Scooter remembered the ear-
to-ear smile on her face when she woke up that
morning and he walked her to the front of the
house, to the awaiting car with a large red bow
on the trunk. Simone meant the world to him.

"Long night, Scoot. I'll see you in the morning," Big Gee said as he and Scooter exited the
car.

Big Gee lived in Scooter's guesthouse, which
was larger than the average suburban middle-class home. Even though he had two other
homes, a condo in Queens and a Manhattan
penthouse, he preferred the guesthouse built
behind Scooter's Hamptons mini mansion. The
house sat thirty yards away from the mansion on
five acres of land. Gee loved the privacy.

"I'll probably be asleep through the day. Wake
me up in the afternoon," Scooter said as he took
careful steps entering the house through the
garage.

As Scooter entered the spacious, ultramodern
kitchen, he was immediately approached by his
short, bubbly, extremely dark-skinned Haitian
housekeeper. She was a middle-aged woman
who had worked for Scooter close to twenty
years now, and she could never seem to wear her

wigs right. They always seemed to lean to one side more than the other.

The worried look on her face made Scooter nervous.

"Scotty, Simone hasn't come home, and Wayne's parents are looking for him," Lillian said with a heavy Haitian accent, which she'd had for the thirty years Scooter had employed her. Scooter looked at his Oyster Perpetual Rolex.

"Did you call her cell phone?"

"I keep getting her voice mail," Lillian answered.

Scooters forehead wrinkled as he raised his eyebrows in surprise. It wasn't like Simone or Wayne to be out past midnight, especially Wayne. His parents were strict disciplinarians. Lillian jumped at the sound of the cordless kitchen phone ringing. She quickly answered. Scooter stared at her face as she spoke to the caller. As the time passed, he became more and more nervous when she covered her mouth with her hand and her facial expression turned from worry to shock. She handed the phone to Scooter.

"It's Mr. Farrow," she mumbled.

"John?" Scooter boomed.

In a tearful, panic-stricken voice, Wayne's father spoke. "Scooter, they found my boy dead. Someone shot him in the head."

"What! Where?" Scooter asked on the verge of panic.

"In the park."

"Did anyone see Simone? She was supposed to be with him," Scooter asked as his heart raced.

"No. No one has seen her."

"John, where are you?"

Scooter then realized that the question was answered by the background noise. Police radios and people talking could be heard. They were obviously still at the crime scene.

"The park."

"I'm on my way." Scooter hung up the phone and suddenly felt sober. As he was walking out of the same door he'd entered, he turned to Lillian and grumbled, "Get her mother on the phone. See what she knows about where Simone is. Then call me right after."

"Yes, sir."

Scooter jumped in the Phantom, not bothering to call Big Gee. The big guy needed rest, and Scooter needed to sort things out on his own. These types of things didn't happen in the Hamptons. He had a feeling that this was not a random act. There was something deeper going on.

***

Scared and confused, Simone still realized there was no use in screaming for help. After driving for what appeared to be an hour, the van stopped. The back door opened, and one of the masked men placed a black bandanna over her eyes and tied it. Her captors then led her into a building that resembled a large, empty factory.

When they removed the blindfold, Simone studied her surroundings more. With the ceiling reaching at least three stories and thick, cubed windows at the top of the linoleum walls, the large space looked to her like some type of hangar, except there were no planes in sight.

They were tying her to a thick, chipped painted pipe when one of the hangar doors opened and a pistachio green BMW 750il entered. Two men wearing black ski hats at the top of their heads came out of the door and walked toward the car. Simone figured those were her captors. Why did they now feel it was okay to reveal their faces to her?

They were evil-looking men. Both dark skinned, with a red, blank, evil glare in their eyes. One was bowlegged, and Simone, despite her circumstances, found his walk sexy. Both had long, shaggy beards.

The occupants of the Beemer emerged. This took Simone by surprise. The driver was one of the prettiest women she'd ever laid eyes on, and the other woman, with long dreadlocks, reminded her of Erykah Badu. But the real pretty one, her eyes were like crystal balls, with a grayish silver gleam. It was like you could almost see through them. To her, she didn't look like the type of woman that would be involved with these dangerous-looking men. There was a kind of aura to her face that spelled innocence. As the women approached, they were followed by the men. Simone's heart began to pound.

"Are you hungry or thirsty? Anything you need, you let us know," the pretty one said. "You will not be harmed, I assure you." She smiled.

Simone swallowed. "Why am I here? Who are you people?" Her voice cracked as she looked at the woman with the pretty eyes up and down, surveying her fashion. She concluded that not only was she pretty, but she also had style.

"Collateral." Simone watched the pretty girl reach for her Gucci purse and remove a cell phone. "Call your mom. Tell her some friends of her friend want their money back. Drop it off at Franklin and Fulton, on the steps of the train station. Tell her if the cops are called, she knows what to expect. Just remember Breeze."

The pretty-eyed girl's voice was filled with threats, even though she was smiling. Simone did what she was told. Her hands shook as she pressed the buttons on the cell phone. Tashy picked up on the first ring.

"Tashy?"

"Simone? Where the hell are you? Your grandfather is looking for you. The lady, Lillian, called here—"

Lillian hadn't informed Tashy about Wayne's murder; she'd just asked if she knew where Simone was, 'cause she wasn't home when Scooter got home. Simone cut her off and spoke in a low, cracked voice.

"Listen! Some friends of your friend want their money. They said to drop it off—"

"Simone, what are you—"

"Tashy, this is serious. I've been kidnapped. They said for your friend to drop the money that's theirs at the train station." She looked at the pretty woman and mouthed, "Where?"

"The steps of the Franklin and Fulton train station," the pretty woman answered into the phone for Simone, with the smile still plastered on her face. Afterward, she gave the phone back to Simone.

"Tashy, they said if the cops get involved, you know what to expect. Remember Breeze."

The pretty-eyed woman snatched the phone from her and ended the call. Tears began to fall down Simone's face.

"You're talking about Ruby, aren't you?"

"You're a smart girl. Hopefully, your mother and Ruby are just as smart." The pretty-eyed girl walked back to her BMW with her female friend, leaving Simone with the two goons.

"Please don't kill me or my mom! I hate Ruby!" Simone yelled. The pretty-eyed woman was halfway in the car when she looked back at Simone and smiled. "Then we have a lot in common. Hopefully, no one else will end up like your boyfriend."

She got in the Beemer and pulled out of the hangar.

When the call ended, Tashy quickly placed a call to Ruby.

"Yo," Ruby grunted after answering the phone on the second ring.

"Ruby, they snatched Simone!"

"What? What the hell are you talking about?"

"That bitch kidnapped my daughter. She said to drop the money you owe her at Franklin and Fulton train station." Tashy's voice was filled with rage. "Ruby, I don't give a fuck who or what happened between ya'll, but the bitch involved me and mines. Make it right, Ruby, 'cuz if something happens to my daughter, I'm gonna blame you." Tashy ended the call.

Chapter Seventeen

In the measure that she glorified herself and lived luxuriously, in the same measure give her torment and sorrow.

—Revelations 18:7

Temperatures in New York were just above freezing the morning Ruby and Mecca walked the empty bike path of Brooklyn's largest park. Ruby hung on every word Mecca said while at the same time thinking how the Italian sun had given her a golden hue. Mecca looked good and healthy. Her once thin face, from lying in a coma for months, was now full, and Ruby could tell that she had put back on a healthy weight. Mecca filled her blue denim jeans by Citizens of Humanity nicely. Ruby noticed how her hair, which was without extensions or a weave, had grown a few inches past her shoulders. Both women walked with their hands in their coats.

Mecca preferred for them to meet at a warm spot, but Ruby felt the park at the time was a suitable place to talk and be out of sight.

"So how'd you know that was Wise's sister?" Ruby asked.

"When I first saw her, I felt she looked familiar," Mecca reported, looking straight ahead as a group of pigeons flew off in fear of their approach. "Then, while I was in Italy, I had this dream. I saw her in my dream. It was a while back, but it made me remember."

"A dream?" Ruby asked skeptically. Mecca glared at her aunt, as if she was insulted.

"Yeah, a dream! The dream just helped me remember. Is that hard to believe?"

Ruby, sensing her frustration, changed her tone. "I'm not saying it like I don't believe you. I just wanna be sure."

"It doesn't take a rocket scientist to figure it out. You know she's behind what happened to Breeze and his family. You said it yourself. She just bounced without a trace."

"Yeah, I . . ." Ruby's response was interrupted by the ringing of her cell phone in her leather bomber jacket pocket. "Yo," Ruby answered, annoyed that her conversation with Mecca had been interrupted. Mecca watched Ruby's facial expression change from a calm one to one that was shocked at the news she received from her caller. "What are you talking about?"

Ruby listened attentively as Tashy revealed the news about Simone's kidnapping and issued a threat. A threat Ruby didn't appreciate. Before she got a chance to respond, Tashy ended the call.

"Who was that?" Mecca asked.

"They kidnapped my girlfriend's daughter. They want me to pay the ransom they said I owe." Ruby had a fearful look in her eyes. A look Mecca couldn't remember ever seeing on her aunt's face.

Mecca sighed. She knew just as well as Ruby that Daphne was responsible for the kidnapping. Only Mecca knew why it was said that the ransom was what Ruby owed. Still, Mecca held her tongue.

"What are you gonna do?"

Ruby stared off into the distance. Unsure of her plan, she answered just the same. "What can I do? I don't know what I owe or where Daphne is."

"I can help you find her. Me and her got pretty close. Give me a day or two. I'll let you know what I find out."

"I don't have a day or two. They want the money tonight," Ruby said.

Mecca paused to think. "Give me your phone," she said. "When they call back, I'll tell them that you're scraping it up. She'll talk to me. Meet me at your crib tonight."

"A'ight," Ruby answered.

Just before they exited the park and walked to their own vehicles, Ruby turned and spoke. "I just wanna know where she's at. I don't owe the bitch shit but a bullet in her skull."

Mecca watched her get inside her truck and entered her own rented car, welcoming the warmth. She removed Ruby's phone and smiled to herself. When she started the car up, she mumbled, "Much smarter than you think I am, Lou."

The Honorable Francis Nicoletti sat behind his mahogany desk in a snow-white shirt with red suspenders and a matching bow tie, reading a sworn affidavit given to him by Detective Levy and Agent Doyle, who sat in chairs, anxiously waiting for him to sign it.

Both Levy and Doyle couldn't read the judge's expression as he stared down at the file of papers they'd both spent long hours preparing. He nodded sometimes, raised an eyebrow, and grunted for what seemed like a lifetime to them.

Levy fidgeted uncomfortably, while Doyle stared at the top of the bowed head of Judge Nicoletti.

Doyle had known him for years; from the time the veteran judge was a federal prosecutor, he was a no-nonsense-type guy who fought every case vigorously. He was a firm believer in the law and the Constitution of this country, and he followed it to a T. He had made a lot of enemies in legal circles due to his stand on justice. If the FBI brought him a case that he felt wasn't convincing of the offender's guilt, he wouldn't hesitate to dismiss it. Agents would storm his office, preaching about how the alleged criminal was a killer, a kingpin who had kids sell drugs out of the school yard, a menace to society, only to hear an even-toned Nicoletti say, "I could have told you about President Reagan, but it would have just been my word. Where's the proof?"

Judge Nicoletti finally looked up at Doyle and Levy with his blue eyes behind rimmed glasses. His pale skin had deep lines, and the double chin jiggled when he spoke.

"The Davidson phone, I'll authorize the wiretap. There's probable cause, but Williams and Carter, I'm denying. Being friends with a target of an investigation is not probable cause, gentlemen. I need more. You got your wire for thirty days. Hopefully, that wire will give you PC on the other ladies. You gentlemen, have a nice day. This meeting is adjourned."

A bulimic, reddish-brown-haired female stenographer packed up her equipment and left the office. Judge Nicoletti removed his glasses and rubbed the bridge of his nose. When the stenographer was gone, the judge smiled at Doyle.

"You owe me a lunch, Phil. I'm starving." The judge gave a sly grin, then continued, "You never know. The right restaurant may get you more wires."

Doyle and Levy stood up, prepared to leave. It was Doyle who spoke first, with a grin. "Never knew you could be bribed."

Nicoletti put on a black blazer, then patted Doyle on his back as they walked toward the office door. "For a plate of lasagna or veal Parmesan, I would have authorized wiretaps to be placed on the Oval Office."

"I knew that dame was bad news. You sure know how to pick 'em." Scooter and Tashy sat in the office of Scooter's bar and grill on the Queens–Long Island border. Tashy raised a disappointing eyebrow at her father's comment. She knew he was exhausted and stressed.

"Don't start," Tashy said vaguely, sitting on a leather sectional, rocking back and forth nervously. Every time her phone rang, she would get jumpy and answer it quickly. A knock at the door interrupted their conversation.

"Come in," Scooter ordered.

The man who entered was someone Scooter was expecting. He stood up to shake the man's hand, which always reminded him of frog's legs. The guy's thin frame and college professor look were a deceptive contradiction to what he was really about.

"Glad you could come at such an early hour, Sonny, but this is one of those 'desperate times calling for desperate measures' situations," Scooter said, gesturing for Sonny to take a seat in front of the mahogany desk.

"I kind of figured it was something that was extremely important for you to call at such a time," Sonny said softly.

Behind the humble, intelligent demeanor, Sonny was one of the most, if not *the* most, dangerous men Scooter had ever met. He was handsome, in a Babyface sort of way, and his brown eyes were direct. He had even features and curly hair that was graying at the temples. His athletically slim body made him look ten years younger than his fifty-three years. Besides him being a stone-cold killer, what made him more dangerous was that he was an ex-marine honorably discharged after serving his country for twenty years. Ten in Special Forces and another ten in the NYPD, which he'd retired from. He was a trained killer who knew powerful people and could get information on any person he wanted. That helped when he was looking for someone, because even if you were hiding in an igloo on the frozen tundra, Sonny would find you.

"You want a drink, Sonny?" Scooter walked over to his personally carved black marble bar and poured himself a glass of Grand Marnier. Sonny waived it off.

"No thanks. Liquor was never a choice breakfast for me." Scooter half smiled at his humor.

"I called you here because some people have kidnapped my granddaughter," Scooter said without hesitation. "This is my daughter, Tashy." As Scooter gestured to Tashy, Sonny nodded.

"I assume it's your daughter Scooter is talking about," Sonny said with a serious expression as he looked at her.

Scooter had used Sonny for many different "services" in the last decade, after he was introduced to him at a campaign fund-raising event for a friend who was running for the state senate.

The introduction was short and to the point when one of Scooter's associate mumbled in his ear, "I want you to meet Sonny Brown. Anything you need taken care of, he can do it. And I mean anything or anybody, you dig?" Afterward, anytime Scooter needed Sonny's "assistance" in dealing with a problem that was considered "expendable" or a "potential threat," Sonny handled it efficiently.

"Do we know who is responsible?"

"Her name is Daphne Carter. She's from Brooklyn. She's affiliated with the Shower," Tashy answered.

"You mean the Shower Posse?" Sonny's eyebrows rose in surprise.

Tashy nodded.

"How did you all get into a run-in with the likes of the Shower Posse?" Sonny inquired.

Sonny remembered that when he worked as an NYPD detective while on leave from the service a case involving the Shower Posse came in. In the eighties, Jamaican posses reeked murderous havoc on many U.S. cities, especially New York, Miami, and places like D.C. Sonny recalled the brutality and savagery of the Shower Posse's murders. They loved to dismember their victims.

"Long story," Tashy said abruptly.

Sonny looked at his Patek Philippe watch. "Long morning. I got time. Need to know what I'm getting into and where to start."

After Tashy gave Sonny the rundown, he simply stated, "We need to talk to your friend Ruby."

Scooter reached in his desk and pulled out a stuffed envelope and handed it to Sonny, who stood up, straightening his Ralph Lauren Purple Label suit. He grabbed the envelope and placed it in his inside pocket.

"Always a pleasure," Sonny commented before exiting the office.

"You sure he can get Simone back?" Tashy fretted.

"He's the best, Tashy. No one can hide from Sonny Brown. That man is probably the only person in this world who could find Osama bin Laden."

"Why doesn't he?" she asked.

"'Cause nobody is really looking for him."

The FBI technicians finished installing the wiretap and electronic listening devices in Ruby's brownstone right before she pulled up in front of her home. Agents sitting in a van with a telephone company logo watched Ruby from the corner of the block. She looked nervous as she exited her Jeep cautiously, looking up and down the block as the sun began to rise. The chilly morning left dew on cars and patches of grass that surrounded small trees enclosed behind small black wrought-iron gates. The temperature got a little warmer as the sun began to rise, promising, at the very least, a sunny day.

When she entered the brownstone, she went directly to the first-floor kitchen to fix a much-needed cup of coffee. When she turned the lights on, she was momentarily startled by the person sitting at the kitchen table.

"What are you doing here, and how the fuck did you get in?" Ruby asked with force.

"I really need to talk to you."

"Listen, Mona, enough is enough," Ruby sighed.

Chapter Eighteen

The suspicion of an ulterior motive is anti-se-
ductive. Never let anything break the illusion.
— Robert Greene, *The Art of Seduction*

Junior McLeod exited the terminal at Miami
International Airport and put a pair of shades on
over his piercing gray eyes. An aqua blue Nautica
deck shirt, white cotton Nautica short pants, and
white track sneakers gave him the typical Miami
everyday look. He wore his long dreadlocks
neatly packed in a red, yellow, and green knitted
cap.

Whenever Junior visited the States, Miami
was the place he enjoyed time in, as it was with
many Jamaicans who came to the United States.
After hailing a taxi and telling the driver that the
Setai Hotel was his destination, Junior stared
out at the familiar landscape of the city. It'd been
a few years since he'd been back in the United

States, as he'd been uninterested in traveling ever since the September 11 attacks, and there probably wasn't a place on the globe he hadn't visited, anyway.

However, this visit was urgent. Urgent enough that the person he was there to see had booked him a room at what was now considered one of Miami's best hotels on Collins Avenue. The Setai Hotel was an oceanfront spot in the center of South Beach, among tropical gardens and pools. The place was top-of-the-line luxury, and Junior's suite put the *l* in *luxury*. Setting down his Tumi luggage, Junior took in the view of the crystal blue ocean from the deck of his room. The ocean smell reminded him of Jamaica. Getting comfortable, he removed his cell phone from its case on his waist and dialed a number. The person picked up on the second ring.

"By the looks of this room, I guess this meeting is more serious than I figured." The accent wasn't lost on the person on the line. A voice and accent the person hadn't heard in years. The feeling was mutual when Junior listened to his response.

"I don't think it could get more serious, old pal. I'll be there in five minutes. I know you don't eat meat, except fish. They got this restaurant on Washington Ave. It's a seafood place. How 'bout we grab a bite?"

"Pleasure, then, brethren."

The line went dead, and Junior went to his carry-on bag and removed a sealed cigar box. Removing the seal, he took out a tightly rolled leaf of Jamaican weed and went to the deck, where he lit it and inhaled deeply. When the potent smoke filled his chest, he held it momentarily, then exhaled a thick white cloud of smoke. Junior felt relaxed.

Thirty minutes later Junior sat in Joe's Stone Crab Restaurant, eating a healthy plate of baked fish, steamed vegetable brown rice, and freshly blended mango and banana juice. Before the dishes were served, he was able to get reacquainted with his host.

"You look like you haven't aged a bit."

"Whatever it is you want, flattery will work in your favor. Too bad I can't say the same for you, old friend. You need to change your diet and habits." Junior smiled.

Agent Doyle shrugged his stooped shoulders at Junior's comment. The relationship between the two men went back years, to when Junior led a vicious attack of the Shower Posse on the streets of New York and Doyle investigated them. Unable to catch Junior himself in a RICO indictment because of Junior's son, who ran the day-to-day dirty work, the FBI decided to indict Donovan and other members of the posse, including Daphne. It was an indictment that led to the raid that resulted in Donovan's murder, Daphne's conviction, and a bloody war on the streets.

Agent Doyle had set up a meeting with the then forty-year-old Junior at a Brooklyn hotel, knowing the murderous reputation he had. Junior commanded a posse that did not hesitate to murder a federal agent, and afterward, Junior respected Doyle even more.

Doyle personally sent a reef of roses to the funeral of Donovan and his condolences to Junior and his wife. He expressed the same condolences at the Brooklyn meeting, where Doyle made the only unethical decision of his long career. It was a decision in which, he felt, the ends justified the means.

At the time, too many bodies were popping up around New York and his caseload was growing because of the posse. So for Junior's promise to stop the war going on in the streets, Doyle gave Junior the names of the informants among Junior's crew. Among those informants were a few people who were responsible for the indictment and convictions.

"A diet? The only thing I need to cut back on is police work. It aged me beyond my years," Doyle said before ordering a huge plate of fried jumbo shrimp, baked salmon with a butter dip, and buttered noodles, which he washed down with white wine.

Junior studied the aging cop and laughed to himself at his style. His white, short-sleeved polo shirt fit loosely around his upper body but was stretched by his protruding gut. The navy blue Dockers were wrinkled, and he wore no socks with a pair of not-so-shiny hard-bottom shoes. The seventies-style Vegas shades made him look even more comedic. After their meals, Doyle got right down to the point of calling Junior.

"Junior, it's like the talk we had twenty years ago in Brooklyn . . . ," Doyle began as he stared directly into Junior's gray eyes. Immediately, he remembered that time when he told his partner that he felt like he was going to pass out after staring into Junior's eyes.

He relayed to Junior everything that had been going on in the investigation of Ruby and the murders. Junior listened intently. When Daphne's name was brought up, Junior's eyes squinted and he folded his arms across his chest.

"Over the wire we placed in Davidson's home, we received information about the kidnapping of Tashy Williams's daughter. Tashy Williams is the daughter of a guy named Scooter Williams." Doyle paused, waiting to see if the name registered. When it didn't, he continued. "This Scooter is a powerful guy with connections high up in city government and the underworld."

The two men paused as a waiter walked over and asked if they needed anything else.

"Let me get another glass of wine," Doyle said, "and the check."

When the waiter left, Doyle looked around at the other tables. They were mostly filled with young, tanned couples having giggling conversations, oblivious to the New York federal agent and the old, dangerous Jamaican gangster who was responsible for at least 5 percent of the homicides in New York in those years.

"So what can I do for you?" Junior asked.

"Talk to Daphne. Tell her to let the girl go. There will be a war bloodier than any of your past ones combined." Again, he paused as the waiter brought his drink and the check.

"And what about the murders already done? Will Daphne have to go to jail for them?"

Doyle sighed. Once again, the ends were justified by the means. "What does she want? I know you know what this war is about, Junior. She still confides in you. This is off the record."

Junior knew he could trust Doyle's word. It was not like Doyle would go incriminate himself and risk ending his career behind the walls he'd put so many people behind, and Junior had enough dirt to do just that!

"Davidson is responsible for the murder of Daphne's older brother years back. She wants revenge," Junior murmured.

Doyle looked into his eyes and, with a serious expression, said, "I give her Davidson, she leaves the country, and the murders go unsolved."

"What about what's on them wires?"

Junior did not know that Doyle had lied about receiving the information from the wiretaps. He'd actually got it from an informant on the street who was a member of Daphne's crew. He had to keep some cards in his hand covered.

"There's nothing on them to implicate Daphne in the murders. If she leaves the country, the kidnapping goes unsolved and there is a statute of limitations on that charge."

"I'll call her," Junior replied.

Doyle sipped on his wine. "Can you guarantee the release of the girl?"

Junior chuckled. "Have the years and bad diet clouded your memory, too?"

Doyle smiled. The world could do without a Ruby Davidson, he thought, rationalizing everything.

Outside the restaurant, before both men went their separate ways, they shook hands.

"I have to go," Doyle stated. "I have a flight scheduled to New York leaving in an hour. So what will you do while you're in the States?"

Junior smiled mischievously. "I still got moves, mon. I'm going to a reggae club to dance with the young people."

"Time for me to take off this Miami attire and get back to the icebox up north. It was nice seeing you again, Junior, and once again, thank you." Doyle chuckled.

"It's nothing, mon. Soon me call you for a favor. I just hope I don't have to book a hotel in Jamaica to ask." Junior nodded.

Too many things were going through Daphne's mind for her to concentrate on a casual sex partner doing what most women would say was a good job at eating pussy. The dark-skinned Taye Diggs look-alike moaned between Daphne's legs while she lay on her back with her legs resting on his shoulders. She had situated herself in the Bronx condo, on a king-size bed in a room that was plush and comfortable. From time to time, he would look up at her between his moans and hard breathing and notice her staring into space.

Her mind was in some other place. It bothered him that she wasn't into it while he was doing her a service, and he wondered how she would act when the roles were reversed.

"Stop. That's enough," Daphne suddenly snapped.

"What's wrong? Did I do something wrong?" he asked. Daphne got off the bed and walked to the armchair, which held her clothes.

"No, it's not—" Interrupted by the vibrating cell phone, she removed it from her jeans pocket and looked at the screen. "Hello," she answered softly.

"Daphne?" the voice hummed.

Daphne instantly recognized the voice as Junior's and looked back at her naked partner and placed her hand by her mouth for him to remain silent.

"You're in Miami? Why?" she inquired.

Junior never came to the United States without informing her so that she could have something arranged for him. Most of the time he would stay at her guesthouse and she would arrange for a car to pick him up and take him wherever he wanted to go. This was unusual.

"I had some urgent business to take care of," he replied.

"Are you coming to New York?"

"Are you on a private line?" he asked.

"Yes."

"Go public and call me at this number," Junior ordered.

Daphne didn't hesitate in leaving the condo and giving her lover a rain check. She had enjoyed the guy's company and he had a mean tongue, so she would definitely be back, but when Junior called and said something, Daphne would stop everything to get it done. Even a bomb-bursting orgasm.

On the way to a public phone, she made a call on her phone, asking if Ruby had made the drop yet. She had already made it clear to Tashy how much she wanted. A quarter of a million in clean, hard cash. When she found out the drop hadn't been made, she was furious.

"They think it's a game? Show them it isn't," she said into the phone, then hung up.

As she parked her car in front of a bar where a group of young guys stood, Daphne studied them before exiting. She realized they had to be hustling in the freezing cold. From the way they were bundled up, they had been out there for hours, and once they saw her, they tried to get her attention. A beautiful black woman jumping out of a luxury car didn't intimidate these young cats.

Ignoring them, she went into the bar and used the pay phone on the wall in the back. Music and smoke filled the bar, which was good. It would mask her and her conversation with Junior from prying ears. Daphne made the call. It was answered on the first ring, and Daphne never had a chance to speak.

"Let the girl go."

"I don't understand what . . ." Daphne's heart skipped a beat.

Junior cut her off. "Daphne, you know what I'm talking about. Forget the money and let the girl go. You can still get what you seek. She is at her home now. Get it over with now. When it's done, there is a flight booked to yard. LaGuardia, tomorrow morning, nine o'clock. Be on it."

"Junior, why are—"

"No need to get into it. Get it done." Junior ended the call.

Daphne hung up the phone, confused and infuriated. Who had told Junior of the kidnapping? Even more confusing was why he wanted the girl let go. Who had talked to him about that? Daphne thought about who she was related to and realized Tashy's father was powerful, but that meant nothing to her or Junior. The Shower Posse feared no one. Except the FBI.

Was Junior in bed with . . . Immediately
she chased the thought from her mind. Junior
would never. She would get to the bottom of it
in Jamaica.

Simone knew it was now or never. She faked
as if she was asleep on the cot while her two
dreadlocked watchers were also asleep on their
own cots. One of them was supposed to stay up
while the other slept in five-hour shifts, but these
two smoked weed all day and night, and after
eating Jamaican takeout, they'd fallen asleep.

The first night they did it, Simone fell asleep at
the same time they did, after catching a contact
high from the weed. Plus, the full stomach of
brown rice and beans, plantains and roti, didn't
help her cause, either.

This time, she stayed up. As one of them
snored, she knew she could tiptoe without waking them. They had made a fatal mistake by
leaving her untied, thinking that fear overcame
her will to escape. They were wrong.

She steeled herself, repeating that she was
the daughter of Tashy Williams and the granddaughter of Scooter. They had learned to take
fear head-on. Slowly, Simone rose off the cot,
and her face scrunched as she got a whiff of her

own body odors after two days without a shower. Though it was light outside, she was unsure as to what time it was and couldn't see the sky through the dusty windows, which needed to be cleaned. There was a door at the far end of the hangar that she knew was open. It was one of those doors with a lock on the outside, but once inside, you could just turn the knob

Still, she could hear her own heart as it drummed within her chest. Opening the door slowly, she stepped out into the cold. A welcoming cold. She took in her scenery and realized that the warehouse was on a long block of other warehouses. At the corner, she saw the Manhattan Bridge and knew she was in Brooklyn. Even though she didn't know exactly where, she was happy to be in the city.

Did her captors assume that she knew nothing of the city since she lived in Long Island? Well, they were wrong, and she was glad that the city was her playground and she knew how to get around it. So she ran. Back in the warehouse, a cell phone rang and awakened one of the men.

"Blood clot!" he barked as he shook his companion. "Fresh, get up! The Yankee gal, where she?"

He looked at his phone's screen to see if he recognized the number, and when he didn't, he calmed down and answered.

"Paul?" Daphne asked.

"What go on, Daphne?" he greeted, as if everything was normal.

"Let the girl go."

Paul thought he heard wrong. "Come again?"

Daphne sighed and growled, "Paul, let the damned girl go. Don't ask questions. Just do it, now!"

Paul couldn't have been more relieved. The kidnapping didn't matter, anyway. He didn't want to think about what would have happened if she hadn't said that. They didn't fear Daphne, but they did fear her connection with Junior McLeod. None of them wanted to be on his bad side; it was an express trip to the grave.

Paul looked at his partner, shrugging his shoulders.

"Who dat? Daphne?"

"Yeah, mon."

"We got to find that Yankee before she return," Fresh said.

Paul shook his head. "Nah, mon. Everything cool. Daphne say let the youth go."

"Just listen, Ruby!"

"Listen to you tell me how you broke into my crib? Listen, Mona, you don't know me that well. I got a lot of things on my plate right now, so don't make me have to beat your ass in here for real," Ruby said in a leveled tone. To accent her point, Ruby pointed her index finger and showed her the rage in her eyes. Tears welled up in Mona's eyes.

"Ruby, someone kidnapped Simone. That's why I'm here!"

"Don't you think I know that?" Ruby snapped. "You sneaking into my house don't help bring her back."

Mona wiped a tear that flowed down her face. "I know, I know, but I think Simone's mother and grandfather are sending someone after you. They're blaming you."

"What? Where did you hear that?" Ruby asked.

"I called Simone's mother, and she told me what happened. She must have been in the middle of a discussion with her father and another man. She forgot to press the end button on her phone, and I heard the conversation. I was worried about you," Mona said in a worried tone.

Ruby was tired of Mona's obsession, but with her revelation, Ruby put that aside for now. Mona might have saved her life with the info. Did Tashy actually think she was behind the kidnapping of Simone? Tashy must think Ruby was petty. Why would she ask for a quarter million when she knew Scooter was worth millions? And she knew Scooter would pay the ransom and would use the whole issue as an excuse for why Simone should stay in Long Island with him. Which would be ironic, since she was kidnapped from Long Island.

"How long have you been in my house?"

"Long enough to hide in the closet and watch some men break in here and put in wires. I think the Feds are listening to us," Mona whispered.

The agents in the van outside went still when they heard Mona's statement. They looked at each other as one picked up a walkie-talkie and announced, "We've been made."

Agent Doyle's voice came through the walkie-talkie, responding to the agent in the van. "Shut it down and get out of here."

The agents left. They did not know Doyle was parked five cars behind them on the opposite side of the street, watching Ruby's home. He was there to make sure Daphne got her revenge with nothing else getting in the way. It would kill two birds with one stone, he figured.

With the murders of Breeze and his family on Ruby, he could say that she was killed in revenge. The murders of the family would be solved while Ruby's killers were on the run. That was Doyle's plan. Unethical, but society wouldn't lose a prominent, productive member, and he wouldn't have to spend his last year on a wild-goose chase and dealing with mountains of paperwork.

"You sure it was the Feds?" Ruby whispered, grabbing Mona by the hand and leading her toward the door.

"It definitely was. I heard things they were saying. They were happy that the wires were in place, and they tested them by speaking to who-ever is somewhere listening," Mona explained.

"We gotta go, then," Ruby mumbled.

"Where are we going?" Mona asked as Ruby pulled her toward the exit.

"Somewhere other than here. I have to think."

Drinking a cup of coffee from Dunkin' Donuts, Doyle waited. He knew Daphne would be pulling up any minute, and the agents hadn't made him aware that Ruby's life was in jeopardy, after hearing what Mona had told her about a conversation she had with Tashy.

They were angry that they had got made and forgot to mention it to Doyle. If he had known, he would have warned Daphne that Ruby knew.

He watched as Daphne, in a green Camry, parked the car across the street from Ruby's house, on the empty block. It was perfect tim-ing. Then his peripheral vision caught some movement, and as he turned, he recognized a familiar face walking up the block. The man was also looking at the brownstone, as if he were searching out an address. Sonny Brown was here to kill.

Chapter Nineteen

But in the end, she is bitter as wormwood, sharp as a two-edged sword.

—Proverb 5:4

Furious that she couldn't put her plan of revenge in play by making Ruby rich, then taking it all away, along with her closest friends, Daphne looked down at her phone as it received a text message from Ruby. The text infuriated her even more as she sat across from her brownstone. It simply said, "Come and get me."

Ruby was taunting her.

She knew she should have killed Simone. Killing her would have definitely made Tashy and her family ready to kill Ruby for their loss. Daphne could have then killed Ruby without anyone suspecting her of the murder. But now Simone had to be let go on Junior's orders.

It was now or never. All the years of planning her revenge and how she would do it went out the window. Daphne had begun to plot and scheme about Ruby as soon as she found out who Ruby was. When she came to the federal prison in Ohio, and they met, the last thing she thought was that she would meet this gangster from Brooklyn that she'd heard so much about, the woman rumored to have killed her brother, Wise.

Daphne had first heard the rumor while she was in middle school, while listening in on a conversation in the girls' bathroom. One girl told another, "That girl Mecca, the light-skin one from Langston Hughes? My cousin said her aunt killed two guys last month. She threw one out the window and shot the guy Wise on the staircase. Her auntie ain't no joke."

The other girl replied, "I don't like that bitch Mecca. She think she all that!"

Just as Daphne walked out of the bathroom stall, the girls stopped talking. They didn't even look at her in the face; they just walked out. She could hear them mumble as they left, "That's Wise's sister."

Daphne knew who Mecca was. She had heard a lot of girls in her school talk about the pretty girl from Langston Hughes whose mother and father got killed while she watched from under the bed. The girl whose aunt was notorious in Brownsville.

Getting to know Ruby while in prison, Daphne realized that if she weren't responsible for her brother's murder, she would have really liked her. She admired her strength, even though underneath the hard exterior there was a woman yearning for true love, a woman who wanted to be paid attention to, and not just because she had a nice body or money. She was someone who wanted to be appreciated for who she really was.

Daphne had sensed that. She saw herself in Ruby, but Ruby was the cause of her pain. She had taken the person who meant the most to her. Daphne remembered how lonely she felt after her brother was killed, how Christmas changed, how abuse from her steppops went unchecked because her strong, fearless brother was gone. And this woman who was now in the same prison as her was the reason for all of her misery.

So she'd plotted.

She didn't understand why Junior wanted her to change her plan. When she was released from prison, she'd told him all about her plan, and he'd told her, "I understand your pain, but why go through all that instead of just getting right to the point?"

Daphne looked him directly in the eyes and replied with steel in her voice, "I want her to feel how I felt. I want her to be happy for a moment, then miserable even longer. I want the people around her to feel pain and blame her. Then I want her to die slowly."

Junior simply nodded. "It is not good to hold that much pain for so long. It could end up destroying you. Before you leave Jamaica, I want you to go see Doc Benjamin."

After she visited Doc Benjamin, her feelings didn't change. Doc Benjamin told Junior, out of earshot of Daphne, "The hatred for her enemies is too deep, brethren. She is driven by it. To try and stop her would be like being her enemy, too."

Junior shook his head and thanked him. He said no more on the topic.

Mecca smiled as she sat in her rented car, low in the passenger seat, watching the drama about to unfold on her aunt's block. It was Mecca who had text messaged Daphne the "Come and get me," using Ruby's phone. Unlike Daphne's, Mecca's plan for revenge was playing out perfectly. She'd even pulled one over on Lou.

Momentarily.

She recalled the dream she'd had last night, where they talked in the airport. Lou was the baggage handler who helped her carry her bags to the ticket counter. He was angry, and she wasn't in the mood for a long speech, so she blocked him out by thinking of being with Miguel. His touch, his smell, his voice covered everything Lou said, until she heard him say, "When you fly on a plane, you gamble with your own life. No fault in that, but gambling with other people's lives is an act of evil. . . ."

Her dream then switched to her seeing her aunt's demise the way she'd planned it. It reminded her to book a flight leaving that afternoon for Italy. She had spoken to Miguel that morning, and he'd informed her that his team won the European championship. She was sorry that she couldn't be there with him to celebrate, and he agreed.

"I know how we can celebrate, though," Miguel stated.

"How?" she asked, filled with a childish excitement.

"When you get back, let's get married."

"I'm coming back today," Mecca said, astonished.

"Good. I'll have everything set up."

"What about my dress and all?" Mecca asked. She wanted her wedding to be picture-perfect and not rushed. Still, it was Miguel, and she knew she was going to do it regardless.

"I know your size. I measure you every night," he replied with a seductive humor.

"You're fresh."

"Don't worry, baby. I'll get the perfect dress by Vera Wang. You'll see."

It was all set, and Mecca couldn't wait to get back to Italy and be in the arms of Miguel. He was her world. She just wanted to witness her former world go away, the same way it had come to her. Violently. So she watched, and something began to happen that wasn't part of what she'd planned.

Agent Doyle got out of his car, with his gun at his side, and approached Sonny Brown.

"Sonny!" he cried out.

Sonny Brown turned suddenly to the voice coming from the street. He smiled at the familiar-faced agent, the same agent who had tried for years to bring him down for murders that Brown was rumored to have committed. Not only had he tried to bring Sonny down, he had tried to link him to Scooter Williams but never could. Doyle told himself that this was one time he could link Sonny to Scooter, but he wasn't here for that, and he didn't want Sonny to mess everything up.

"Agent Doyle," Sonny said, looking at the gun in his hand, "what brings you to Brooklyn?"

"I was about to ask you the same thing," Doyle said, approaching Sonny to pat him down. From the corner of his eye, Doyle saw Daphne walking down the sidewalk, looking at Ruby's home.

Daphne glanced at Doyle and Sonny Brown curiously. She didn't know the two men, but the white man and the black man looked out of place. In fact, to Daphne, the white one looked like a cop.

Then the sound of a door being unlocked came from Ruby's brownstone. A second later, Ruby and an unidentified woman came out. Ruby immediately saw Daphne and reached inside of her coat, drawing a gun, as Daphne did the same.

Doyle looked up at Ruby, and the second he took his eye off of Sonny Brown, he heard a loud boom and he felt a blow to his chest that knocked the wind out of him, leaving a burning sensation. He couldn't breathe. He felt hard, cold ground beneath him and blacked out to the sound of gunfire erupting all around.

Ruby immediately aimed her .40 caliber at Daphne and fired repeatedly. It roared on the quiet block, causing people within their homes to frantically dial 911. Ducking behind a car, Daphne aimed her silenced .45 at Ruby.

It sputtered softly, shattering windows and splintering doors all around Ruby. Both women were too busy shooting at each other to notice Sonny Brown shoot Agent Doyle, who lay dead on the sidewalk as a pool of blood began to form under him.

Mecca watched in amazement and confusion. Who was the black man, and why did he just shoot that white guy? And why was he now aiming his gun at Ruby and shooting?

Ruby pushed the woman that was at her back into the vestibule of the brownstone as she screamed. She then turned back to Daphne and unloaded her .40 caliber at Daphne, who hid behind a parked car. Then her body jerked from Sonny's 9 mm Beretta bullet tearing into her shoulder, and she looked at him, shocked. She turned her aim toward him, and before she could get a round off, Sonny sent a slug into her chest.

Mecca watched as a spurt of blood ejected out of Ruby's open coat.

Daphne saw Ruby drop. She was confused because she knew it wasn't her bullet that took Ruby down. She got up from behind the car and watched the black man walking away from the scene in a hurry. She quickly walked up the steps to the wounded Ruby and kicked the gun out of her hand.

"Hey, Ruby, don't look too good, bitch!" she grumbled, bending down over her.

People were now looking out windows at the scene. Mona sat in the vestibule, in the corner, with her legs to her chest, crying. Daphne heard her sobs and aimed her gun at her and put three bullets into her face. Somewhere in an apartment, someone screamed.

Ruby couldn't move. The bullet had gone through her chest and out her back, shattering her spine.

"Fuck you, bitch," Ruby mumbled between labored breaths. "Your brother died a scared bitch."

Before Mecca had revealed who Daphne was, Ruby had had suspicions at one time. It was customary for inmates in prison to show other convicts they were acquainted with photos of family, friends, and themselves on the streets. Once Ruby got to know Daphne, she showed her many pictures in her photo albums, most of which had been sent by Mecca, of her and Shamel.

Daphne never showed her one.

When Ruby inquired about it, Daphne told her, "I don't want to be reminded about what I am missing."

It was a reaction that Daphne had when Ruby was showing her pictures that gave Ruby her first suspicions. She had a photo of her and Wise that they took together in the famous club in the Bronx known as the Fever. The couple had posed, holding each other from behind, with Wise's arms wrapped around her waist and holding her hands against her stomach. Both of them had matching gray sheepskin coats, while Wise wore a hat, and Ruby had her hair out in a Jherri curl. As soon as Ruby turned to the picture, Daphne looked away, as if she hated seeing it. She played it off, as if something else had caught her attention, and walked off of the bleachers in the prison yard.

"I'll be back, Ruby. This chick Karen been owing me for months."

Ruby saw Karen across the yard, and her suspicions of Daphne became doubtful, because it was a fact that Karen owed Daphne money. Eventually, she made Ruby forget about it, and when she told Ruby she would put her on when she got out, that got her attention.

The next time Ruby became suspicious of Daphne's relationship to Wise, things had already began to happen. The robberies of the spots, then her sudden disappearance, brought those old thoughts back to the forefront of her mind. She wanted to act on those suspicions, but she never realized that she was being rocked to sleep, as she did with Mo Blood.

Now, lying paralyzed on the steps of her brownstone, the same one Daphne put down a payment for, she looked into the face of a woman hell-bent on avenging her brother's murder, which took place twenty years ago. Ruby had to respect the way she'd sought her vengeance. It was the most cunning, well-planned, patient plotting and acting she'd ever witnessed a person do. She had to admit, Daphne was a dangerous enemy.

Daphne chuckled and watched the mist form from both of their breaths in the cold weather. She watched Ruby's eyes blink as she struggled to hold on to her life force, which was slowly leaving her body. Tears rolled down her face as her life flashed before her.

"That's what I always admired about you, Ruby. You're a fighter. Even lying here, dying, you just have to get the last word in. You're the toughest bitch I ever met," Daphne said as sirens roared in the background.

"Get . . . it . . . over . . . with . . . mufucka," Ruby panted.

"For the record, if my brother died a scared bitch, no one will ever know that but you and

God," Daphne announced as she pointed her gun at Ruby's head. "Now go tell God and my brother how scared you were."

She squeezed the trigger.

Wrapping her Burberry scarf around her mouth and nose, and fixing her Dolce & Gabbana shades, she quickly walked to her car and sped off to the airport, leaving the city of her childhood, a city she loved more than any place on earth, for good.

Mecca drove up and watched Daphne pull off and parked in the same space. She jumped out of the car and ran toward her aunt, screaming.

When the first police responded to the call of shots fired, they saw Mecca bending over the still corpse of Ruby, crying and hugging the body. The officers noticed Agent Doyle a few yards away, lying in the gutter but not moving. The blank look in his eyes indicated he was gone. People who lived in the neighborhood began to emerge on the street, still in shock at what had taken place in their peaceful, cozy, middle-class neighborhood.

When some of them were questioned, the police received a bunch of jumbled stories of what took place. Unfortunately for the investigators, no one got a good look at Daphne's face, which was covered by a scarf, or at Sonny Brown, because most of their attention was directed at Ruby, the neighbor they all recognized.

One knockoff version of Spike Lee told the police, "I don't know her personally, but I know she wasn't your average middle-class woman. I saw her in *Don Diva* magazine. She's a tough chick." Afterward, he pushed his oversize glasses up the bridge of his nose, played one of his favorite hip-hop songs on his iPod, and rode off on his mountain bike.

Within minutes, the Brooklyn block was flooded with ambulances, cops, and law enforcement officials from various agencies. When the news went out that a federal agent had been killed, everyone except for the director of the FBI showed up. The only thing Mecca shared with the investigators who questioned her as they sat in the back of an unmarked Crown Victoria was, "She's all I have. I have no family besides her, and now she's gone. I don't know who did this."

And the tears flowed. Happy tears. As chaos tore through Ruby's neighborhood, Tashy and Scooter found peace when Simone's voice came over Tashy's cell phone.

"'Ma, come get me please. I got away from those people. I'm at the mall on Fulton Street in Brooklyn!"

Tashy and Scooter arrived in his Phantom as quickly as they could, almost getting a speeding ticket on their drive to Brooklyn. When they pulled up in front of Albee Square Mall, a teary-eyed Simone ran out to the car and jumped in.

"Take me home."

Scooter dropped them off in Harlem.

When Daphne reached Jamaica and inquired about Junior's decision for her to kill Ruby immediately, he told her everything he and Agent Doyle had discussed. He told her about the deal they'd struck years ago and how it related to her. "If it wasn't for that agent, you would still be in prison, Daphne. His influence is what got you that sentence. You were supposed to get fifty years."

Nodding, she looked out at the street from the chauffeured 600 Benz and wondered. "So who was the guy who showed up and killed the agent?"

"I'm not sure, but I'm willing to bet that girl's family sent him there to get your old friend. He and Agent Doyle must have known each other. Maybe he was sent there to kill anyone who was around, and Doyle wanted to save you," Junior answered. "Did he see you?"

"Yes, he did."

"Then I guess we'll never know." Junior shrugged.

"Will there be anything else?"

"No, thank you so much." Mecca grabbed the cup of water and aspirin from the Jennifer Aniston–looking stewardess on an Alitalia flight bound for Italy. She sat alone in her first-class seat, listening to the CD player on her lap.

Realizing she had no useful information to give the authorities about her aunt, Mona, or Agent Doyle's murders, they'd let her go. Mecca told them she had just returned from Italy with her boyfriend and had seen nothing. Before leaving, she told them if she found out anything else, she would call them immediately. She told them she wanted to know who her aunt's killer was.

She realized she no longer cared how Lou felt about her deceiving him. He wasn't there in real life, experiencing the emotions that she experienced from the betrayal. How much did he really care, anyway? Why was he so fixated on trying to put her life in order, but not on putting the people around her in check? Why didn't he try to convince Ruby not to set up her father to get robbed? Why didn't he tell her aunt not to have sex with Shamel? Why didn't he stop Tah Gunz from shooting her, or Karmen from sleeping with her man and him cheating himself?

She didn't want to see or hear from Lou anymore. She didn't need him. She'd got what she'd come for, and if she had to pay in the hereafter, so be it. She'd been through it all and might as well enjoy heaven on earth with Miguel.

"So, your hands are washed of me?" Mecca was startled by the voice of Lou, who now appeared in the empty seat next to her. She knew she wasn't dreaming.

"How did you—"

"That's the least of your problems, my love. The question is, why? Why would you deceive me? Deceiving me means you've gained control of yourself. Use that control more positively and you'll get further in life." He paused and looked around. "But you didn't use that control properly, and life has a way of getting its own revenge. This you will see soon."

Mecca didn't like Lou's tone. As she thought, the plane began to shake violently. She immediately gripped the seat tighter, and her heart thumped loudly in her chest. She felt the sharp descent, and the pilot's voice came over the intercom.

"Passengers, this is your captain speaking. We are experiencing some difficulties. Please remain calm, and follow the instructions given by the flight attendants."

Mecca looked at Lou, who sat next to her with a self-serving smirk. The stewardess who had served her earlier rushed to the seat across the aisle and fastened the seat belt with a look of panic across her face.

"The plane is going down too fast," she said and looked over at Mecca. Mecca looked at Lou.

"Lou, I'm sorry. Please stop it. I'm a changed person, I swear."

"I would fasten my seat belt if I were you," Lou responded.

"Lou, don't do this. I'm getting married. I plan to live a positive life with my husband. I'm going to raise a family, and I'm not going to raise my children how I was raised. I swear!"

The pilot's voice came over the speakers again. "Ladies and gentlemen, please fasten your seat belt and duck your head in your lap."

"This is it, Mecca. The end of it," Lou said as their bodies jerked from the plane's rapid descent.

Tears rolled down her face. She took one more look at Lou before she ducked her head.

Lou looked her in the eyes and said, "It's done."

The impact of the plane awakened Mecca. Instead of being on a crashing plane, she was looking up from her bed into the eyes of her favorite doctor as a white woman in a long white coat opened up the blinds in the all-white room, letting in the sunlight.

"'Today is a beautiful day, Mecca. It is also your day, remember?" The handsome black doctor held her hand.

Mecca nodded. "What time is it?" she asked while wiping the cold out of her eyes with the back of her hand.

"It's seven-thirty. Your hearing is at nine o'clock. You should get ready now."

The doctor left the lady in the white uniform in the room. Mecca looked at her, and she smiled through puffy red cheeks.

"Good luck, honey. I hate to see you go, but you deserve to leave this place."

She waited until the lady left, and got off her bed and looked at herself in the room's full-length mirror. She smiled at her own reflection.

"Yeah, today is my day," she mumbled. "I'm going home."

Epilogue

Lest you ponder her path of life—her ways are unstable; you don't know them.

—Proverbs 5:6

Family court, Brooklyn

The small courtroom fell silent when the tall, broad-shouldered, bespectacled judge Norman Pastel entered from a door situated behind the bench.

"All rise!" the bailiff announced.

Once everyone stood, the judge responded, "You may be seated."

Mecca looked down at the judge. He reminded her of Marlon Brando in *The Godfather*. As she sat down, she turned, looking at the spectators' section, smiling at her aunt and friends of her aunt that she didn't know but saw every time a court hearing took place.

The judge's voice was a deep, rich tone. "I understand this is a hearing on a report and recommendation from the staff at the psychiatric facility in Bronx County."

A slim woman of six feet stepped up to the podium situated in the middle of the courtroom, between what would normally be the tables for the defense and prosecution of a criminal defendant. This wasn't the case of a criminal; the hearing was to determine Mecca's madness.

"Michael T. Moore, Your Honor. I'm here on behalf of Miss Sykes." The pale-skinned guy pointed to Mecca, who was sitting next to a black woman and a man dressed impeccably, while Mecca wore a plain white dress shirt, blue slacks, and black leather loafers with two-inch heels. Her hair was pulled back into a ponytail.

"Are you her attorney, Mr. Moore?" the judge asked.

"Yes, Your Honor."

The judge folded his hands and placed his elbows on the bench desk. "Proceed."

"Your Honor, this is a twenty-year-old case that I will bring you up to speed on, being that you're new to the case. A case that's been heard over and over for many years by the now retired Honorable Stanley Doyle." he paused to look down at papers he had on the podium. "In 1988 . . ."

Brooklyn, 1988

Fourteen-year-old Mecca watched as her aunt surreptitiously placed a snub-nosed .38-caliber revolver handgun inside an empty sneaker box and placed it in on her closet shelf. Her aunt Ruby didn't notice her niece, who she'd taken in when she was eight years old, after her parents were murdered in their Brownsville apartment in 1982.

Mecca and her aunt lived in a Coney Island apartment in the same building as Ruby's friend and lover Monique Johnson and Mecca's half sister, Dawn. Monique and Mecca's father had an affair while Mecca's father and mother were together. It was no secret in Brownsville that Dawn was Bobby Sykes's daughter, because the news had spread like wildfire. Mecca's mother was infuriated at the news but didn't bring it up to Bobby, because she was in love and it was a fling when they broke up.

When Mecca's mother saw Monique's baby, she had no doubt it was Bobby's. She hated Monique, but she didn't take it out on the baby. She was mature enough to invite Monique over so that their babies would know each other.

When Monique moved to Coney Island, it was Ruby who made sure that the girls grew up together as sisters. At first, the girls got along wonderfully, but after the murder of Mecca's mother and father, Mecca's attitude toward Dawn and Monique changed. They got into fights often because Mecca initiated them.

Despite their problems, Monique still loved Mecca as if she was one of her own. Mecca clung to Monique to make Dawn jealous. It was revenge for Mecca, because Dawn had tried to steal Bobby Blast's attention when they were younger.

Then, one day, while Mecca and Dawn fought over a Barbie doll that they both claimed was theirs, Dawn told her, "My daddy bought me that. He loved me more!"

That was when Mecca started to plot her demise.

It was years later, when the girls were fourteen and had started to blossom, that Mecca carried out her plan. One day, when Ruby was out and Monique slept in her bedroom, Mecca retrieved Ruby's gun from the sneaker box, grabbed a pillow, and walked up to a sleeping Monique and shot her twice in the head. She walked out of the apartment and down the hall to the apartment Monique and Dawn lived in and knocked. Dawn answered.

"Mecca, what's up, girl?" she asked, looking at Mecca, who had a strange look on her face, with her hands behind her back.

"Nothing."

Mecca walked into the apartment when Dawn turned to walk to the bathroom. She was in the middle of curling her hair with a hot iron when two shots rang out through the complex. Dawn's body slumped to the floor.

Mecca stared down at her, smiling. "Hey, Dawn, don't look too good, bitch. See if Daddy loves you now."

The shots were heard by the neighbors in the building, and they opened their doors, looking into the hallway as Mecca walked by as if she didn't see them. The gun was still in her hand at her side.

She climbed into the elevator and rode it down to the first floor and sat on the steps in front of the building. She was arrested and taken to the police station. When Ruby arrived, Mecca told her interrogators, "Those bitches got what they deserved."

After a psychiatric evaluation by defense and prosecution experts, it was determined that Mecca was unfit to stand trial. She suffered from various mental illnesses. One doctor testified, "When she was a very young child, she suffered head trauma when she fell in her neighborhood playground. This concussion went untreated, resulting in brain damage."

Another psych testified, "Her head trauma, coupled with the emotional trauma of watching her parents being murdered at such a young age, only worsened her already unstable mental condition."

On the recommendation of both defense and prosecution experts, and subsequently stipulated by both attorneys, Mecca was committed to a psychiatric facility for the criminally insane. Every year she would have a hearing on her condition.

It was later decided that she would never be tried for the murders, but she could be released from the facility only on the recommendation of the staff of the facility. Those hearings would be held every year.

"Your Honor, I call my first witness, Dr. Paul McLeod, Jr.," Mr. Moore announced.

The courtroom was hushed as a well-dressed man who appeared to be in his fifties walked to the witness stand. He wore his dreadlocks in a ponytail. Mecca recognized the gray-eyed man as he stated his name for the record and told the court his occupation and dealings with her.

"I'm a clinical psychologist who has worked with Mecca Sykes for the last five years," he said with a Jamaican accent.

"And you have with you your report and recommendation. Is that correct, Mr. McLeod?"

"Yes, I do."

"Can you tell the court your recommendation?" Mr. Moore asked from the podium.

"Yes. It is my professional opinion that Miss Sykes's treatment is complete and she is ready to reenter society as a fully functioning, mentally fit adult."

"And you base your opinion on what?" the judge asked, looking over his glasses.

"Your Honor, in the last five years Mecca has shown so much maturity that she even helps the staff counsel other patients when those patients suffer psychotic episodes. The patients practically trust her more than they do us, and under our watchful eyes, we even have her give them the medication when they don't want to take it from staff."

The judge nodded his head, and Mr. McLeod was excused.

"I would like to call Dr. Benjamin Mason, Your Honor," Mr. Moore announced.

A thin, wiry man in his midforties walked to the witness stand with a slightly stooped posture.

His complexion was olive toned and dull, and he had brown, bold eyes. He was clean shaved and had short graying hair on his head.

Dr. Mason was born and raised in Senegambia, West Africa, and moved to the United States in the 1970s, after earning a degree in psychology at the University of Cairo, Egypt. Once in the United States, he got a job at Bellevue Hospital in Manhattan, where he worked until 2000.

He was subsequently offered a job at the Bronx facility, with the promise of a salary close to a hundred thousand a year, as a senior psychologist who would train college students who were majoring in the field of behavioral science. He had testified at over a hundred trials, mostly for the state and only a handful of times for a defense lawyer. He was accomplished in what he did and made sure that everyone in the room new it.

As he sat on the stand, Mecca didn't bother to look at him and instead looked at the lawyer paid by Ruby to represent her. Dr. Mason had opposed her release at her last hearing five years ago, where he'd simply stated, "It is my opinion that Miss Sykes's behavior and mental condition deem her unfit to function normally in society." Now she wondered what he would have to say.

After explaining his credentials to the judge and informing the court that he had had the occasion to work with Mecca for the last seven years, he expounded on their relationship by stating, "A lot of my time with her was short. She isn't on my caseload. Dr. Parker has worked with her for the twenty years she has been at the facility."

"Surely enough time for you to render a report and recommendation, correct?" Moore asked.

"Indeed."

"And your recommendation is?"

"Contrary to the one five years ago, I must say," Dr. Mason remarked with a smile, "today a different Miss Sykes sits before you. Not the manipulative, impulsive young girl I saw seven years ago. With Dr. Parker to credit, assisted by the staff who testified prior to me and others, what you see today is a mature, mentally developed woman ready for a productive livelihood among society."

Mecca couldn't believe her ears. She turned to stare at a man she'd come to hate. A man other patients at the facility called "Doc Devilman." Her eyes watered, and she felt strange inside.

When he walked off the stand, he passed by her and smiled. "It's your time, Mecca. Make the best of it. Good luck." With that, he left the courtroom.

"Your Honor, I call Daphne Carter."

Moore's voice was followed by the double doors of the courtroom opening, and a heartbreaking, lovely, statuesque, golden-brown-skinned woman with beautiful, pale hazel dreamy eyes strutted in. Her knee-length black Versace dress showed her dancer's legs. Her perfectly done hair surrounded her oval face, with a ripe mouth under her small, pudgy nose, which she applied makeup to smartly. Every man in the room stared in awe, while the women glared as her Chanel No. 5 perfume filled the room. The sight of the woman brought a smile to Mecca's face. Daphne Carter took the stand and crossed her legs after stating her name for the court. She went on to explain her job at the facility and how it related to the treatment of Mecca.

"I am a mental health counselor. I've been working at the Bronx County facility for ten years. I have counseled Mecca every two weeks in her anger management groups and have had one-on-one talks with her on many occasions."

"I understand your staff deals with a small amount of patients. How does that affect the patients?" Moore asked while sipping on a glass of water that had been placed on the podium.

"With a small amount of patients, it affords us more time to deal with the patients' needs individually. Mecca is on Dr. Parker's caseload, and Dr. Parker keeps me informed of her progress before she comes to groups or sessions with other doctors. This is so we know what type of individual we are dealing with."

Her voice was smooth and gentle on the ears and had captivated every man in the court.

"Miss Carter . . ."

"That's Mrs. Carter," Daphne corrected him.

Mecca smiled, as if she was in on a secret that no one knew about. Daphne was married to her childhood sweetheart, Donovan. He was an American-born Jamaican who she kept a picture of on her desk. He was very handsome, and once in a while he came to the facility to pick Daphne up. They lived in Brooklyn together, and she told Mecca that Donovan was a master chef who ran two Jamaican restaurants in Brooklyn.

"Tell us about Mecca's progress, Mrs. Carter."

Daphne smiled, looking at Mecca. She was a twenty-three-year-old woman when Daphne began working at the facility. Well, she appeared to be a woman, but when Daphne became involved with her, she realized this was still a little girl in emotional pain, trapped in a woman's body. She'd walked in on Mecca unaware when she was having a conversation with herself in the voice of a small child. Then her voice changed to her regular one.

She would listen to Mecca speak to herself as if she really was speaking with another person. The conversations were mainly about seeing no reason to change her life. Mecca seemed to blame her behavior on the death of her parents. Most memorably, Daphne heard her say, "How am I supposed to feel after my mother and father were killed in front of me? Am I supposed to just forget that? How did you expect my life to turn out? This life is all I know!"

Daphne's heart went out to her. Besides Dr. Parker, Daphne was the only other staff member that had established closeness with her beyond the call of duty. She treated Mecca like a daughter. As her condition improved, Daphne shared a lot of personal things with her. She told her about how her brother was murdered and how much it hurt her. The abuse she'd witnessed her stepfather administer to her mother. Things Daphne told Mecca made her sad but gave her strength.

"We can't let these things control us, Mecca," she'd told her. "We have to pick up the pieces and put it back together and make our lost loved ones happy by doing good in life."

She'd watched Mecca grow over the years. There were setbacks when she became angry and had psychotic episodes where she had to be sedated, but those incidents gradually became a thing of the past.

"She has made the best progress I've seen in any patient since working at the facility," Daphne testified. "She is very ready, sir."

"Thank you, Mrs. Carter."

As she walked off the stand, she stopped at Mecca's table and reached over to hug her. Several tears had fallen from Mecca's eyes, and Daphne wiped them away.

"I love you, Mecca."

"I love you, too, Daphne."

She left the courtroom, wiping her own tears away with a handkerchief.

"I call the last and final witness, Your Honor. Please bring in Dr. Louis Parker," Moore announced.

In walked a man standing six feet, with a glowing dark brown skin tone, penetrating black eyes, a mole at the corner of the left eye, a close-cropped, sharply lined graying beard, cut-glass cheekbones that made him incandescently handsome, and a perfectly rounded, short Afro with graying temples.

His presence was commanding. He walked with an air of authority. He was in charge. He looked expensive in his tan suit by Ralph Lauren Purple Label, white Dior Homme dress shirt, and silk tie. He'd complemented his suit with a pair of brown suede Hermès bit loafers and a rose gold Breguet watch. His scent of Attitude Armani overshadowed the scent left by Daphne. This man looked serious.

"Please state your name for the record," the judge commanded.

"Louis Parker."

Moore went into action. Dr. Parker was his most important witness. Even though the other staff members' testimony was compelling, Mecca's release from the facility depended on Dr. Parker's opinion and recommendation.

"Can you tell us your occupation and duty at the facility, Dr. Parker?"

As serious as he looked, to those who knew him, he was a kindhearted, devoted Christian man who genuinely cared for the patients under his control. He treated everyone fairly, and he made his patients feel as if they were in a family setting more than in a psychiatric institution.

"I am a clinical psychologist, a professor of behavioral sciences at Columbia University, and author of two books on psychiatry. I am the managing director of the Bronx County psychiatric facility."

Mecca stared at the man who for the last twenty years had been like her father, brother, mother, friend, and sometimes foe and watcher. She had a love/hate relationship with the man, who was caring, but at the same time stern in administering discipline when she got out of hand. This was the only person alive that knew everything about her. He had her life down to a science. He knew when she was in a bad mood, a good one, or just sad. He knew her thoughts, her weakness, everything.

She was brought to him a broken-down, lonely, angry, frightened fourteen-year-old who wanted to prove to the world that she was tough. He saw right through it all. From the beginning they argued daily. She screamed that he knew nothing about her.

"Those files don't mean shit, motherfucker!" she would yell.

He would remain calm and wait it out. Their arguments turned to long conversations about her growing up without parents after watching them being murdered. Conversations that were tearful for her, and for the first time in his career, someone's story brought him to tears. Mecca became Dr. Parker's personal task.

"Dr. Parker, tell us about Mecca Sykes and what it was like working with her for twenty years," Moore said, taking a seat next to Mecca. Dr. Parker smiled, showing a set of perfectly white teeth.

In 1998 officials from the Brooklyn family court and juvenile facility literally had to strap down a young teenager to a hospital gurney and wheel her into the Bronx facility. Dr. Louis Parker and his staff were awaiting the new admission. They were forewarned by her attorney that she was not a happy camper.

The staff wasn't shocked by her behavior; they'd seen it all before. Nobody wanted to be admitted to a "crazy house" involuntarily, especially a teenager. Mecca was immediately sedated and put on suicide watch for her first week. Once she was calm, Dr. Parker paid her his first of many visits in a dimly lit padded room that brightened after he walked in. After introducing himself, Mecca simply stared at him.

"Double homicide? Wow, you're a real mean young lady." He leaned against the padded wall.

"And what?" she growled. Mecca sat on a chair that had been bolted down and was connected to a plastic desk on the wall. She rolled her eyes.

He held up his hands. "I'm not your enemy, dear. I'm here to help."

"I don't need your help," she snapped.

"Obviously you do. I mean, the average fourteen-year-old girl, as pretty as you are, usually doesn't kill two people and something isn't wrong."

"Maybe they deserved it," she mumbled, rolling her eyes and neck simultaneously.

"I doubt that," he stated. "But let's talk about that for a minute."

Mecca studied the gold nameplate on his white coat. "Listen, Dr. Parker . . ."

"Call me Lou. That's what everyone calls me."

Within a two-year period, Dr. Parker was able to break through Mecca's tough exterior, which he called a "defensive front." At her first five-year hearing, Dr. Parker felt they were making progress, but still opposed her release. He had determined that she was not ready and was still showing antisocial behavior.

Then, at the last hearing, he again opposed her release but explained in depth about her condition and treatment.

"Under hypnosis, Mecca has imagined an envious version of herself living a life of crime where she is the heir of a drug-dealing empire headed by her aunt, who I know personally as a hardworking woman in the Department of Corrections. More strangely humorous about this life as a big-time drug dealer who controls her Brownsville neighborhood is that her other characters are me, my staff, and her fellow residents at the facility. She envisions some of them as her close friends who became her enemies. Enemies she is seeking revenge on."

"Who does she envision you as in this imaginary tale?" the judge asked Dr. Parker.

"A cross between the Devil and God."

"Dr. Parker," Moore continued, "at Mecca's fifteen-year hearing, you informed the court of this imaginary tale of a life of crime, which she shared with you under hypnosis. How did you go about dealing with that?"

"With the help of staff like Dr. Carter, Mason, and McLeod, the progress begins by digging beneath the emotional scars and anger to bring out the good that all humans have subconsciously within them and that they suppress with the emotional baggage. We knew from the start that her problem started in childhood, with the murder of her parents.

"I presented her with different scenarios in problem-solving sessions called Thinking for a Change and Anger Management. For example, one scenario that I presented her with was, what if she found out her aunt was responsible for her parents' murders?"

People in the spectators' section all looked at Ruby, who was embarrassed by the comment.

"We wanted to know how she would deal with it," Dr. Parker continued.

"Initially, she wanted to seek revenge on her aunt, and when other scenarios were introduced, such as characters in her imaginary tale betraying her, she wanted revenge on all of them. Within the last five years, she eventually began to see the foolishness in her tale. A psychologist from centuries ago, named Sándor Ferenczi, termed when another person becomes part of a person's ego, internalizing that other person's character introjections. Mecca's character in her imagination was her father. He was a drug dealer in her Brownsville neighborhood.

"Another way I dealt with her was by replaying her childhood to her. I had pictures of her as a child, along with family and friends, up to her teenage years, prior to being admitted to the facility. Under hypnosis, we traveled back to those days.

"I found out that she wanted answers as to why things happened that made her sad. The untreated head trauma only added to her condition. Fortunately for her, she was a young lady when the trauma occurred, and her brain had not fully developed. The trauma only caused her development to slow down, so at fourteen she actually had the mind of a nine-year-old, one who felt anger and felt unloved by everyone. Along with growing up in Brownsville, her mental state fueled the feelings of rejection and depression."

Moore stood up and walked to the podium. "So today, twenty years later, what is your recommendation, Dr. Parker?"

He sighed and looked at Mecca as his eyes filled with tears. Sniffles could be heard throughout the courtroom. His testimony was emotional for many, even the judge.

"Mecca is ready to go home."

"Surprise!"

Mecca's friends at the facility cheered as she returned from court accompanied by Dr. Parker and Ruby. The recreation room was decorated with balloons and glittering banners that read FAREWELL, MECCA!

Mecca smiled as she took in the faces of all the people she'd grown to love over the years. Her friends and fellow patients who had put up with her mean attitude and treatment of them.

"I should have never stolen her nail polish," Tamika told herself.

"Listen, everyone!" Dr. Parker announced. "Mecca's aunt is here to take her home. We have a podium set up so everyone can say their last words and good-byes. Miguel, make it short, and don't be up there giving a sermon."

Miguel was a young Puerto Rican patient who happened to be Mecca's best friend. Mecca sat next to Ruby and Dr. Parker in a metal folding chair as her friends walked up to the podium one by one and said their good-byes.

Karmen, her sometime friend who had been at the facility since 1990 for killing her boyfriend, who had smacked her in the face for yelling at him, got up to speak. She had cut his body into pieces and had fed them to her pit bulls. She'd kept his head in the freezer. It wasn't unusual to see the two of them competing for the interest of the boys within the facility. As she spoke, she rubbed one of her braids that fell over her shoulder.

"I know we were at each other's necks, Mecca, but all in all I admire you. You're a real chick. I'll miss you."

Karmen walked away. Next came a brown-skinned girl two years younger than Mecca, named Tamika. For years, they'd hated each other, after she found out that Tamika had stolen nail polish from her makeup kit. When Mecca found out from Karmen, who wanted her to do something so Mecca could get into trouble, Mecca got a razor and slashed Tamika while they played in the rec room. Tamika needed thirty stitches to close the wound. Afterward, she was placed in a rubber room for a week, and when staff found out Taheem had given her the weapon, he was transferred to another facility.

"I never said I was sorry for stealing your nail polish. I'm sorry, Mecca." Tamika walked toward her with her arms out, and Mecca stood to hug her. "You deserve this more than any of us," she told her. Tamika was there for killing her baby by dumping her newborn in an incinerator.

Next, a tall, handsome, athletically built man three years older than Mecca rose to speak. He was admitted to the facility a year after her for chopping his younger cousin's head off in an East New York building.

He told the cops, "That motherfucker stole my bag of weed."

Shamel was Mecca's first crush. He was placed in the rubber room for a week when he beat up Taheem for giving Mecca the razor to cut Tamika. He knew Taheem did it so Mecca could get into trouble.

Mecca had told Dr. Parker that Taheem hated her, which was why he'd given her the razor. She explained he hated her because she wouldn't be his girlfriend. Dr. Parker understood why in her imaginary tale of crime, Taheem shot her, placing her in a coma for three months.

In his cool tone, Shamel spoke. "I'm gonna miss you, Mecca. You know how we do. Stay up. I love you."

Shamel walked over to hug her.

"Oh, boy!" Karmen said as Miguel began walking to the podium. Everyone laughed.

Miguel was the most talkative guy in the facility. All he talked about was how he was a street-ball legend from Bushwick, Brooklyn. He bragged and showed pictures of him at Rucker tournaments. He had articles about him being one of the best high school players in the country. He would talk for hours. It was Mecca who loved to listen, though. Miguel was her second crush once she found out that Shamel was messing with Karmen.

Miguel was admitted to the facility in 1997, after he stabbed and killed his father and then shoved a broomstick up his dead father's ass. Miguel's father had molested him since he was seven years old. Basketball was his escape from his horrible home life. His mother died of a drug overdose a year after his father first molested him. He immediately fell in love with Mecca when he got to the facility. He didn't care that at first she paid him no attention when he sent her cards he'd drawn of beautiful landscapes. He was an extremely good artist. He wrote her notes of how he wanted to travel the world with her, go to places like Paris and Italy. He said he would become a basketball star and spend the money on making her happy.

Eventually, Mecca began speaking to him. She found him to be cute. It didn't matter that he was talkative. Mecca put his stories into her imaginary tale. Every day she sat with him, listening to him talk about growing up in Bushwick and being the neighborhood star. He never talked about his personal life.

"I hate to see you go, Mecca, but I'm happy that you get to go. I don't know what I'm gonna do now. I look forward to our talks. Can I call you?"

"Oh God, don't do it," Karmen joked.

"Shut up, Karmen," Miguel said. "Anyway, I love you, Mecca. You're my best friend, and you will always be that. I never had—"

"Okay, Miguel," Dr. Parker interjected. He knew Miguel was about to go into one of his speeches.

"A'ight, Dr. L. Bye, Mecca. I love you." Miguel went over to a crying Mecca, and they hugged tightly.

Dr. Parker walked Mecca and Ruby out to the parking lot. Before they exited the facility, the old, stooped-shouldered, bald-headed janitor they called Stone came over to them.

"Hey, Mecca. You leaving finally?" His voice cracked.

"Yes, Stone, I am." Mecca walked over to hug him. For twenty years she had watched him clean up blood, vomit, feces, and other human body fluids from off the floor of rooms and the halls. He was a nice old man who treated the children like his grandkids. He snuck in candy to give them. Mecca was one of his favorites. He reached in his old uniform and pulled out a picture.

"She would have loved to see this day."

Mecca grabbed the picture, and a tear dropped from her eye. The picture was of an old black female patient all the people called Nanna.

Nanna had spent thirty years at the facility, after killing her two sons, who she believed were possessed by the devil. She told the judge, "My sons, Kaheem and Brian, were sent here by Satan to tempt me. The Bible say, 'Don't tempt the Lord thy God.'"

In 2002 Nanna died of a heart attack. She was seventy-seven years old.

"Good-bye, Stone." Mecca hugged the old janitor.

Outside, Dr. Parker hugged Mecca. He prayed Mecca's behavior, which had made him recommend that she be allowed to reenter society, wasn't an act. He had seen plenty of patients act as if they no longer suffered from mental illnesses. They "introjected," as psychologist Sandor Ferenczi called it, other people's character. They acted normal when they really weren't. He felt strongly that Mecca wasn't acting. If she was, she was one of the best actors he'd ever seen. Hollywood would definitely be her calling.

"Remember, if you feel you need someone to talk to, or you're feeling stressed or depressed, I'm a phone call away," Dr. Parker said as he wiped Mecca's tears with his hand. Mecca hugged him tightly.

"I'm gonna call even if I'm not depressed," Mecca responded.

Ruby shook his hand. "Thank you for everything."

"It was my pleasure. Mecca made me realize this job was worth taking."

With that said, Mecca and Ruby got in Ruby's '07 silver Range Rover. Mecca waved at Doctor Parker as they drove off, and he returned the gesture.

They drove in silence for a while, and Ruby looked over at her now thirty-four-year-old niece. She looked like the spitting image of her mother, Big Mecca.

Tears fell down Mecca's face. Ruby fought to hold back her tears. She had to show strength for her niece. She was extremely happy that her niece was finally going home. She had spent thousands of dollars hiring lawyers to help her niece get released. Only to have her hopes crushed every year.

Every opportunity, she'd visited Mecca for twenty years, witnessing the change in her. At times, she'd even admitted to herself that Mecca wasn't ready for the streets. Mecca was an emotional wreck, and Ruby knew why. She also knew that what helped her somewhat in her process of getting better was something that Ruby told her during one of their visits.

As Mecca looked out the window at the passing cars and the homes and buildings of the Bronx, the clouds seemed brighter than anything she had ever known.

"Thank you, Ruby."

"What's that for, baby?" Ruby asked.

"For killing the guys who killed my parents."

ORDER FORM
URBAN BOOKS, LLC
97 N18th Street
Wyandanch, NY 11798

Name (please print):_____

Address:_____

City/State:_____

Zip:_____

QTY	TITLES	PRICE

Shipping and handling: add $3.50 for 1st book, then $1.75 for each additional book.

Please send a check payable to:

Urban Books, LLC

Please allow 4-6 weeks for delivery